CW01508479

DEDALUS

Dara Kavanagh is a writer, academic, translator and poet. A
native of Dublin, he spent more than a decade working in
Africa, Australia and Latin America before returning to settle
in Ireland. He is the author of several books
and poetry collections.

Dedalus has published his three novels *Prague 1938* (2021)
Jabberwock (2023) and *Scorched Earth* (2025).

DARA KAVANAGH

SCORCHED EARTH

Dedalus

Supported using public funding by
**ARTS COUNCIL
ENGLAND**

Published in the UK by Dedalus Limited
24-26, St Judith's Lane, Sawtry, Cambs, PE28 5XE
info@dedalusbooks.com
www.dedalusbooks.com

ISBN printed book   978 1 915568 81 6
ISBN ebook   978 1 915568 94 6

Dedalus is distributed in the USA & Canada by SCB Distributors
15608 South New Century Drive, Gardena, CA 90248
info@scbdistributors.com   www.scbdistributors.com

Dedalus is distributed in Australia by Peribo Pty Ltd
58, Beaumont Road, Mount Kuring-gai, N.S.W. 2080
info@peribo.com.au   www.peribo.com.au

First published by Dedalus in 2025
Scorched Earth © *Dara Kavanagh 2025*

Printed and bound in the UK by Clays Elcograf S.p.A.
Typeset by Marie Lane

A C.I.P. listing for this book is available on request.

FOR THE PALESTINIAN PEOPLE

TABLE OF CONTENTS

CAST OF CHARACTERS

2nd Lt Frederic 'Fred' Hart, a volunteer turned deserter, who returns to Ireland after ten years' exile under the assumed name 'Jimmy Cade'.

Katherine 'Kit' Hart, Fred Hart's younger sister who is an amateur artist.

Edmond Hart, Fred Hart's older brother, who has assumed the running of 'the Elms', the Hart estate in Co. Roscommon.

Charles Hart, the nominal head of the family, who has suffered from debilitating depression since the death of his wife, Frances 'Fanny' Montagu.

Cpt Jack Montagu, a retired officer. Fanny Montagu's uncle.

CAST OF CHARACTERS

Reginald Orr, the Hart family solicitor, who undertakes to find Fred Hart.

Dominic Foley, a Dublin-based barrister whom Orr enlists to assist him in his search.

Cressida Fitzsimons, a mute stained-glass artist, companion of Katherine Hart.

2nd Lt Albert 'Bertie' Nuzum, a fellow officer in Fred Hart's unit during the South Africa campaign.

2nd Lt Padraic 'Patch' Kinkaid, a fellow officer in Fred Hart's unit during the South Africa campaign.

Elspeth 'Cissie' Kinkaid, née Hamilton, widow of Patch Kinkaid.

Tom Kinkaid, Patch and Cissie's son. He is thirteen at the time of Fred Hart's return.

Aloysius 'A.T.' Wall, a freelance journalist embedded in Fred Hart's unit during the South Africa campaign.

Cecil Havelock-Saunders, a retired Major standing in the 1910 Westminster election.

Sgt Caleb Judd, a henchman of Havelock-Saunders and Fred Hart's sworn enemy.

CHAPTER ONE

S hrill of a whistle. A jolt; a clank. The carriage rolled backwards. Instinctively the man reached forwards, into vacant space. He glanced to the corridor, to ensure he hadn't been observed. When he saw that he hadn't been, he again consulted his fob. Three minutes past. He nodded. It looked as though he would have the compartment to himself.

As the train gathered speed out of Kilfree Station, Reginald Orr LL.B. unbuttoned his kid gloves, laid them on the seat beside a dove grey homburg, and removed a package from his breast pocket. Perching a pince-nez on the bridge of his nose, he undid the ribbon, royal blue, and slid the envelopes apart. Five. Five, together with a photograph; a crushed flower of unknown species, faded to ochre; a picture postcard with a Portuguese stamp, dated *Outubro 1900*. Also a newspaper clipping, far too recent to have yellowed.

It was the last of these which had set him on this fool's errand in the first place; had lent the decade's old correspondence a patina of urgency. Not that he was the man to lend credence to a mere report, not without testing the evidence. If it turned out a fool's errand, he winced, then he might well prove the perfect fool to have rushed in to accept it.

A lost brother. A biblical ring to that.

Reginald Orr arranged the envelopes by postmark as best he could—all were from the same year, the last full year of Victoria's reign. End of an era. *Ind Imp* the coinage declared, a temporal title to lay alongside *Fid Def*. Rendering unto Caesar. Well, wayward Edward had come and gone since then, and it was her grandson who now sat on the throne imperial. Would historians of the future refer to an Edwardian age? That remained to be seen.

How do you assess a monarch? Imperial measure! That was one for the club, later.

Orr extracted the first of the letters and smoothed it out on his trouser leg. The pages had been frequently unfolded, refolded. A childish hand slanting downward, scored with unruly corrections; with the kind of slapdash punctuation he frowned upon. The ink had blanched over the years.

The letter itself was undated, Orr noted without comment.

Well, Kit, it's finally happened. There's no going back now!

Impossible, quite impossible, to think of her as 'Kit'. She was Katherine. The name fitted the woman she'd grown into. It was solid. Assured. He never cared for the habit Edmond and her own father had of docking it to Kate, as though she were some wench out of a Shakespeare comedy.

Peculiar, to think she'd ever been, what? Fifteen? Sixteen at a push. Which would have made this Freddy character…? Nineteen, he supposed.

There was quite the ferment along the quay to wave us off. Mothers, sweethearts. Flags and bunting, colourful as any public holiday—though we made rather a drab show of it in our Indian khaki. After the previous scrap down there, which didn't end well, it seems they've finally dispensed with the scarlet. And there's no such thing as risking the regimental colours in battle, either. Down the quays, the DMP (bless 'em!) did their bit to keep the jeers and protests away (and yes, my dear, I do know we don't see eye to eye on this one!)

Hard, not to be caught up in the sheer noise of it all. It quite fills one until one's entire ribcage hums like a bell. It had me skittish as a colt. And then, the regimental bands were making such a holiday prom out of the whole affair. "Goodbye Dolly I must leave you, though it breaks my heart to go". *Then the same skittishness twice over as we mounted the gangways into the belly of the giant liner. The feeling of being caught up in something huge and inevitable. The wheels of the mighty Juggernaut.*

Then the baritone blast and resonance of the ship's horn…

I knew you couldn't be there; besides everything else Father would never have allowed it. Still, I scoured the crowds. Felt a pang of real disappointment that somehow you hadn't slipped away from "The Elms" to make it across to Dublin. The dock was thronged with cheering families, wives holding up infants, teary sweethearts. Do you know—you'll laugh at me—if you had been there, I believe I'd have let on to the chaps you were my very own Dolly Gray, waving me away?

Now that was a rum thing to say.

Because I'm still not at ease sporting an actual uniform, and I can't help but think the others sense it. I'm a little afraid of them, truth be known. Oh, not so much the officers—they're the sort of chaps you might encounter out on a jaunt down to Fairyhouse with Cpt Jack. But the men. The way they look at one—or am I imagining it? Not so much hostility. Derision? God forgive me, but there are one or two of them whose low physiognomies wouldn't look out of place in a set of Lombroso's illustrations.

Those months I spent playing at soldiers in the cadet corps seem as artificial and remote now as the Portora Royal boarding school. The bottom line is I feel a fraud. Like the dwarfish thief who stole the giant's robe and feels it hang loose—now what's that from? And I can't help but think...

Orr examined the photograph Katherine had entrusted him. The young man didn't look entirely out of place in his officer's uniform, gazing out with those dark eyes so like hers. Youthful, certainly. But callow? Pale. Slight build. It was the fair moustache, perhaps, that most failed to inspire confidence.

14

And I can't help but think it must show. I mean to say, Edmond was always the warrior of the family. Always so much more robust than I. Rugby. Boxing. Polo. Which of our names is inscribed on pretty much every medal and cup in the trophy cabinet? And who used draw up columns of tin soldiers, meticulously painted, across the study table, playing out the battles of Balaklava and Inkerman any time Cpt Jack would visit? I was only ever roped into those, you know.

Of course Father would never have allowed the eldest to enlist, that goes without saying. The son and heir. Not that Edmond would have wanted to, that's not what I'm saying. And then Mother, God rest her, always had her heart set on the cloth for her Freddy. Some living or other in a shady glen, like a scene out of Trollope. I think in the end, Father felt he ought to go through with her wish for form's sake, never mind that I've never had a head for scripture. The pageantry of it, yes. Stained glass and hymnals. Candlemas. Christmas. But that's all so much theatre. The irony of course, it was Edmond who showed all the promise when it came to theology. Look at his grades at Trinity! But you know all this. Sorry if I'm wandering.

Orr yawned, watched the staves of telegraph wires fall and rise, fall and rise, and beyond, the monotonous midland plain scarcely moving. Parallax, that was called. Opposite him was a route map, *M G W Ry*. He wondered idly where precisely they were. Somewhere between Dromod and Inny Junction, presumably. He glanced at the fob. Problem you might set a geography class. A train sets off from such-and-such a station at such-and-such an hour at such-and-such a speed…

He'd always liked mathematics. The slide rule, for its invention; the log tables, for their precision. Compound interest. Trigonometry. The axioms of Euclid. Something satisfying, there. Eternal truths. If it hadn't been for a nagging fear that one day he might wind up as a chalky pedagogue, he might well have read mathematics at university. But there you are. Law was the safer option.

His forensic eye returned to the photograph. In Portora Royal, he'd been the year behind Edmond Hart. All-round sportsman. Head prefect. And hadn't he been a Trinity "Schol"? All that potential, just to take upon himself the running of a decaying estate eviscerated by the Land Act and devoured by death duties. When he could have made his mark in any one of the professions. When the Dublin parliament was finally restored to this benighted island—and all that was required for that was for the Parliamentary Party to hold firm and demand of Asquith, as a price of their support, that he finally curtail the power of the Lords—there'd be sore need for statesmen of Edmond Hart's calibre.

Gone to seed, rather. Run to fat, too. Why, the man might have been another Edmund Burke if only he'd gone in for law.

No memory of the missing younger brother, who'd have been, what? Four years behind? From the photo, he had that same chestnut glare that Orr found so disconcerting when Katherine looked hard at him. Into him. Sensitive, yes, but with all the smouldering conviction of the martyr. Now the letter had mentioned it, the picture wouldn't have been at all incongruous if Frederick J Hart had been army chaplain.

Sorry if I'm wandering. But even if Father had tried to forbid my enlisting, I mean to say, what could he have actually done? Even if I wanted to join the Royal Inniskillings as our beloved grand-uncle suggested, the days of Cpt Jonathan "Jack" Montagu of the 88th, the "Devil's Own", are long gone, when a commission was there to be bought and paid for.

What I suppose I'm saying is that, beneath all the high spirits and derring-do, which really are infectious you know, I have this constant grind in my gut that, sooner or later—and probably sooner—I'm going to be found out for the imposter that I am. I know it'll sound crazy, but I fear the men—I mean the rank and file—rather more than I fear the enemy. Though chances are, by the time we finally arrive down there, the whole affair will have blown over.

That's all for now, Kit. I looked back at Dublin Bay earlier this evening as we gradually thrummed out to the open sea—the entire ship really does vibrate like a top—and as my eye followed the sweep of land down beyond Bray Head, I think for the first time I really did wonder will I ever see this land again. Not that I wish to sound maudlin. I daresay anyone leaning on a stern rail watching the wake churn backwards is visited by the like feeling. And then, one really does feel one is sailing out to meet the new century! What wonders that is likely to usher in, Kit! To borrow from the immortal Burke, "Bliss it was in that dawn to be alive; but to be young was very heaven."

At this point the writing broke off, leaving the latter part of the third page empty. Reginald Orr looked to the next. 'Day 4' it was headed, to the right hand side. He glanced back to the opening leaf but found no comparable heading.

Day 4

Do you know, it never crossed my mind that I mightn't simply dispatch these musings as I pen them? As though each morning a mail boat might magically draw up alongside. At this rate I'll end up keeping a log of the entire voyage! Though my musings won't finally make the post until we arrive in Cape Town or Durban or wherever it is we're to disembark. Unless word comes that Kruger has backed down, in which case we can all go home! That said, a tar told me we'll likely stop in on the Gold Coast to take on coal. Perhaps I'll get shore leave and the chance to post it on to you then?

Oh—you recall, when I joined up, I mentioned a chap from Enniskerry, Kinkaid? You remember—he's RC. Militiaman. I told you about the almighty rumpus he kicked off when he eloped with the daughter of the Hamilton estate? Yes? So anyway, turns out I'm bunking with Padraic—"Patch" everyone calls him—and a third wheel on the tricycle name of Bertie Nuzum, whom Patch knew when they were growing up. Father a Justice of the Peace, and a big noise in the Wicklow Militia by all accounts. He's one of the few subalterns with actual leadership experience, even if it was just with the same militia. Nuzum fils *is six three in his stocking feet and forever banging his head. Because everything aboard ship, and I mean literally everything, is positively Lilliputian. The three of us share a cabin about half the size of Nana's linen closet, and twice as clammy. Wherever he sits or bunks, Bertie Nuzum's great big toes in their holey socks poke up everywhere! Though at least we officers are accorded a modicum of privacy, you should see where the rank and file have to string their hammocks, not to say do their business. Though even they have it easy compared to the devils in the infernal boiler rooms, begrimed like blackamoors as they feed the great Baal of a furnace.*

Incidentally, do you know how the horses are accommodated? I'd never really thought about it. Well, it seems they're stowed below decks on their transports, stood upright with hammocks slung beneath their bellies so they never get to lie down or skit about—so Nuzum informed us, though I'm not entirely sure I believe him. Looking at the big toe poking out of his sock, Patch Kinkaid said all in all he'd prefer to be down with the horses! Funny thing, I don't think he was entirely joking. There's more than a bit of old Lemuel Gulliver about Patch. Still, it must be pure Bedlam there if the sea gets up.

Speaking of which, we've left sight of land entirely. It's a disquieting sensation, nothing but our tiny convoy in the vast expanse of ocean. Though I daresay we must have lost sight of land for a while that time Father took us on that foray over to the Isle of Man—what year was that? I want to say '92. I remember Cpt Jack was less than impressed. I can still hear him muttering: "Bah! If Charles was so keen for you all to see Douglas, he might just as well have taken you down to Bray and saved the boat fare!" He was far more taken with that old Manx speaker he found—do you remember? She sold us those toffee-apples, and was about twice as old as Methuselah.

Of course if even one quarter of his stories can be believed, Uncle Jack has seen Bengal, Ceylon, Siam, Shangri-La! Remember that yarn he used tell about the Chinese mandarin and the monkey? I wonder was it that Isle of Man trip that made me promise myself to see something of the world? Incidentally, did I ever tell you what Edmond advised, when I told him? "If you're serious, Freddy, you might try out for the Indian Civil Service. Oh and cancel your subscription to Blackwood's, yes?" As if sweltering in some fly-infested office in Delhi as a 'competition wallah' might be anyone's idea of seeing the world! Besides, it was <u>his</u> subscription to Blackwood's. I just had Father renew it every year when it came due.

The concluding lines were in a darker shade of ink, and had the look of an afterthought.

That's all for the present. Much love to Father and Nana— and tell Cook I'd give anything for a jar of her gooseberry preserve. Oh, say to Edmond if he asks, I could find no one among the brass by the name of Lennox. Might be on another of the transports, of course.

Much love,

F.

PS I hope you've left off cheering on the Boer, now they're soon to be taking potshots at your brother?

Orr looked up. Vision of Katherine Hart, that evening at Musgrove's, playing a John Field nocturne. That was the night he'd won them a grand slam in spades at auction whist, and she'd tapped his nose with her fan, 'Clever Reggie!' Had she really cheered on the Boer? Even at the tender age of fifteen it was difficult to imagine, for all that she could be quite a vociferous advocate for women's education and the vote. A thing or two to say about the condition of the tenants, too. Refused outright to ride sidesaddle.

Favoured a gamine hairdo, of course, though that scarcely made her a bluestocking. Suited her, rather. She would have gone herself on this Dublin adventure at the drop of a hat but for the trip out to Achill. To that artists' colony or what-have-you, to close it up for the winter. Had been prearranged months ago. Couldn't simply drop out, apparently, though he was damned if he could see why not. Case of *force majeure*.

They were slowing into Mullingar Station. Here, a Catholic priest entered the compartment with a breviary and a civil nod; then a wheezy woman upholstered like a chair, bearing both an enormous handbag and the myopic scowl of a governess. Unhurriedly, the family solicitor replaced the pages into the envelope and retied the bundle, which he slid, together with his pince-nez, into his inside pocket.

Then, sitting back and closing his eyes, he dozed out the remainder of the journey.

CHAPTER TWO

H is back to the vacant desks, Br Colman watched the dusk thicken over the rooftops. It was his favourite hour, the corridors silent, the clamour of another day spent. The evening air was palpable now, the smoke of a thousand chimneys settling in tawny strata, obfuscating the domes and spires of the city beyond. What was it Swift had said on the subject? 'Burn everything from England but her coal.'

'D'you say something?'

He was surprised not so much by the appearance of young Kinkaid as by the fact that he'd given voice to the thought. 'The immortal Dean,' he pronounced, without turning from the mansard window. He frowned so as to recall the quote correctly. 'Burn everything that comes from England except *their people* and their coal. No doubt your friend Mr Griffith would approve of the sentiment.'

'Wouldn't know, Brother.'

He turned about. 'No?' Was it an effect of the failing light that intensified the boy's pallor? Perhaps it explained his recent absence. In previous years, the school library had been a refuge of kinds. 'You've been unwell?'

'Me?' There was a new shyness, an avoidance of eye contact. 'No, Brother.'

'Then I can only assume our humble *scriptorium* has lost its charms.' He wiped his spectacles on his cassock and approached, screwing his eyes. 'You've been back in the wars, I see.'

Tommy Kinkaid's hand touched defensively jaw and temple.

'The rough tribes of the inner city. They're every bit as fierce as anything in Fenimore Cooper.' He angled the youth's head up with two fingers. Some discolouration. A light swelling. 'They treat you differently. Not one of their own, you see.'

'Wouldn't know, Brother.'

A memory came to him of Mrs Kinkaid. An elegant woman. Genteel, though she did her level best to conceal it. Not quite coarsening the accent; seasoning it with terms picked up locally. 'Your mother's family is from Wicklow, I think?'

'Enniskerry, Brother.' Then he added, as though bothered by it, 'Originally.'

'Well there we are.' Colman O'Kelly nodded, slowly. An only child. The mother a Gaelic Leaguer, too, if Br Aodhán was right in his deductions. Published occasional poems in their ᴄᴌᴀɪᴏʜᴇᴀᴍʜ ꜱᴏᴌᴜɪꜱ under a pen name, what's this it was? He'd have to play that card carefully. He didn't want to chase the young scholar away, now that he'd finally found his way back upstairs.

There was something else he'd heard about the Kinkaids. Military people. What was it, now? Cissie Kinkaid was a war widow. Husband an officer, killed fighting the Boer. Though that on its own wouldn't explain the descent into the north inner city. Had there been some whiff of scandal? Hold on now. Was she a convert, was that it? Or was he mixing her up with somebody else. All a long time ago of course…

Tom Kinkaid was looking up at him.

'What brings you back to my particular eyrie?'

The youth's expression was difficult to read. It lay somewhere between guilt, candour and defiance. When he failed to find words, he reached into his satchel and dug out a book. Staring hard at the floorboards, he proffered it.

A novel. The spine was split, the dust jacket torn. A number of sheaves had come loose, threatened now to spill out. 'I'm not sure I follow.'

'We had confession, earlier on,' muttered the pupil. He seemed to consider it sufficient explanation.

'Go on.'

'I was told to give it back.'

'I see.' He examined the book more closely. On the reverse of the frontispiece, the stamp of the school:

Leabharlann Naomh Eoin baiste
Scoil na mbráichre Críoscaí

Opposite, a dedication to Br Aodhán ó Murchú, in the hand of the author.

'You borrowed this?' he said, doubtfully. 'I've no recollection.'

'I fecked it, Brother.'

'Ah! *Et lux erat.* No remission of sins without first a restitution.'

'Sorry it got kicked asunder. They grabbed it off of me and started flinging it around.'

The Christian Brother laid his fingers alongside the bruises, but this time the youngster flinched as if repelled by the show of empathy. 'And that was what St Augustine would term the *casus belli*?'

'They wouldn't give it back. They kept thrunnin' it from one to another until they made a right bags out of it.'

'Throwing,' he corrected, mildly. 'And so you took an equal battering. Who was the ringleader? Master Kelleher, I have little doubt.' The boy stared hard at the floorboards. 'Schoolboys' code of honour; Mum's the word, eh? And all the while that blaggard gets away with blue murder.' Seeing the flush darken dangerously, he made a show of angling the book, *The Riddle of the Sands*, to the dying light. 'A few stitches and some gum Arabic will see this chap right. Tell me, how did you get on with Davies and Carruthers?'

The boy shrugged. Then, when the silence extended the interrogation, 'I thought it was a bit far-fetched, to be honest with you.'

Br Colman threw his head back and laughed aloud. 'Was it, bedad? Clever, all the same, or wouldn't you agree?'

'Yeah?' The tone suggested he wouldn't agree.

'His use of the word "riddle". A riddle is of course a puzzle, an enigma. But it is, furthermore, a sort of sieve, you

25

see. They use it to separate out the stones from the finer soil… I can see you're not convinced.' He examined the youth. Almost his own height now, but drawn, unnaturally skinny. A diet of thin food and poisonous air. 'What age are you, Tom?'

'Goin' on fourteen, Brother.'

'Are you? Going on fourteen! Well, I wouldn't let Br Aodhán hear your opinion on the plausibility of plot. Mr Childers is a particular friend of his from his time in Kilburn.' He laid the book on a nearby desk. 'I can't condone a theft. But I daresay I can understand the impulse. At your age I was a very devil for adventure stories.' He gripped either hand behind his back, swayed pendulously, frowned as though he were a stage pedagogue. 'What I don't understand in all this, Mr Kinkaid, is what made you "feck" the blessed thing in the first place? Couldn't you have asked leave to borrow it? Isn't that how we operate here?'

A clumsy shrug. 'Don't know, Brother.'

'What don't you know?'

'I couldn't ask to borry it.'

'Oh?'

A flush, visible even as the light died in the room. 'It wasn't the only one I took, Brother.'

'I see.' Br Colman passed the student and, glancing once down the dusky corridor, shut the door. A feeling akin to dread was settling in his stomach. He removed his spectacles and began to polish them needlessly in his cassock. 'Best come clean. How many?'

A shrug.

'Three?' Silence. '*Four*?'

'Maybe a dozen?'

'A dozen!' Taken aback, the old librarian pivoted about and interrogated the bookshelves. 'I had suspected several copies of Sɽᴀɪméᴀɽ nᴀ Sᴀeᴏhɪʅse had gone astray. A Maths primer, perhaps. *The Love Songs of Connacht*. A Wilkie Collins, I think?' He turned back, troubled. 'But a dozen! You're quite sure?'

Another shrug, this one an affirmation.

'You intend to restore these lost sheep in their turn, I hope.'

For the first time, the youth's grey eyes met his own and held them. Again, they were lit by that peculiar mix of candour and defiance. 'I can't, Brother.'

'Oh? And why is that?'

'I sold them.'

'You *sold* them!'

The eyes were back to the floorboards.

'But where? How? I don't understand.' Too many images were cascading through the old man's mind. 'No point in inquiring as to *why*, I suppose.'

'I needed the money.'

'I daresay. For what, pray?'

A third shrug. An angry snort. He'd have to be cautious. 'But you sold them to whom, for heaven's sake?'

'To a booke seller, Brother.'

The entire affair was ludicrous. Had it been anyone but young Kinkaid, he'd have suspected they were taking a rise out of him. 'What "*booke* seller"?'

'Fella who runs a stall. Down under Merchant's Arch, it is.'

'And this *booke* seller, as you term him… wasn't he

bothered that these books were stamped with the school logo?' Unnecessarily, the Brother opened the returned novel and tapped the identifying brand. The silence confirmed his suspicion. 'A scoundrel, then. That's receipt of stolen goods. Tell me. The truth, mind. Was it he put you up to it? Because I've a good mind to march down to your friend the bookseller and confront him with the evidence.'

'He does only be there weekends.'

Never mind the grammar, the tone implied something. 'You mean to say you've done this more than once?'

'One other time, Brother. About a month back it was.'

'I see. And how many…?' He was reluctant to go on. This was too fantastic.

'Twelve is the total, Brother. Twelve not counting the one I gev you back.'

'And a good thing you did. A gift from the author to Br Aodhán. I'm glad to see your conscience at least baulked at that much.'

Was the flush one of shame or resentment? 'It's just I wanted to have a read of it first.'

'Well I have to say I'm surprised. You of all people, Tom Kinkaid.' Twelve books stolen. On two separate occasions. Still, he hesitated to come down hard. 'I'll need, at the very least, a list of the missing sheep. Can you furnish that, do you think?' A new thought took the Christian Brother. A new concern. 'You mentioned these earlier thefts in your confession?'

A nod, penitent.

'Then we'll say no more on the subject.'

The youth nodded harder, still avoiding eye contact, and

was on the point of leaving. 'For your penance, once I've run a few stitches through it, I've a good mind to have you read this chap again, cover to cover and write an essay on its merits.' The quip brought up the hint of a smirk. 'Which reminds me, will you be joining Br Aodhán's excursion on Sunday? He assures us the weather is set to improve.'

For a second time that evening, the boy appeared to flinch.

'A foray back to your native province, near enough? I understand they're meeting up with a couple of other troops at Westland Row Station in time to take the ten twenty-five to Bray. Pity it's not a better time of year. In spring you have all that gorse in full bloom.'

A deep breath. Sharp. 'I won't be going.'

'But why ever not?'

'It's the ma. Dead set against it, she is.'

'Oh?' Might he risk a hint of what Br Aodhán had unearthed? 'I understood your mother was all for the Gaelic revival?'

A guarded look, evaluating. 'She is. But that's as far as it goes.'

'Well then?' Colman O'Kelly could scarcely conceal he was taken aback. Surely Cissie Kinkaid could see the effect the Dublin tenements were having on her son's health? The poetess who'd written of a winter sunset—and really, the case had been strongly made that 'eiLis RuA' was she; after all, she had published that children's book about Dublin's colourful characters—: 'mAr A bheADh LAsADh nA heicinne Ar LeiceAnn nA cAthrAch'. As you might say, *like the flush of a consumptive upon the city's cheek.*

Could the boy be tubercular? It was endemic in this

decaying capital. 'I'd have thought Br Aodhán is the very man for pushing the old language. Isn't that what his excursions are all about?'

'What she's against is all that Baden-Powell stuff goes with it. Marching and drilling like we were soldiers.'

'But the fresh air! The exercise! Perhaps if I had a word with her?'

'Wouldn't do any good. With respect, Brother.'

Should he point out that at least the CBS boys wouldn't be marching behind the Union Jack, whatever other flag Br Aodhán might have them follow? But then, if the father had been killed fighting the Boers…

He dropped his voice marginally. 'If it's a matter of the train fare…'

A mistake. Kinkaid's head tossed upwards like an angry colt's. 'I've to go. I'm sorry for flogging your bookes.'

Br Colman put out a conciliatory hand, but the boy had already departed.

CHAPTER THREE

Reginald Orr glared above his pince-nez at the waiter noisily clearing the plates off the adjacent table. He'd been out of sorts since he'd discovered he'd left his gloves on the train. This gloomy November weather would play hell with his chilblains. Besides, it would necessitate a trip to the Lost Property office.

Foley must have been held up at Kings Inns. Distastefully, he compared his fob to the wall clock. Five minutes' difference. He held the half-hunter to his ear, was reassured by its miniature pulse.

He began, for the umpteenth time, the second of the letters. Undated.

Day 13 (?)

Do you know what Africa is, Kit? Shall I tell you?

Never mind the Daily Mail *map which, I feel sure, Edmond will have spread over the study table, the dark continent resembling a great pork chop stuck with little flags. Africa, my dear, is an endless strip of olive green laid out upon the horizon to separate sea from sky. I'd say that it slips silently by to port (LHS of ship!) except that one has the sensation it never moves. Or it's we who never move. Really, we're insignificant as water fleas attempting to traverse Lower Lough Erne. For three days before we called into Freetown, and for three days after, the continent's coast lurked a steady two leagues off. Most afternoons, it is brooded upon by a heavy armada of thunderheads in battleship-grey, whereas out here the sky remains clear blue. I daresay there's some meteorological explanation—Edmond would know.*

A most unpropitious sight met us after we entered into the harbour, which is something of an archipelago. I hesitated whether to tell you about it. It was just before dawn, our flotilla was at anchor, I was above decks. At about a cable's length, on one of the transports alongside, my attention was drawn to some activity on the deck. Several large bundles were being hoisted up from the hold, then shunted clumsily to the side and dropped overboard. It was the tar beside me explained what these bundles were—horses which had broken limbs the previous day—a wind had got up as we approached the archipelago, delaying our arrival. "They'll make short work for the 'arbour sharks," he informed, with grim satisfaction.

'Patch' got to go on the launch onshore. Said to the C.O. he wanted to pick up some sort of toy or gewgaw for his youngsters—they had the croup before we left, did I mention that already? I trust he got my letter off safely— although the way he described the settlement wouldn't exactly inspire confidence. Everything gone to rot on account of the climate. Natives indolent and watchful, and treated with the utmost contempt by gin-soaked colonials with bloodshot eyes in sweat-soaked linen. I'm not saying he doesn't have an axe to grind, mind. Must be tough leaving a young wife and two "chislers" (sic) behind. And then, I've always suspected ole Padraic has a touch of the Fenian in his blood. Rarely has a good word to say about the Empire upon which the sun never sets. Though I think that's partly to get a rise out of Bertie Nuzum. Bertie's all about how the Empire brings medicine and the law to the uncivilised. Still, it is hard to gainsay the old leprous fort I saw through binoculars on one of the harbour islands, sorry relic from the days of the slave trade. To brighten up those of us stuck on board, an entire flotilla of canoes came alongside, offering every conceivable shape of bizarre and improbable fruit.

One tends to forget—or maybe it's that one never really appreciates—that when it's winter in our part of the world, somewhere else it's high summer. Of course we haven't even begun to arrive down there as yet. But yesterday, we crossed 'the Line', an occasion marked by a bit of a free-for-all. High jinks and horseplay. I was surprised at how tolerant the brass was about it all. Apparently it's a venerable naval tradition. Things grew boisterous as any music-hall burlesque, not to say lubricious—I won't describe what louche use was made of the coconuts! Two weeks spent sweltering in the hold's infernal heat meant there was quite a deal of steam to blow off. The rank and file are only allowed above decks a couple of times a day for exercise and drill, and that strictly by rote, by Company (ask Edmond if you can't remember!). Poor blighters don't even get target practice, which might be of some use against the Boer sharpshooters—it seems the Empress of India is something of a niggard when it comes to her men at arms squandering ammunition.

Now, there's another thing I rather misjudged. To begin with you'll remember I was more than wary of the men. The hoi polloi. *Of course, so far as I'm aware, one does rather rely on the RSM and the NCOs to keep them in line. Did I mention we're sharing the transport with a battalion of regulars—the Dublin Fusiliers? Those corner boys fire fine leers at us mere Yeomen, I can tell you. Ill-concealing their disdain.*

But I think I also told you about two lowbrows assigned to my own Platoon, or should I say Troop (ask Edmond!), who always seem to be sizing me up—one with stuck-out ears and eyes set close together, the other ginger-headed and sly, somewhere between fox and rodent? O'Byrne and Molloy (her Privates, they!). Mea culpa! *It turns out foxy is an apprentice farrier, jug-ears a Trinity student, though I've no recollection of our paths ever having crossed in the quad during my own brief sojourn there. Both well spoken, all things taken into consideration. It took Bertie Nuzum to point out that that's the essential difference where the Imperial Yeomanry is concerned. I knew already that most of the top brass were right toffs— the Earls of Longford and Leitrim, to say nothing of Sir Power's Whiskey himself! It's the Captains and Majors who are on secondment. As for the regular men, far from the dregs and riffraff that traditionally swell Her Imperial Majesty's ranks for a bob a day, when not militia, these recruits have rallied to the flag from out of the aspiring echelons of society—second sons, fox hunters, students, postal clerks, postilions, ostlers, journeymen, jarveys— just so they know their way about a horse! Not that some of them don't curse and swear like tinkers, though one senses that, with them, it's all so much bluff and swagger. Hard to say what precisely motivated them, I daresay each has his own story to tell. But I have to say, it came as quite the relief to find it so.*

Orr blinked about him. They were lighting the lamps. Still no sign of Foley.

He motioned to the waiter for another pot of tea, but even when he wasn't engaged with the gas jets, the blaggard was a past master at avoiding eye contact. Too bad he'd left his portfolio at the boarding house out in Chapelizod. There were plenty of papers for the Land Commission he could have been getting on with.

His eye skipped down half a page to the succeeding entry.

Day 16 (17?)
Quite the buzz about the ship all day. Word is—and the

irony of course is that you'll know all this up in Boyle with far more clarity and detail than any of us poor soldiers actually on our way there!—that Redvers Buller has been stepped down. "Reverse" Buller, Nuzum calls him, which really is rather good. I shouldn't be at all surprised if he has been dismissed. To divide one's force in three, and then have each third part suffer a humiliating defeat, all within the space of a week, that must break all military records! The responsibility for the Colenso fiasco in particular has to be laid squarely at the old duffer's feet. Lost a damn sight of good Irishmen, too. Though the question we're all trying to get our heads around—what might it mean for us? For the campaign? We had been told we'd be operating like dragoons, riding to battle but then fighting on foot. Now it seems there'll be a great deal more scouting and reconnaissance, because that's what let them down in the 'Black Week' engagements. All rather daunting, when you consider that none of us has ever hunted a quarry more dangerous than a fox, and I've yet to meet the fox that could handle a German Mauser!

It's a curious game, estimating how long it'll be before you receive this, Kit. And how much more all of you back in "The Elms" will already know by then. No chance to send it off now before we arrive in the Cape Colony, which is apparently another five days' sail. Then what? Three weeks more for the return voyage? I have this vision of thousands of soldiers' letters gathering on the African coast like migratory birds to wing their way to England and Ireland.—'allo Daphne, blimey it ain't 'alf 'ot round these pa'ts, in parficulah any time the Bore lets fly with his Mauses. Still, mas'n't gramble, eh? best of, your Alf xx.—*As Daphne reads these immortal words, who knows if her beloved Alfred hasn't already 'caught one'—like the light we see from stars which have died thousands of years ago.*

Incidentally, I've been thinking a great deal about what you said re the Dublin Metropolitan School of Art. It strikes me, Kit, you could do a lot worse than

Orr, aware of a minor commotion toward the door, glanced up to see Foley's bowler hat and muffler bearing down on him. He'd brought in with him a whiff of damp and smog from the streets. 'Sorry! Sorry!'

The lawyer smiled thinly, noticed with a modicum of envy the proffered calfskin glove. 'Please,' he said. 'Take a pew.'

'Couldn't be helped,' wheezed Foley, unwrapping the muffler. He really was quite out of puff, would want to keep an eye on that high complexion of his. Too close an acquaintance with *John Jameson*, that was the thing. Too fond by half of the *nunc est bibendum*. Still, they say it's many a good man's failing. This time, Orr did manage to secure the waiter's attention, mimed out two more teas. Darjeeling, yes.

'So?' Foley laid his gloves daintily atop the bowler which he'd balanced on the table. Flopping into the chair he blew out comically, mopped with handkerchief his wide expanse of brow. Thinner on top, perhaps, but the garland of curls about the ears was luxuriant as ever. Flat, pugnacious nose. All told it was a patrician profile which Orr considered wouldn't be out of place on a Roman coin. Quite the reputation about Kings Inns for devilling. RC. What they termed a Castle Catholic.

'So what's this all about?' he gruffed. What appealed was that the man was never one to beat about the bush.

Orr nodded slowly, permitting a thin smile as he pushed across the table the photograph. His colleague lifted it, then queried him with candid eyes made all the bluer by the high complexion.

'Hart, Frederick James.'

'And this was taken?'

'1899. Early 1900.'

Foley examined the cap insignia. 'Imperial Yeomanry.'

'Did well. Mentioned in dispatches. A rising star, by all accounts.'

'Until?'

'Until he went walkabout. Somewhere in the Transvaal.'

'Prisoner, perhaps?'

'Not a prisoner. Absconded. The father received a letter from the C.O., though he couldn't put his hand to it when I asked. The letter talked of disgrace. Dishonourable discharge pending.' Foley's gaze invited him to elaborate. 'If there was a court-martial it was conducted *in absentia*.'

'Charge?'

'Absence without leave?' the lawyer shrugged. 'Then there's failure to obey an order. Conduct unbecoming, at the very least. Seems as if one night he simply rode off. Never returned.' He paused to allow the waiter set down a fresh teapot, then to fooster punctiliously with cups, saucers, teaspoons. The pugilist's mien across the table remained a challenge to read. 'Exhibit B,' his index pushed the picture postcard slowly across the table, 'would suggest the fugitive made his way to Portuguese East Africa.'

'Following in old Kruger's footsteps,' suggested Foley, paying the postcard a cursory inspection—a sepia image of a tramp steamer in a colonial port identified by the photographer as Lourenço Marques; and on the obverse, besides name and address, the single word, '*shameful*'.

'It's the identical hand to his letters,' the family solicitor interjected.

'Kit Hart is his wife, I expect.'

'Sister.'

Foley nodded, grimly. 'A deserter, then, pure and simple.'

'That's what I want you to find out. See under what heavy sentence he lies. One imagines the ultimate penalty would no longer apply.'

Foley looked supercilious. Amused. 'Unless one might consider ten years' hard a death sentence.'

Orr smiled in the manner of one issuing a receipt. 'Service records. Campaign Medal lists. Who do we know in the War Office?'

'Duggan,' shrugged Foley. 'Hendrick.'

'Good.' The solicitor gave the tea a slow stir before pouring. 'One imagines the *Freeman's Journal* will have put in its pennyworth.'

Foley indicated with his brow, 'And the letters?'

'Hart's. They predate the affair.'

'Then why read 'em?'

'One wants to understand one's quarry.'

'A legacy issue.' Foley sat back, tapping his fingertips. The candid eyes were on his, irony illuminating them. 'What's your client's interest in this Hart character?'

'I never mentioned a client.'

Foley hoisted his eyebrows in an interrogatory fashion. Rather than answer the implied question, Orr selected the newspaper cutting, slid this across the linen. 'This would suggest it's not quite old history.'

"'*Fracas Interrupts Liberty Hall Meeting*,'" read his companion.

'Less than a week old, as you see.' Orr's hand, ungloved, invited him to read on.

> "'*There was quite a to-do in Liberty Hall last night when, after Major John MacBride had concluded, the speaker purporting to be Lt. 'H', veteran of the Anglo-Boer campaign albeit from the opposing side, was invited to take the stage. Whether or not it was the officer who had been 'dishonourably discharged' (so the handbill proclaimed, as though it were a singular honour), might now never be known. For the speaker wasn't allowed to speak a solitary word. Before he had the chance, jeers, heckles and whistles arose from a boisterous faction that had evidently been planted in the audience in advance. It took an intervention by the police to restore order to the ensuing mêlée, by which time our presumed Lt. 'H' had absconded—and not for the first time, it would seem! It is suggested the interlopers were supporters of Cecil Havelock-Saunders DSO, who is to stand in Dublin's College Green constituency on the Unionist ticket in the upcoming Westminster Elections.*"

Foley sat back, one eye closing as though the better to take aim. 'A veteran *purporting* to be "Lt H."?'

'Hart, one assumes.'

'Quite,' the junior barrister concurred. 'Scarcely constitutes irrefutable evidence. I mean to say, how many served in that imbroglio in the end? A quarter of a million?'

'Officers?'

'Very well. Shall we agree one tenth the sum? One in *twelve*? That would still leave tens of thousands of candidates whose surname might begin with the letter "H".'

'Ah, but in the first place this man absconded "not for the first time". And in the second, there is the testimony of an eyewitness.'

'Objection! Counsel is introducing new evidence previously undisclosed.'

'Overruled. Though in this case, the witness' account is, shall we say, rather less than conclusive.' Orr sat forward, as though careful not to have their exchange overheard. 'If it is Hart, I suppose he'd face imminent arrest?'

'I seem to remember a general amnesty as part of the peace treaty?'

'For the Boer fighter, yes. It would hardly extend to deserters.'

'I'm not so sure. Do the same rules apply to the Imperial Yeomanry? I understood theirs was a temporary stint.'

'I should imagine the identical rules would apply in wartime.'

'But ten years on. Statute of limitations?'

'Shouldn't like to have to depend on it.'

Foley shrugged. '*De minimis non curat lex*.'

'Meaning?'

'One imagines the Castle has bigger fish to fry.'

'I daresay they have. It's the Provost Marshall I was thinking about.'

'In the wake of all the unpleasantness that Quaker woman unearthed, one would have thought they'd adopt the maxim, "Least said soonest mended". Foreign press had quite the field day.'

'That's figuring without the British Army's talent to shoot itself in the foot. Unless our new King intends a general amnesty. Draw a line under the whole nasty business.' He raised the teacup, set it down untried. 'Damn it all, that MacBride blaggard and his confederates are walking around scot free, aren't they? And what they did was a damn sight worse than desertion. That's treason, in any man's language.'

'And yet,' came the other's rebuttal, 'there are those who call the new Fusiliers' Arch up at St Stephen's Green "Traitors' Gate".'

'Do you tell me so?' Orr made no attempt to conceal his displeasure. 'Fenian agitators, I shouldn't wonder.'

Foley nodded slowly, as though weighing the submission. 'What was it Talleyrand said about treason being a matter of dates?'

Orr eyed him. 'I never took you for a *Sinn Féiner*.'

Foley turned on him one of his shrewd, assessing looks. 'I still fail to see what's your concern in all this.' Had the lawyer winced?

'Let's just say I've a family interest.'

'Indeed?' Coming to a decision, Foley pushed the teacup aside with the back of his hand. He'd scarcely tasted it. 'Have you eaten?'

Orr replied that he had not.

'Splendid. There's a new chef over at that club of yours whom all Dublin is talking about. Paris-trained, by all accounts.' He abruptly rose. 'Shall we?'

CHAPTER FOUR

The boy shrieked aside the sheet of corrugated iron that served for a door to the cellar—probably it had once been a coal bunker or a lumber room, extending as it did under the main building. Smell of dank, of habitation. He heard a whimper, felt a dog's wet nose thrust against his hand. 'Hey, old fella.' A paw pushed out eagerly against his thigh.

He entered on all fours, tentatively. It was difficult to see inside—the single, recessed window, scarcely bigger than a schoolbag, was pasted over with old newspaper. But the tobacco-coloured light filtering through was sufficient to make out that the mattress was unoccupied. The boy tousled the dog's rough mane. 'Where is he, fella? Where's he at, huh?' His eyes took in the kitbag; the shaving mug. The shard of a mirror dully luminescent, a river at twilight. 'Where's he gone, old boy?'

Old hessian sacks carpeted the floor. On wet days the vagrant would throw one over his shoulders. He stooped down by the tea crate that served for a table. A tin mug; a pewter plate. A wine bottle ivied with wax was a makeshift candleholder. From his pocket he drew out several candle stubs. These he laid out—there were three—then a stack of coppers that amounted to the princely sum of $9\frac{1}{2}^{\text{d}}$.

He glanced behind him toward the doorway, but the only eyes upon him were canine. He then went to the mattress and knelt. Tacky smell, as though something acrid had been smoked. He lifted a corner and patted underneath until his palm encountered an envelope. This he withdrew, angled it to the light from the doorway. Manila, foolscap, containing a number of sheets closely and messily written. He opened his coat, tucked it beneath his shirt, buttoned up the coat. Before he left, he took from his satchel a pencil stub and a scrap of paper. He licked the lead, considered, then returned pencil and paper unused. Time enough. 'Tell him,' he said to the dog as he was replacing the corrugated iron sheet, 'tell him I'll see him again, yeah?'

It was dark by the time he got to the flat above the huckster shop on Lower Dorset St. Though he'd had his own key from the time he'd entered secondary school, he found the door on the latch. She was always doing that! He closed it behind him, shot the bolt, listened as the patter of the typewriter upstairs came to an attentive halt. 'That you, Tommy?'

'It's me, Ma.'

What was it she wrote, that she kept it locked away in a drawer? She'd never give him a straight answer. Beside the Underwood typewriter sat a copy of Edward O'Reilly's

45

Irish-English Dictionary. But why all the stealth? She was the last person who'd be involved with a secret society. When he was small, she'd written a book which bore his name in the dedication. *Tales of Old Dublin Town.* You'd still find it in Eason's in the run up to Christmas. Stories of Zosimus, the blind street-bard; of the Hellfire Club; of Copper-faced Jack; of Billy in the Bowl. But his favourites had always been the ones she'd dreamt up specially for him: how the Northside gang consisting of Brogans, Gogans, Logans, Hogans, Grogans and Wogans always outwitted the Southside gang of Borans, Morans, Lordans, Forans, Dorans and Horans. He loved those, though he'd be loath to let on now to any of his classmates.

He waited for her to appear at the top of the stairs. Perhaps a minute passed before she did so. 'Where have you been?' She had that faraway look, as she always did when the writing was flowing. 'Down bothering that oul tramp, I suppose.'

'I wasn't.'

'I told you. I don't want you going next or near him. Do you hear me?'

'I wasn't,' he repeated, with more conviction.

'Go on with you.' He could tell her mind was elsewhere. 'There's the mutton stew from yesterday in the pot. Put it onto the stove, love.' She turned, then added, an afterthought, 'I'll be in in a minute.'

He removed from under his shirt the envelope, which he slipped into his satchel. He then climbed the stairs, traipsed into the living area, dropped his satchel onto the table. The room was in shadow, but he hesitated to light the oil-lamp. He'd always found something in semi-darkness that was agreeably disquieting. The half-light, Mr Yeats called it. That was from 'Aedh Wishes for the Cloths of Heaven', one of his mother's favourites.

With a tongs he opened the door of the stove. Mound of pale ash. How like her! He combed through the grey bitter feathers until he'd discovered a glow-worm, cherry red. This he fed with newspaper and kindling until he'd coaxed out a flame, a wing of light emerging from a dull chrysalis.

'What are you doing, moping there in the dark?' His mother advanced into the room, made directly for the lamp. 'Giv'us over a light there, would you?'

'With all your writing, Ma, you let the fire go out again.'

'Smart Alek! For your information it wouldn't have gone out if you'd've been home when you were supposed to be.'

'We were having confessions.'

'Confessions, if you don't mind.'

'Well? Didn't yous Protestants have confession and you growing up?'

'Aren't you terrible clever?'

Warmly, he handed her a lit taper which she touched to the wick of the lamp, then replaced the soot-streaked chimney. He admired how the growing yellow gilded her features. With her copper hair, she was still a handsome woman. 'That's what has me late, anyhow,' he said. 'The remission of sins.'

'You didn't go looking for our friend after, I suppose.'

'I didn't see him, no.'

'You promise.' She looked directly at him. 'Tommy? You promise me?'

'I'm hardly going to lie to you and I only out of the confession box.' He bit at the quick of his thumb. 'I just don't see what's so *wrong* with talking to him, is all.'

'Don't you now? Because I said so. Isn't that reason enough for you?' She lifted the lid of the pot, broke with her finger the white film of grease on its surface.

'When he knew Da. Mam? He was actually *there* when Da died.'

'Is that what he told you?'

'That's what he told *you*.' Her back was to him. 'That's what he told *you*, Ma.' No reaction. 'I was sitting over there when he said it, so I was.'

She lifted the pot between her forearms, manoeuvred it onto the stove.

'It's cold,' he sighed. But she wasn't paying any heed. 'It's cold, Ma. You have to give it a chance to catch.' Then, trying to keep his tone casual, he queried, 'you're going out tonight, yeah?'

'Meeting's tomorrow night, love' she said. 'I told you that.'

His voice, in asking, had given nothing away. 'You think that stew might be warmed up by then?'

She ignored this. 'Look Tommy.' She straightened up, her hands pushing into the small of her back. 'I want you to steer clear of that man. Anyway, you shouldn't be going anywhere next or near that part of town. I told you that a hundred times. There's bad people lives there.'

He sat up, brightly. 'You mean prostitutes, mother?'

'Don't get fresh! But promise me. You won't go down there. You won't try to see him any more. Alright?' She turned. 'Alright, love?'

'But you still haven't explained to me. Why not?'

'Because I said so.' She shook her head. 'Because he's

only an oul sponger is all he is, scrounging around after hand-outs.' Her eye narrowed. 'Don't think I don't know what happened to that steak and kidney pie last Sunday.'

'What do you mean?'

'Oh, innocent Amy! Only letting on to eat it, you were. Don't think I don't know where the rest wound up. Inside that bloody layabout. Him and his bloody mongrel.'

'He's no layabout, Ma. For your information, he takes any sit he can get so he does. Night watchman when he can get the work.'

'Aye. Throwing drunks out of the shilling houses on Purdon Street. Is that a job?'

'He's down the docks any morning there's a collier needs unloading. He just has to wait for the nod from the gaffer like everyone else.'

'Is he, 'faith? Then why can't he go by his real name? Why does he gad about letting on he's Joe or Jim or whatever the hell he calls himself?'

'There's enemies he has to lie low from.'

'Aye. Creditors would be nearer the mark.' She opened the stove door, flung in a shovel load of lignite that erupted a billow of fine grey dust into the gloom.

'Wait, can't you? You'll put the bloody thing out.'

'Don't you "bloody" me, Tom Kinkaid!'

He waited for the space of two breaths. 'You have to wait until it catches.'

'Look. Just do it for your oul wan, and leave it at that. Can you do that much for me?'

'But he knew Da.' She wouldn't meet his eye. Always a warning sign. 'They were in the army together.'

'Well?' She was readying her dart. 'And if they were? Because I'm telling you, I won't stand by and have anyone filling up your head with notions. Isn't it enough your father was killed in the war without you following after him?'

'No one's following after him.' She was close to the point, he could tell. The point where she'd march off into her room, and for days after he'd be on the receiving end of her silence. 'There's no one following after him, Ma.'

But she wasn't quite there yet. 'Look at Bertie Nuzum, came home with his face put back together like a jigsaw puzzle. Is that what you want? To be stuck up in a bedroom with the curtains drawn, afraid to go out until after it's dark?'

'Mother.' He spoke quietly, could hear his own breath rise and fall like an agitated sea. 'There's no one following him anywhere.' Her gimlet stare was upon him, daring him to go against her. 'It's just, I'd like to know what kind of a man my father was. What's so strange about that?' He peered at the top of the Welsh dresser where stood, alongside the photo of baby Nancy, the honeymoon picture taken in Skerries harbour. 'What's so terrible in that? D'you know something funny, I've never seen a single photo of Da in uniform. Why *is* that?'

She frowned into the twilight. 'You're such a boy.' She lifted the lid. She replaced the lid. She felt the stove with her palm. She took away her palm. Evidently, the stove was still cold. The chill of November had begun to muster in the shadows flexing about the room. Or, it was only now that they were aware of it.

'I've told you about your father. Tom? I've told you about your father.'

'Yeah.'

50

'Everything that's worth knowing,' she insisted. In the lamplight her eyes were aglint with the familiar memory. Her head moved from side to side as she recited. 'Patch had such a way with horses, I think that's why my father was so fond of him. Why he took it so bad, when... He'd taken him on as a stableboy when he wasn't that high. Used to play at hussars and the seventh cavalry with my brother, Billy. And young Bertie Nuzum, any time he was over from Delgany. When my father had him race his first point-to-point, he was younger than you are now.' Her breath snagged on the retelling. 'Horses were always his first love, he could never stand to be away from them for long. We only ever came a close second. If we can't go out to Enniskerry to see my people so they can tell you what Padraic Kinkaid was like, I'm sorry. Truly, I am. But that's how it is. That was the choice we made. Mine as much as his. My father made that much abundantly clear. We made our bed. Now we may lie in it.'

He considered for a moment. 'But why...'

'Please!' In the lamplight her face looked drawn, the fine lines etched with a heavier hand. An image came to him, how, when first she was promoted to front of house from the workshop at the back of the milliners, she used come home wearing the most outrageous and elaborate hats. How she'd put on the accents and manners of everyone who came into the hat shop so as to entertain him—she was a ferocious mimic. Once, when he was maybe four or five, he'd gaped in wonder at the shop window. She'd told him it was filled with exotic birds escaped from the aviary in Dublin Zoo.

'Please, Tom. Can we leave it at that? For this night of our Lord, can we leave it at that?'

He rose, gave her a tired hug. Her arms remained by her sides. Then he made a show of feeling the top of the stove and, letting on it was red hot, he shook his hand and blew on it.

'I suppose the jaunt out to Bray on Sunday with the school is out of the question?'

CHAPTER FIVE

At the Pillar his companion took his leave of him.

Reginald Orr was unused to the glow inside. The general sense of...? Unreality. Wooziness. Foley really was a martyr to the ball of malt. Called to the bar, one might make a pun of that. Would want to watch it all the same, else he'd find he'd acquired a reputation that would be the very devil to shake.

From the shadowed portico of the GPO eructated the bawl of a drunk, some ballad about how he'd bested the recruiting sergeant. Orr was glad of the silent company gathered around the Pillar awaiting their rides home. He looked up the thoroughfare as far as the Rotunda, taking in the wires stretched overhead, past the scaffolding where they were putting up their monument to the Chief. All was empty, compared to the clang and clamour of earlier. The city really had changed from the time he'd been a law student. Motorcars, for one thing, were common enough now that they no longer startled the horse traffic. And the trams hummed and sparked. Whatever else you might say about William Martin Murphy, he was a man of energy. Had the vision to amalgamate the tram companies. And with his grip on the newspapers, he had the guile to get that vision across. Now, if they could just get the parliament back, that'd inject some real life into the place. Landed money, and all that went with it. Never mind that they abutted some of the worst slums in Europe, after all, Kings Inns was squeezed between the King St tenements on one side and Henrietta St on the other. If he had Dublin clients, he'd be advising them to invest around Rutland Place, Mountjoy Square, Great Britain St, North Great George's St. All those less than salubrious addresses that once upon a time had been so respectable.

He peered at his half-hunter. Ten fifty-two. Not so bad. Tram would have him back in the boarding house this side of half past eleven. He rubbed at his long fingers, which had begun to itch. Those damned gloves. He'd have to call in at the Lost Property on the morrow. A pang seized him, a belt of wind. Too liberal with their damned garlic. Never agreed with him. A laugh echoed, female, and for the briefest moment he felt it was aimed at him. But it was just a couple, out for a late stroll. Then over beyond Clery's, English accents. Ricochet of coarser laughter. Tommies on their way up to Monto.

Soon enough, the city's underworld would begin to emerge. Be a rum thing, a chance encounter with this Hart character. There'd be a story to bring back to Katherine! But then, would he recognise him after a decade of vagabonding, there was the point.

Turning back around, his tram was there.

In Chapelizod, he was shadowed along the pavement by a cat. A tin can rattled down an empty side street, though there was scarcely wind enough to drive it. He shivered, and it wasn't merely the cold rising up from the river. Every cat is grey in the dark. Who was it had said that, now? Wilde, he supposed. Or Bernard Shaw?

He'd had the queerest sensation as the tram rattled past the Royal Barracks on Albert Quay. A premonition? Effect of those whiskeys, more likely. He wasn't used to them.

The landlady, who'd waited up, suggested a cocoa, which given the chill would be most welcome. He settled into an armchair by the hearth in the guestroom to await its arrival. In the grate the greying embers were still warm. As was the room. All chintz and china, too fussy by half. He leaned his head back into the antimacassar and he must have dozed because he was woken by the landlady's hand on his forearm. Marvellous. Thank you. Very kind.

As much to stop himself nodding off as anything else, he reached into his pocket for the pince-nez and bundle of letters. The photo he had, for the present, entrusted to Foley. It took several iterations to locate the paragraph where he'd earlier left off.

the light we see from stars which have died thousands of years ago.

Incidentally, I've been thinking a great deal about what you said re the Dublin Metropolitan School of Art. It strikes me, Kit, you could do a lot worse than have a tête-à-tête with Auntie Vickie, next time she's home from

Brittany. Father might dismiss her as a "Sunday painter and dilettante", but I imagine that's because she always carries in with her that aura of scandal and independence. You do know she took lessons with Sarah Purser? Anyway, just a thought, though I still maintain the Royal Irish Academy of Music would be playing to your stronger suit.

Vickie Bowman. Not their aunt, of course. Their late mother's first cousin, was it? He'd been introduced to her at that exhibition. That gallery in Carrick, what's this it was called? Time they'd made a day of it. Had she an aura of scandal about her? Independence, yes. But any moneyed spinster dressed in tweeds exudes an aura of independence. Perhaps, ten years ago...

He recalled not thinking much of the paintings. Too out of focus for his taste. Altogether too free with the palette. No sense of control, which is surely the first thing one looks for in a work of art.

He rubbed his eyes. Stifled a yawn. Landlady really had loaded the cocoa with sugar.

the light we see from stars which have died thousands of years ago.

Read that before. Really, his concentration was wandering.

What hadn't been determined, of course, what hadn't been thought through, was what precisely he was meant to do if and when he did come across this Frederick character. Convince him to make the trip out to Roscommon? How was he expected to do that? There was the small matter of the legacy, but all in all he'd rather leave news of that to Katherine. He might ask him at the least to write home, even if under an assumed name? But then, if he was minded to send such a letter, he hardly needed to be coaxed to do so. Would all rather depend. What was it he'd done, that led to that word, *shameful*?

He glanced at the newspaper cutting. A telegram had alerted Edmond to it: *irish times bottom page three*. Same character who'd sent a letter the week before, saying that they thought they'd spotted 'Fred' shambling along Sir John Rogerson's Quay. There was another visit he'd have to make.

Tickle at the end of his nose. He sniffed, daubed it with a handkerchief. Now that would be all he needed.

Foley had said something of interest. It was after their meal. That new chef with his French fads would play havoc with his digestion by-and-by, but for the present, the second tumbler of whiskey—one could scarcely call it a *digestif*—had suffused him with a fiery sense of wellbeing. Foley confided, dropping his voice because the Kildare Street Club was such a nest of die-hard Unionism and he was, after all, a Catholic Orr had had to sign in, that he'd recently had a number of encounters with Cecil Havelock-Saunders. He of the newspaper article. Councillor, collector of cess and of bad debts, and one pitiless bastard. Look into his eyes, they're the dead eyes of a pike. Major Havelock-Saunders, retired, Fifth (Irish), though he couldn't swear to the regiment. Unpleasant character from head to toe. A bully and a bigot. Maybe not quite another Major Sirr, but no compunction whatsoever when it came to not sparing the rod. All sorts of unsavoury rumours had followed him home from the war. The point being, if it was his coterie who'd been planted in Liberty Hall to prevent 'Lt. H' speaking, what did that say?

Well, that was one for the morrow. Orr took a final sip of tepid cocoa, to make some sort of show that he'd appreciated it. A shiver racked him as he stood. It really had turned cold.

The following morning, over breakfast, he resumed his reading. He selected the third of the letters. Undated. Of course it was.

A drip on his nose and a ticklish throat. Be-damned if he wasn't coming down with something.

Well, Kit, finally I'm seeing something of the world!

The view on the approach to Cape Town is really something to behold. Imagine a proscenium arch with the entire backdrop taken up by the most marvellous mountain. Think Ben Bulben, but on a truly epic scale. For however long I get to live, I doubt I'll forget that image. Another thing I hadn't expected—for about an hour after we'd disembarked, it was as though the land under our feet were in constant motion; it was the ship that had been steady.

I have to say I've begun to pity poor old Kruger. Seems as if the entire British Empire has been assembled in the port to put him back in his box—troopships from Australia, New Zealand, from India, Canada, and the deuce knows where. We must outnumber the poor farmers ten to one, with wharves and sheds stacked to the rafters with boxes of ammunition, crates of provisions, spare wagon wheels, fodder for the horses. I've even seen great bales of barbed wire. Nothing is being left to chance this time round, that's for sure.

The rumours were true about Landsdowne giving

Buller the old heave-ho, by the by. Seems he took another pasting on his way to relieve Ladysmith. A ridge called 'lookout', or Spion Kop—old news by now of course, I imagine Edmond will have it marked on the map? So the Grand Old Fool marched his men up to the top of the hill, but when he marched them down again he left hundreds lying and dying where they fell. Advanced in the dark, but dawn found them in plain sight of the enemy, with not so much as a rock or a tree for cover. It's one thing to make your name shooting down the Zulu with their spears and shields of animal hide, quite another to try it against a foe armed with the latest German Mausers and Krupp's field artillery. A right bloody shambles, by all accounts.

It's not quite as hot as I'd been led to expect. But then, I suppose we're past the height of summer down here. It was far hotter along the Gold Coast, that much I can vouch for, particularly on days when there was little or no wind. That said, we've been told in no uncertain terms, once out in the field, however hot and dry it gets, the men are 'not' to be permitted to take untreated water from riverbeds or waterholes. It must be boiled first, then left to cool. Rife with parasites and enteric, it seems. I wonder if the same applies to the horses.

Which reminds me, I've a piece of gossip for you! I know you've never actually met them, Kit, but I feel as if you do actually know them. I mean of course Patch Kinkaid and Bertie Nuzum. I think I told you Patch had been all his life a stableboy? I should think Cpt Jack would give a great deal for an hour's chitchat with him; he knows the form and the pedigree of every racehorse in Ireland!

So yesterday, Sunday, we had a day's leave. But even so, Patch actually 'volunteered' to remain with the horses; those that had received cuts and strains and bruises in the course of the long voyage. He really has quite a way with them, and the C.O. was delighted. That left Bertie and myself free to take out a couple of geldings for the day. We took them up the flank of Table Mountain—my God, Kit, the view out over the Southern Ocean, which seems to stretch on for ever! Agreeably cooler, too. But that's not what I wanted to tell you about.

It was the first real chance I've had to chat with Bertie on his own, and my goodness, the man can talk for Ireland! You remember I told you he and Patch grew up together? By which I mean, as kids they knew each other. Played jousting knights and "cowboys and injuns" on occasions the Nuzums were visiting the estate. So now it appears they were both sweet on the same girl! Lt Albert Nuzum was altogether open about it. And not just any girl, either. It was Elspeth Hamilton—you remember, Kit! She's the girl Padraic Kinkaid ran off with, that gave rise to all that hullabaloo! Bad enough she was the daughter of his employer. But, as I'm certain I wrote you, Patch is RC. And so 'she's' the Mrs Kinkaid he's left behind him, looking after the two 'sick chislers'! He's always referred to his missus as 'Cissie', so it took me a minute to make the connection.

Bertie never mentioned if he'd ever made his feelings known to her, by the by. Though he did say that Patch was aware. Naturally I was loath to ask. But do you want to know the cream of it? Have a guess who served at their wedding as witnesses! Nuzum himself and his sister Dorothy. And the cherry on the cake is that it was Bertie's old man, Stanley Nuzum SC, who made the necessary arrangements for Patch to get fast tracked into the Yeomanry. He'd been pretty much Bertie Nuzum's factotum in the Wicklow militia, but never an officer. There! Now you won't be able to complain I never send you any gossip. Why, there's enough in that for a novel by your Emily Lawless!

I can't tell you what it was precisely—and perhaps the wonderful view had its part to play—but Nuzum's story filled me with a sense of elation. I've never had a girl of course—you, my dear, would have been the first to know. But there was something in his story, in the vagaries of it and the manner in which they'd navigated those choppy waters, that stirred me with a feeling akin to love for these rough companions I've been thrown together with. I tried without much success to explain it to Edmond in his letter. I've had another couple of days to chew it over since then.

Funny, it hadn't occurred to Orr that Fred Hart might have written also to Edmond at this early stage. To Charles Hart too, probably. Later on, she'd said, after he'd left off writing to her, their father would receive and read out a dry, monthly missal. But would they have held onto correspondence from a disgraced brother and son for the better part of ten years? That was more a woman's part, an adoring little sister's.

I told you before that I felt an imposter in this uniform and I'm afraid I haven't managed to shake that. I've looked more closely at my two companions to ascertain what it is about them that inspires confidence that 'here be soldiers'. Officers, too. An eye of cold command, isn't that what Shelley calls it? Older than me by a couple of years, but beyond that? Kinkaid is every inch the horseman of course. Gentle, but a tough build backing up his gentleness. Muscles like knotted rope. Not a character you'd want to go ten rounds with I can tell you. Whereas at six three, Nuzum is ungainly for a rider. And skinny as a Quixote! A "pull-through for a rifle", Patch calls him. So why is it that he, too, is every inch a soldier?

I realise it scarcely applies—I did turn twenty on the voyage, though I managed to keep that one under my hat for fear of the high jinks that might ensue—but I always seem to come back to that maxim Cpt Jack came up with. You might be too young to remember? It's the time Father was lost in a slough of despond, the year after Mother died. I can still see it clearly, can still smell the sweet smoke from Cpt Jack's briar. They were in the music room, Father standing by the piano, and I remember Edmond was there. 'Charles,' said the Captain, in that fine, thespian voice of his, 'it's high time you stopped behaving as a man who thinks "I've never been this old before", and began acting as one who realises, "I'll never be this young again".'

I do hope you like the orchid? It reminded me of the plant we came across that day in the Botanic Gardens up in Belfast.

'Are you alright for another drop of tea, sir?'

Orr looked up.

'Another cut of toast, maybe?'

Beyond the landlady, he took in that the breakfast area had emptied long since. A tickle; a snuffle. Vexed, he reached for his handkerchief.

'I hope you didn't catch a dose and you out last night, sir?'

Orr blew his nose, waved away the suggestion with the hanky.

'D'you know what I do take for that? A powders in hot water with a teaspoon of honey.' She squinted an eye, approximating a wink. 'Only I do put a sup of gin in with it.' She was leaning in just a little too familiarly over the table. 'Will I fix you one, sir? It'd be no trouble.'

His eye ran to the Dresden clock on the mantelpiece. 'Rather early in the day, no?'

'That would of never stopped my Harry, God have mercy on him. He took a snifter first thing in the morning every day of his life he did and it never done him any harm. Never missed a day's work in his life. Swore by that snifter, he did. He'd be alive today God have mercy on him if he hadn't of stepped out in front of an omnibus and he going to cross the North Circular Road. That's what finished him. Nineteen hundred and three that was.'

She remained uncomfortably proximate. She appeared to be waiting for something. Should he extend his sympathies?

'Well? Will I fix you one, sir?'

Orr waved a hand over the debris of his breakfast to intimate he was finished, and made to rise. A wave of dizziness broke and ebbed. 'Perhaps later.'

CHAPTER SIX

The old soldier in the long scarlet tunic looked every inch a Chelsea pensioner. Ramrod straight despite what he wryly termed 'the accumulation of *anno domini*'. They were seated on a bench not far from the Magazine Fort. The trees of the park were still touched with late autumn. Far too cold today to provide hidey-holes for courting couples.

Remarkably, his eyesight had remained so clear he required spectacles neither to peruse the letters he'd been handed, nor to admire the view across the valley to the Royal Hospital Kilmainham. Swore he could make out the time on the clock face, though Foley suspected there was more than a touch of Baron Munchausen about this gent.

First contact with the enemy! Not with the kommandos *of the field, though. One never sees them apparently—so*

veterans have informed us with grudging respect—firing
from out of dikes or behind rocks and kopjes with their
confounded smokeless ammunition. Or sending volleys
out of the elephant grass before melting like smoke back
into the veldt. No, this contact was with a couple of
extended families, seated by the side of the track. Silent
as statues. Watchful. No men. No males at all, if it weren't
for one toothless old-timer (who sat stock still in a rocking
chair!) and behatted youngsters with faces stern beyond
their years. And a gummy granny with a pipe stuck in her
gob and skin like tobacco leaf.

*They don't quite look like us. I don't know what it is.
Snub nosed. Eyes wider apart. Fair-skinned and blond, but
with all the accumulated effects of wind and sun and hard
living; with their dour Calvinism and guttural speech,
and enormous waggons drawn by a dozen oxen. But do
you know the strangest thing of all, Kit? The headgear
of the women! It's every bit as elaborate as those Breton
women that Auntie Vickie Bowman used to paint. Like an
apron piled up in a sort of double tier, as striking as any
nun's wimple. And antique, as though they'd stepped out
of a Dutch genre painting by—who is it again you're so
keen on? I must see if I can locate a photograph to send
you when finally we get to Bloemfontein. Our hosts have a
most discourteous habit of ripping up rails and wrecking
bridges, so that sometimes we're held up for days on end.*

*The country too is like nowhere else. Not that we
ever stray far from the railway. Everything is so vast. So
wide—the land, the sky. The trees are different. Tougher,
I think, and sporadic, and stratified like those clouds you*

sometimes get lying in layers across a sunset. I haven't seen any of the big beasts—lion, elephant, giraffe. Sometimes, startled by our clamorous approach, skittish deerlike creatures will dart away from the stunted thorns and shrubs they chew on, and yesterday I did see a comical warthog lead a trail of tiny mechanical piglets from a waterhole. Our horses won't eat the scrub that grows here in place of grass, that's one of the reasons we can't stray far from the supply trains. The other of course is water. Though trying to stop the men from lapping from any muddy 'stroom' or 'meer' we happen upon without first boiling the water has proved a task beyond Hercules. That's just one more advantage the Boer farmer enjoys— his ponies are to the manor born, bred out of this parched scrubland, freeing the kommando *to wander it at will.*

The farther into this vast land we venture, the more I incline to your view, Kit. After all, what the deuce do I know about the 'Zarps' and 'uitlanders' and their blessed rights? To listen to Patch Kinkaid (and there's scarcely any avoiding that!) the whole sorry affair comes down to a shameful grubbing for gold—after all, prior to the Rand gold rush and in the wake of the last scrap, Transvaal and the Orange Free State were granted full secession rights. He puts the whole imbroglio down to imperial hubris driven by the vaulting ambition of Chamberlain—whom I seem to remember Edmond once dubbed 'Chichester for an age of steam and steel'. You should see him taking off old Joe Chamberlain, with a halfcrown stuck in his eye for a monocle! Funny as any Punch *cartoon. And here in Africa, as Patch says, all roads lead to Rhodes.*

SCORCHED EARTH

Incidentally, you remember Messers O'Byrne and Molloy? The student and the apprentice farrier I was so wary of? Well Pvt O'Byrne, he of the close eyes and stuck-out ears who was reading Earth Sciences at Trinity before heeding the call, has developed into quite the confidant, so much so I'm putting him forward for the rank of Lance Corporal. Soft spoken chap, hails from Mullingar originally. Very interesting on the geological history of this vast land, can read layers of rock the way you or I might read pages of a book, and a book a great deal older than the Bible, at that. A most interesting way of seeing the world. Coal, for instance. He told us that coal was laid down by ancient forests, millions of years ago. So that when we burn coal, we're actually releasing sunlight that has been trapped there in the rock for aeons. Think of that! Anyway, have a guess how he says the men of 'B' Company refer to us? I mean by 'us' of course the subalterns: Nuzum; Kinkaid and myself. So we're the Three Musketeers, it would appear. Now I wonder which is Porthos, which Athos and which Aramis?

Not exactly everyone's idea of a d'Artagnan, but we have temporarily acquired a fourth musketeer. A little hop-o'-my-thumb with wire-framed glasses and hair that stands on end like the Last of the Mohicans. Seriously, I doubt he's more than four foot eleven, though round as a turkey-cock and every bit as ferocious! Name of Aloysius Terence Wall. No such thing as calling him Al or Terry. Though he will permit "Ay Tee", as though he wants to be taken for another "Tay Pay" O'Connor! War correspondent. Freelance, he proclaims with belligerent pride, though Cpt Plunkett told us his expenses are picked up by the Pall Mall Gazette. *Which is curious—he's no more English than I am! In any event, he's been handed over to 'B' Company, "the Dublin's", for safe-keeping, until such time as we march into Bloemfontein, and who knows, maybe onward to Pretoria and the relief of Mafeking. I only hope he can ride a horse!*

He has regaled the three of us with a number of accounts he's had from veterans on rotation or recuperating from their injuries. One in particular will amuse you. It involves a couple of Scottish Highlanders. It seems they were on a picket, somewhere north of the Orange river. Just before dawn they were surprised by a section of Boers. Now what do you think those rough fellows did with them? You must take into account, they weren't in a position to take prisoners along with them. So they had the two Highlanders strip as naked as the day they were born, and then, once the sun came up, they had to walk barefoot back as far as their lines, with not so much as a tam o'shanter to spare their blushes! Well, Kit, what do you think of that for military justice? One can only hope that story hasn't made the Illustrated London News*!*

Foley examined the old soldier as he read, his lips moving silently as prayer. It was a principle of his to be as generous as possible when it came to proffering trivial and extraneous material. Helped to foster trust, a sense of reciprocal obligation. Of *quid pro quo*.

He'd exceeded the allotted biblical span of three score

and ten. So he had declared right at the outset, with a wryness that scarcely concealed some sort of challenge that underlay it, as though he dared you to believe yet would be disappointed if you did. "Nothing left now to look forward to but the 'age of the slippered pantaloon'." Fine head of hair all the same, colour of old ivory. Long face, lean as a greyhound's. Whiskers curled up like musical notation.

'Meant to ask,' he interrupted him. 'A chap you might know from the Kildare Street Club.'

'Kildare Club?' The eyes, incongruously childish, opened wide. He drew from his pocket what he'd termed earlier his 'briar', and all the time he was talking, his thumb worked carefully to tamp down fibres of tobacco into its bowl. 'Did you ever hear the story of a famous billiard game took place there? You didn't? Around the time all that fuss was being made over the Light Brigade. Which was an out and out disaster, when looked at with a cold eye. This game of billiards was between myself and a chap name of Stanhope. Daniel Stanhope. "Black Dan" they called him. Card sharp. Bit of a rogue. Rumour was, he'd fought a duel, right here in the Phoenix Park. Had to take a year out on the continent until the affair blew over. I'll get to the point. Cut to the chase.

'We'd had a falling out, myself and Black Dan. Girl at the back of it. Actress. No need to go there. What the wager came down to—the stake on our famous game, I mean: one of us would have to quit the field. And to make quite certain of the victor winning the day and the spoils that went with it, the loser would join up. Take a commission. There was quite a deal of excitement in the air at the time.' His free hand began to beat out a tattoo, '*Half a league, half a league, half a league onward, into the Valley of Death rode the six hundred...* Now, when word of the stake got around, the entire club crowded in to watch. Elbow room only, and scarcely a breath of air, so closely were they packed in to watch. Atmosphere tense as any cockfight.

'Of course, what I hadn't factored in, a bit of a dead-eye when it came to wielding the cue, old Stanhope. "Abandon Hope", I should have called him. Pretty soon it was cannons to the left of him, cannons to the right, I can tell you.'

'Very good!' Foley rewarded the quip with a full and resonant laugh. '*Veerry* good!' The principle of generosity extended to laughter. Simultaneously his mind was running a calculus. Did the dates stack up? Balaclava would have been, what? Fifty-five years since?

'I was no slacker myself. Made a decent showing. But to cut a long, involved and rather dramatic story short, two days later I caught the train to Sligo—it's where my people hail from. And that's how I came to serve. Connaught Rangers; the 'Devil's Own'. Still talked about in the Club, I shouldn't wonder. Can't say if Stanhope wound up with the girl, I never cared to find out.'

Foley nodded his impressive head, a show he appreciated a good anecdote. His story concluded, the raconteur put a match to the bowl of his briar and drew severally until the fibres had caught. 'I'd imagine you still have an idea of the membership? This man I was referring to...'

Captain Jack Montagu emitted a sound that was curiously like a whinny. 'Can't help you there, I'm afraid. Blackballed, you see.'

'Really?'

'Oh yes! Back in ninety-two.'

'May one ask why?'

'Little disagreement over an ivy leaf in my lapel.' He inhaled meditatively, the briar emitting a curlicue of blue smoke.

'I see. Well, perhaps you came across this character in military circles? I'm referring to Cecil Havelock-Saunders.'

One eye narrowed. 'The politico?'

'*Ecce homo*. Retired Major. DSO.'

'Is he?' The old soldier considered this. 'Knew the father. Managed a couple of estates for absentee landlords up around Sligo, Fermanagh. Cute as a Kerry fox. Sold a deal of horses to the regiment down the years, and knew more tricks than any tinker, I can tell you. But he ran those estates with an iron fist.' The old man's fist came down onto his thigh. 'Reputation for utter ruthlessness. Rack-renting. Forced evictions. Nasty piece of work all round.'

'It's not far from the tree the apple falls.'

'How so?'

'The son. Cute as a Kerry fox. Nasty piece of work all round.'

The retired captain gave him an ironic look, as though he suspected the rise were being taken out of him. 'Who did you say your colleague was?'

'Orr. Reginald Orr, *Legum Baccalaureus*. As I say, he's indisposed.' This much was true. A message-boy had brought a note to Kings Inns the day before, summoning him. When he called out to Chapelizod, the lawyer was bedbound. 'Came down with quite a chill, I'm afraid.'

'Orr,' the old man considered. He clicked his fingers. 'Son

of William Orr, the land surveyor.'

'That's the man.'

'Illustrious ancestor, also William Orr. United Irishman, hanged by Justice Yelverton, who shed crocodile tears as he pronounced sentence. Reginald, you call him? Yes, it could be Reginald. Took over from McSharry not so long back as family solicitor. Represented the Hart interest in that business over the millrace. Handled it competently, by all accounts. Hard to warm to, all the same. Constantly fussing, if not at his cuffs, then at the ends of his waistcoat. I'm not the least surprised to hear he's indisposed. Bloodless character. Wants a good dose of iron. Always has a washed out look to my eye, as though he's been sent once too often through the laundry.'

Foley threw back his patrician head and laughed aloud. He waited to see if his companion was disposed to go on. After a minute's silence, 'Tell me about the family,' he invited. Because the phrase this washed-out solicitor had used intrigued him—*let's just say I've a family interest.* Could old Reggie have developed an interest in the girl, Kit? Always had been one for playing his cards close to his chest.

'What do you wish to know?'

'Charles Hart is your nephew, is that it?'

'Poor old Charles! No. Frances was my niece. Fanny. Fanny Montagu.'

'Ah. Yes, that makes sense.'

'Poor old Charlie. Never really recovered, after she died. Had to pack it in as magistrate. Had a series of mild strokes. Tipped him into a melancholy out of which he's never really pulled himself. Not for longer than a few months at a time. That said, he's possibly more of a danger to the estate at those times he's feeling elated! Ready to embark on all sorts of madcap projects, moves on to the next before the first is halfway done. That's why Edmond has had to take the helm. Place would have gone to pot entirely. Pity. On a losing wicket if you ask me.'

'You think so?'

'Not a doubt about it. He's quite right, what he says in the letters here. It was always Edmond was the soldier of the family. Freddy was more interested in daydreaming. Nose permanently stuck inside some book or other. Cut a theatre out of a biscuit-box one Christmas, little cardboard figures he painted just so. Used to put on shows he'd dream up for the family, that sort of thing. He only joined the cadets to escape from that damned boarding school. Bullied there, by all accounts.' There was a softness, a vagueness about the old man's features as he reminisced. 'No. It was Edmond was cut out for a soldier.'

'And the girl? Kit?'

'Kate, you mean? Oh, they were always thick as thieves, she and Freddy. Always hiding behind curtains, whispering together. 'The Whispering Alibis', I used call them. Came as quite a shock when he told me he intended to join up, I can tell you! Cadet corps hadn't suited him either, so far as I'm aware. So I told him, Frederick, I said, there is simply no point in half measures. Imperial Yeomanry be hanged! Go for the Inniskillings! Fine old regiment. Can trace its lineage back to the Williamite Wars. But would he listen to an old soldier, do you think? Bah! You may be sure Edmond wouldn't have messed about with the Imperial Yeomanry.' He straightened. 'Never told him, of course, but it was I smoothed the path for him to be taken on as an officer. In those days I still had contacts, you know.'

'And this figure you ran into, down on the quays. You're quite certain it was him? Ten years is a long time.'

'Not the blindest bit of doubt! It may have been ten years, but some things you can't change. This figure might have been a beggar, the way he was dressed. Though he had something of the corsair about him, too. Windblown, moustache like a horseshoe. A gypsy's kerchief tied round his head. But it was the eyes. Same eyes as young Kate, like two polished chestnuts. Fanny had them too, you see.' He was lost for a moment in the memory, and then he started, as though wakened. 'And then, the manner in which he shambled away from me, when I spoke his name. Like a guilty thing. Why would he have done that, if it wasn't he?'

Why indeed. 'It's not the first time you saw him.'

A narrowed eye. 'How d'you mean?'

'I understand, three years ago you sighted him. In Cork, was it?'

'Bah! That was far from certain. Mizzling, you see. Figure seen from a dogcart shuffling along the Mardyke. Couldn't be sure.'

'All the same, it led to Edmond and Katherine spending a week there.' He assessed the colour rising to the man's bony cheeks. 'And didn't you once spot him at the Galway Races?'

A dignified pause. 'I don't care for your implication, sir.'

'No implication! I'm simply assessing how the land lies.'

The retired captain emitted something between a harrumph and a whinny. It was time to shift tack. Foley allowed calmness to return between them. 'Tell me, Captain. Do you know if there was a court-martial?'

'Now, Edmond would never give me a straight answer on that point.'

'There was a letter. Is that right?'

'There was!' The ramrod back gained a further inch. 'Well. Now. There was something a bit rum about that.'

'Oh?'

'It warned Charles straight out that if his son ever made contact with the family, they should tell him in no uncertain terms to steer clear. Not by any means to return to the country, nor put his head over the parapet wherever he might be hiding out. Under heavy sentence and so forth.'

'What's unusual in that?'

'Well, it's simply not done! The C.O. taking it on himself to warn a relation. Shows he must have thought pretty highly of him, all the same.'

'I don't suppose you know what happened to that letter?'

He flushed pink and pivoted, as though accused. 'How the deuce should I know that?' Then he softened. 'Really, you should ask Edmond.'

'Not Charles?'

'I believe there was a brief exchange between the brothers. Perhaps two years on? Exchange of wires, no more than that. Half sentences telegraphed in Morse. Can't quite recall where he told me Freddy's cable came from. Cairo, perhaps?'

'Hmmm. What made him do it, do you think?'

There was a pause, as though the old man hadn't quite followed. 'Ah! Why did he do a bunk, do you mean? Blamed if I know. Tired of burning out farms, I shouldn't wonder.'

'Apart from that wire, the last correspondence the family

got from Frederick, so far as I'm aware, was the postcard from Lourenço Marques. That word, *shameful*. Any thoughts?'

'Shameful. Shame. Man alive, the entire empire was founded on the principle! Couldn't operate without it. In every port, in every outpost, you'll find just such desperate characters, looking to outrun their past.'

CHAPTER SEVEN

The boy tugged at the man's arm, gave the shoulder a firmer shake. But the head merely lolled sideways and backwards. Beside him, the mongrel whined, pawed at the prostrate body.

The candle was throwing restless shadows about the cellar, magnifying every object into its sinister parody. The acrid smell, something burnt or smoked, was stronger than the day before. Where the head had lolled the mouth gaped wetly, a gargoyle's.

The bandana had fallen away, and he saw that the skull, round as a cannonball, was covered with a fine stubble. Behind one ear, the top of which was cropped, a scar glimmered like a seam of quartz. He kept it concealed, like the twitch in his right hand. It was a tremor which could spasm when he tried to do anything fiddly—a blemish he had the knack of hiding in a pocket. The result of trapped nerves, he'd said, when with the boldness of youth, Tommy had asked.

'I suppose you're hungry to see the world?' the man had gone on. 'I know at your age I was. Your old man, too. But remember old Aesop's warning: Be careful what you wish for, lest it come to pass. I've seen the world, now. And I'll tell you. It's a hard and shoddy place. Filled with vice and roguery.'

He loosened the filthy rag around the man's throat. The eyeballs were visible, but rolled up to their whites. With two fingers he gentled the eyelids wider, held the candle nearer. They were dead to the world, though the chest intermittently rose and fell. There was something snakelike in the pinpoints of the pupils.

It wasn't the first time he'd seen the vagrant—the fugitive—in this state. This wasn't the ague from which he periodically suffered, the sweats and shivers that might last for days on end. Once, through a gap in the boards, he'd witnessed him firing, in the bowl of a long clay pipe, a marble-sized ball of tar.

It might be hours before he came round.

He touched his own shirt, slipped two fingers between the buttons. The question was, what to do now with the typescript concealed there. It was incomplete—shot through with gaps and doubts arising from the close-written pages he'd picked up the day before, its handwriting anxious and spidery and vitiated with second thoughts. Initials stood in for proper names, as though the whole thing were hurried, or in cypher. His heart had quite literally skipped about the base of his throat when first he'd scanned it. Although the man, gripping his arm and eyeing him directly, had said the story was just a story, it had the ring of truth about it. Of first-hand testimony. If it was true, it marked him for a deserter.

Another time, the ex-soldier had growled: 'Think you want to see the world? Follow the flag? The Butcher's Apron, your own father called it. I've seen things done in its name, my friend. I wouldn't wish those images on anyone.'

He'd hoped they could go through the scribbled pages together, that he could make precise the detail of the fearful incident. It wasn't every evening his mother was out at a Connr̄aoh na Saeohilse meeting, so could be relied upon not to return home before midnight.

Should he leave the typescript here? Slip it under the mattress?

But when he finally woke from fevered dreams and discovered the envelope, what would he make of the effort, patchy and inadequate? Tom Kinkaid had promised to bring him what his mother termed a 'fair copy'. And in duplicate— he'd told him about the old chocolate box on her desk where she stored sheets of carbon paper. She kept only the pages of her manuscripts locked in a drawer, whatever it was she wrote these days. He looked at the prostrate fugitive. Jimmy, he called himself. Jimmy Cade. If this was his best attempt, Jimmy'd think him a mere schoolboy, all hot air and promises.

And then, would it be safe, lying under there? His Ma was quite mistaken, he felt certain of that. It wasn't creditors this man was hiding from. Could the manuscript be in some way dangerous? That would depend. Could it all have happened as he'd described it? And if it had, did anyone else know of the pages' existence?

What to do? The problem was, there was no one he

could ask. In school he was a loner. How was it Br Colman put it? The tribes of the inner city sensed he wasn't one of their own. So true. When you were bullied, everyone shunned you. Mimicked your accent. He had his Ma to blame for that, despite her rather laughable efforts to blend in. But he could hardly talk to her. Mention the former soldier and she saw red! He'd played with the idea of approaching Br Colman, when first he'd seen what the manuscript contained. But no. If there was any danger, it seemed wrong to involve the old librarian.

Br Aodhán would be the obvious candidate. Always blowing off about John O'Leary and 'who dares to speak of '98?'. It was he organised the annual jaunt down to Bodenstown. It was said that over the bed in his cell hung a picture of Robert Emmet in the dock. A great man for the 'beıoh feaṟ móṟ ƚe ṟá aṡainn maṟ aoı aṡ an cıonóƚ maıoın amáṟach', and if the 'aoı' wasn't some big buck from the GAA, it was Willie Pearse talking up Scoıƚ Éanna and the Celtic heritage, or one of the Fays out of the Abbey Theatre. 'These are exciting times, boys. Exciting times! Éıscıṡı anoıṡ! After a hundred years of sleep, the Irish nation is once again stirring. Aṟ aṡháṟóh ƚıbh, a bhuachaıƚƚı Cáım ın éaⱱ ƚıbh. I envy you your youth. And never forget this. If Ireland is to take her place among the nations of the earth, she must first prove to the world that she *is* a nation.'

His orations, his bluff delivery, were naturally a favourite target for schoolboy parodies. Though there was no doubting his zeal. But if Tommy Kinkaid was a keen enough history student, he was no great shakes at the Irish, both of which were the man's subjects. And he was worse again at sports, which was Br Aodhán's real passion. Besides, he'd had something of a cavalier attitude towards attendance of late—it was one way of steering clear of his tormenters. And mitching off class was one of the Brother's particular bugbears.

He pulled his fingers back out from his shirt. Too risky concealing it in the room when the man was in this state. Anyone could walk in and pull the place apart. Even the mongrel's barking wouldn't wake him.

He rose, looked beyond the corrugated iron to the rubbish-strewn yard. It was still early. He'd left the Dorset St flat shortly after eight. It could hardly be more than nine, now.

As he walked along Great Britain St, he thought back over the six weeks in which he'd known the man who called himself 'Jimmy', but in a manner that inspired little confidence it was his real name. True, in the man's jacket, he had once seen a much folded Merchant Navy Certificate made out to one '*James Cade*' of '*Bristol*'. If it was his, why did Tommy's mother insist he was going about under a false name?

He'd arrived home early from school one afternoon in late September to find a stranger seated at the table. At once his mother was uncomfortable, on her feet. Her restlessness made the man rise, too. The boy took in the teapot and cups, the buttered cuts of barmbrack. Also, a redness about her eyes.

'You're not supposed to be down at your hurling?'

'Cancelled,' he shrugged, throwing both hurl and satchel into the corner, his gaze never leaving the stranger. In his sailor's reefer jacket and headscarf there was something of the seadog about him; much as he pictured Martin Eden when the misfit first entered his friend Arthur's house. He had no inkling, then, it was one of the novels he was soon to flog. If he'd had, the premonition would have fascinated rather than appalled him.

81

'Thanks again for dropping by,' said his mother in a tone that made it plain the visit was at an end. And when the figure hesitated, she added, 'I'll see you out.' He noticed she was using her posh voice, the one she used when she was front of shop in the milliner's on Henry St.

The man hovered at the top of the stairs, peering back. 'He has the look of him, you know. It's there around the eyes.' The voice was educated. Genteel, even. Out of all keeping with his rough appearance.

'Who?' Tommy had called, already suspecting the answer.

'Your father. You have his look.'

And that was all. His mother was impatient to get the visitor outside. From the banisters he watched as, at the door, she took a half-sovereign from her purse. 'For your trouble,' she said. The man's refusal held little conviction, and when she pushed the gold coin into his jacket pocket, he didn't retrieve or return it.

'Who was that?' he'd asked, when she was back upstairs.

'That was nobody.'

And sometimes it was precisely like he was nobody. There would be a vacancy about him. An empty stare. A mouth that chewed on nothing.

Other times he was cantankerous. Short tempered.

Dublin being no more than a town, and Tommy Kinkaid an old hand that year at doing a bunk from school, it wasn't long before he encountered the tramp a second time. That was when he discovered he and his father had been in the army together in South Africa. Not alone that, the man claimed he'd actually been present at his death. Though all he would say, as they stood at the railings outside Mountjoy Square, was that death was an obscene thing. Inglorious. Attended by neither meaning nor dignity.

In fact, there was very little he'd managed to ascertain since that chance encounter that pertained to Africa, or to any of their time together in the army. Once, when he was in expansive form, this 'Jimmy' character told him that, in the days after they'd disembarked in the Cape Colony, a competition had been organised between the subalterns of the various mounted companies. And how he alone, Patch Kinkaid, had succeeded in snatching all eight of the silks from the tips of pointed stakes without knocking any of them askew, thereby winning glory for the 'Dublin's'. Later that afternoon he'd said, 'I thought there were meant to be two of you.'

'I don't follow.'

'Patch Kinkaid talked about two "chislers", as he called you.'

'Baby Nancy. My sister. She died when I was three. She never even made her second birthday.'

'I'm sorry to hear that.' The man's brown eyes contemplated him. They were eyes like the oil painting of the Spanish monk in the school oratory. This day he was lucid. Fully human. 'You mustn't blame him, you know.'

'Why would I blame him?'

'Leaving you. Abandoning you.'

'I'm not.'

'It was his way out, you see. To ensure his young wife a steady income. He'd never again have got a position as a groom, you may be sure of that.' In the wan sunlight, a rare smile lit the vagrant's face. 'Do you know how he banged out a living, prior to joining up? He'd sell tips. He told me

83

himself how he used put together a throwaway he'd flog at the race meetings at one and sixpence a throw. Leopardstown. Fairyhouse. Setting out the pedigrees, the form, what to look out for. What jockey was good over what distance. Who it'd favour if the going was yielding. Who was new to blinkers. He had his regulars, he said, but at the best of times it made for a precarious living. Having to hawk his wares well out of sight of the stewards. It was no career to raise a young family on.'

Another day, glancing the ring of bruises under Tommy's shirt sleeve, he took and examined the arm. 'You're being bullied.' He gazed directly into his face. 'I was packed off to a boarding school. Portora Royal, you won't have heard of it. I was utterly miserable there. Picked on something awful. A school full of toffs, mine was, but human nature doesn't change.

'I was a bit of a loner. No more than yourself, I expect. No use at all at sports. I think they saw me as effeminate. This one fella, Cassidy his name was, had it in for me. He and his cronies.' He allowed space for Tommy to speak. When no reply came, he resumed. 'I'd always heard that bullies are cowards at heart. The way to defeat a bully is to stand up to him. It was Edmond's mantra. My big brother. No one bullied him. So this one day, I decided I'd had enough. I put my forehead down and I charged this Cassidy chap from all the way across the dormitory. Like a ram gone mad. Butted him right in the ribs.'

'What happened?'

'What happened? He was winded. Once he got his breath back, he handed me the worst beating of my life. That's what happened!' He laughed. It was infectious. They both laughed. 'Landed me in the infirmary. But I never turned tattletale. That was a point of honour up there. There was nothing lower than a snitch. Hadn't the men of '98 been betrayed by spies and informers? Funny thing, though, the bullying eased off after that. I want to believe it was because he saw I hadn't dobbed him in it. But I think what it was, he'd simply got bored of tormenting me. In any case, not long after, I left. Headed to the army cadets of all things. The curse of the second son.'

But lucid days, human days, were few and far between. He'd hoped, at last, that the manuscript scribbled down in the wake of the fiasco at Liberty Hall might contain some clues about his Da. But the events it described, if they'd happened at all, had taken place months after Patch Kinkaid had been laid to rest. And for some reason, Tommy always held back on asking him directly.

So why these furtive visits. Why the subterfuge? Why the sin of disobedience, when his mother was dead set against them? Why the sin of stealing books so as to pass on a few bob, when it was clear he'd only squander them on laudanum or opium or whatever dope it was he was addicted to?

Perhaps it was that, finally, Tommy Kinkaid had begun to feel like a character in one of the novels out of Br Colman's library.

Arriving back at Dorset St, he saw in the window that the lamp was lighting. The Gaelic League meeting must have been cancelled or curtailed. Immediately, his mind began to sift through its store of plausible excuses—it was far from the first time he'd been caught out away from home.

Mounting the stairs, he became aware his mother wasn't alone. His back to the stove, a man stood in an unbuttoned ulster and outsized bowler. Though he seemed about average height, there was something slight about him. He had scarcely a chin at all, and as though to compensate, a waterfall of a moustache to rival Douglas Hyde.

Tommy looked to his mother. 'Who's this?'

'Never you mind who's this. Where have you been?'

'Out.'

'I know you've been out. What I'm asking you is out where?'

He shrugged off the query. 'Who's your man?'

The latter shifted his weight. 'Are you going to answer your mother?' An oddly deep voice, too phlegmy to be baritone.

'What are you meant to be? A G-man out of the Castle?'

The way the man exchanged a bemused glance with his mother, he might well have been. Instinctively, the boy's fingers touched his chest. This visit had something to do with the manuscript. To throw them both off the scent, he kneeled to untie and retie a lace. He could feel a flush rise to his cheeks, a pulse hammer at his throat.

'That oul vagrant that was here that told you he knew your father,' said Cissie Kinkaid. 'Do you know where he hangs out?' He stared directly at the man's boots. 'Tommy?'

'What? No.' He looked up, tossed his head petulantly. 'I told you. I haven't seen him.'

'There you are, sir,' said his mother, stepping from the table. 'He hasn't seen him.'

'Hasn't he?' The man teetered forwards, backwards. 'Goes by the name of Jim Cade.' His moustache wiggled, almost comically.

Emboldened by his mother's unexpected support, the boy

looked up squarely at the intruder and shrugged with what nonchalance he could muster. 'Can't help you.'

'Can't you indeed.' Suddenly resolute, the man stood away from the stove. He buttoned his coat. 'Well, that's that then.' Tipping his hat to Mrs Kinkaid, he strode from the room and marched down the stairs. They waited until they heard the front door detonate.

'What the hell was that about?' he asked.

'I told you already and I won't tell you again. You stay away from that man.'

CHAPTER EIGHT

*T*oday *we buried Patch Kinkaid.*
It's too easily said. A mound of earth. A rude wooden cross. Later, they'll replace it with something more permanent. 2nd Lt Padraic "Patch" Kinkaid of Her Majesty's Imperial Yeomanry, died of Enteric Fever, 13th April 1900, "Requiescat in Pace". *But what will that say? Where, the husband and father? Where, the groom who at twelve won his first point-to-point? For now, there are simply too many in need of urgent burial. Five, six, every day. It's taken something of the shine off the surrender of Cronje's army at Paardeberg, I can tell you.*

It truly is a frightful thing to witness, how rapidly young life can be snuffed out. He was so robust, twice the man I'll ever be. A bare week ago, all of these men were bantering, laughing, riding. And it's a squalid death, Kit. I don't know how much you remember of Mother's last few days? Her gauntness, her breathing ragged and difficult. But even that was pretty in comparison to the hell of the field hospital. Fever and delirium. The stifling heat, the endless groans. Dehydration, sweats, bloody diarrhoea. A biblical plague of mosquitoes, of blowflies and maggots. And always, the appalling stench.

I promised him I'd write his wife. But what can I possibly say to her? How I watched, helpless, as he turned into a corpse in the space of a week? How he died delirious, crazed with thirst, croaking aloud with mad eyes to 'save the horses' as though he were seeing a stable burning?

Nuzum has taken it hard. Of course they knew each other as kids. But he's grown silent over the last week. Clammed up. He goes for long rides, alone. By rights it's he who should be informing Beth Kinkaid. Cissie. But he refuses. Says he feels damnably responsible for talking Patch into joining up. It was his father the barrister who secured Kinkaid his commission.

The situation appears to have plucked the flight feathers out of our friend Aloysius Terence Wall, too, though at least it's given him plenty to write home about. I hadn't thought about it, but he sends 'copy' from Bloemfontein P.O. to London directly via the telegraph, so everything is clipped right back to the bare bones of words. You should have Father try to pick up a copy of Pall Mall so you can see how he writes.

That's all for the present. Really, this whole ugly

business has quite taken the wind out of my sails.
My love to all,
F.

Foley looked enquiringly at the figure in the dressing gown, a number of pillows stacked behind him. Beside the bed, a mug of beef tea was cooling.

'That's it,' declared the prone figure by way of reply. 'That's the last of 'em.'

'At least this one bears a date.'

'Perhaps. But it's still many months before our chap goes absent without.'

'Indeed.'

The man in the bed swiped at his raw nose with a handkerchief. 'There were other missals. Directed to the father, Charles, dutifully, on a monthly basis. Dry. Factual. He'd read them out at table, by all accounts. But these are the only ones that have physically come down to us.'

'I see.'

He sniffed, wiggled his nostrils. 'How did you get on with our friend?'

'With Montagu? You were right, I'm afraid. What we term an unreliable witness.'

'Ah!'

'So what happens now?'

'Well that's just it. I was fully prepared to stay put to sweat out this cold or flu, while you perhaps attempted to track down this Nuzum character. See is he still in the army. And Beth Kinkaid, the widow. See if our chap has made contact, there.'

'But?' prompted the other.

'But, that wire came first thing this morning.' The intermittent prelude to a sneeze caught the family solicitor as he motioned with his brow toward the bedside table, on which lay a torn envelope. Foley's raised eyebrows enquired as to the contents.

'It seems Katherine Hart is determined to come... *raaaaff!*... to come to the city herself. Cut short her sojourn in Achill. Thinks she'll simply... smell him out if he's here, I expect. With a... a... *raaaff!*... a sister's intuition, I shouldn't wonder.'

'When is she due to arrive?'

'Didn't say. But she's one determined young lady. Once she's made up her mind... *raaaaflaahh!*' This third sneeze appeared to have defeated the patient. He collapsed back into the pillows, buried his nose in the damp kerchief, and motioned with a flick of the forehead that the other could go.

Several days later, Orr stood in Amiens St Station awaiting the arrival of the Sligo train. In greatcoat and muffler and with a permanent drip tickling the tip of his nose, he was out of sorts. He'd had to invest in a brand new pair of kid gloves. But that wasn't it. It was that she, Katherine, was to arrive imminently. Six days he'd been in Dublin, and he had nothing to show for it. Not a blamed thing, beyond a couple of addresses for leads that were ten years old. When the whole point of his embarking on this fool's errand was to try in some way to impress. As though he, a Bachelor of Laws, were some knight of old out on a quest for his lady's gratification. Tilting at windmills would be nearer the mark. Why, he hadn't even dropped in as envisaged to McDowell's at no. 3 Sackville St.

To date, he'd only corresponded by post, most recently on the eve of his departure.

One thing he had determined. He would *not* inquire as to what had made her cut short her sojourn at that artists' colony. He had his own views on that place, and the sort of characters it attracted.

Orr winced as the chamber echoed with a metallic shunt and shriek. Sharp sounds grated on his nerves. The engine coughed and huffed laboriously into the station, throwing out great skirts of steam. He watched with distaste a damp cloud billow along and then down from the murky glass ceiling. Would do his chest not one bit of good, that went without saying.

The passengers had begun to alight, to pass him in dribs and drabs. Why did she linger so by the end carriage? She was reaching to help down a large, wheeled portmanteau, surely not her own? No. Chap following it down. Folded mackintosh. Rust-coloured suit brash and squared like graph paper. Now, who the devil was he? Some chance encounter on the train, most likely. Would be just like her, chattering with a perfect stranger.

When she was about ten yards from him she looked up. Brimless hat, cobalt blue. She'd picked it up on her Paris trip. What was this she called the style? *Cloche,* wasn't that it? French for a bell. Belle of the ball. 'Reg!' her face lit up. She laid a dove grey glove on his forearm. 'How marvellous of you to be here.' She turned. 'This is… I'm so sorry, I've forgotten your name.'

'Doran.' The man raised hat and eyebrows as though a string ran between them. 'Marty Doran.'

'Mr Doran is a commercial traveller. You'll never guess. Turns out he sold Father that threshing machine back in... *oh six*, was it?'

'I believe it was *oh seven*, miss.' Broad, toothy smile. A toad's mouth. Forever toadying. Dryly, Reginald Orr touched with two fingers the brim of his homburg, 'Delighted, I'm sure.' He then switched abruptly to Miss Katherine Hart. 'Shall we...?'

They walked along Great Brunswick St in silence, Orr carrying the lady's valise. At Townsend St the commercial traveller at last took his effusive leave.

'Thought we'd never see the back of that character. You're staying at the Imperial, I imagine?' the solicitor inquired.

'No. With Cressida Fitzsimons.'

'Cressida?'

'Fitzsimons. Does all that wonderful work with stained glass. The Sons of Usnach? No? Then you might remember, Cressida was my companion the time I travelled to Pont-Aven to visit Vickie Bowman. In any case, she's renting a small place out in Ranelagh.'

'Ah. Let me think. Ranelagh. Tram from College Green, I expect.'

'No need. I told her I'd meet her at the Municipal Gallery on Harcourt St.'

'But in that case,' frowned Reginald Orr, making a direction with his right hand, 'we should simply have gone along Nassau St and then at...'

She stopped, causing him to stop. 'How are you, Reg?'

'Humph! Precious little to report, I'm afraid. Tracked down that Nuzum chap mentioned in Frederick's correspondence. No longer serving. Invalided out, some time around the relief of Mafeking.' He watched with disapproval as from her handbag she produced matches and a cigarette, then proceeded to strike up right there on the street. Pure affectation of course. 'Living back on the family estate with a spinster sister, by all accounts. Delgany, in County Wicklow. Father a senior counsel turned judge, though we haven't crossed paths. Now, the war widow, Elspeth Hamilton Kinkaid. Her whereabouts were proving a trickier nut to crack. That is, until I remembered Thom's Directory, which as you know…'

Head back, she exhaled a provocative scarf of blue smoke. Then she composed a smile, as one might for a child. 'Yes, but how are *you*?'

He motioned with a glove about the muffler, the nose. 'As you see.'

'Dear Reg,' she teased. 'You haven't changed one tiny bit, have you?'

His eyebrows arched, surprised. 'In the space of one week?'

CHAPTER NINE

As he emerged on all fours into the unlit chamber, rough hands bundled him inside, thrust him flat against the wall. A palm was clamped across his mouth and fingers pressed into his windpipe. From the darkness beyond emanated a low but continuous growl. He could feel hot breath on his face. 'Did anyone follow you?'

He shook his head, no.

'You're sure?'

He nodded, vigorously. The hands eased. By the crate, the growl gave way to a whine.

'They're circling,' the man, Jimmy Cade muttered, turning his back. 'He's closing in.'

Massaging where the throat had been gripped, the youngster squinted about the unlit room. 'Who is?'

The vagrant, the fugitive, ignored the question.

'There was a man asking after you.'

He spun around. 'What man?'

'Last night. When I got home.'

'What did he look like?'

'I think he might've been from the Castle.'

'What did he *look* like, damn you.'

'Like a detective out of a vaudeville. A big moustache he had, and hardly any chin to speak of. And a bowler hat was a full size too big for him.' It was too dark to distinguish how Jimmy Cade had received this, though there was light enough to make out that he had exchanged reefer for donkey jacket and, in place of the bandana, a cloth cap such as a docker or carter might wear, pulled down past the ears. 'You think he might be a "tec"?'

A grunt suggested Jimmy didn't think so. 'It was a mistake to show my mug at that meeting,' his low growl sounded. Tonight, any refinement in his accent had disappeared.

The silence extended. To interrupt it, the boy asked, 'Who's Judd?' Instantly, the hand was back at his throat and his back hit the wall.

'Who told you about Judd?'

He felt his eyes bulge. 'You did,' he croaked. The grip tightened. The face loomed huge. 'Where did you hear that name?' Unable to speak, he rocked his head from side to side. At last the grip loosened, and his lungs gulped the musty air.

'Where did you hear that name, Judd?' The voice was calm now. Measured. The accent not so coarse as before.

'You said it, over and over. That time you were delirious with the fever.' The vagrant's eyes glittered as he considered this. 'Who is he?'

'He's the Devil.'

A protracted silence followed this, broken only by the boy's laboured breathing. Then the voice asked, 'Did you bring it?'

Automatically, Tommy Kinkaid touched his shirt. 'Some of it, only. There's bits I couldn't get.'

'Couldn't…?'

'There's some bits I need to go through with you. I couldn't make out the writing.'

His eyes had begun to grow accustomed to the dark and he could see the man make a ball of his right fist. This he brought to his mouth, and momentarily he gripped, between white teeth, the hand that was prone to shake. 'That's why I need it typed up,' he growled. There followed a coarse sound, the scrape of a match, another. On the third strike the match caught, throwing fickle light about the chamber. He snatched up the stub of a candle, lit it, screwed it into the neck of the wine bottle. 'Give it here,' he said.

About an hour later the boy emerged into the evening. He had all his wits about him.

If one part of him felt an imposter, like this was all some sort of schoolboy lark, Jimmy Cade's jittery anxiety had infected him. Every footfall, every silhouette in a doorway might constitute a threat. Who were these demons who were circling, closing in? Led by Judd. *He's the Devil.* Had they to do with the manuscript he was now at least in a position to complete, just as soon as he could sneak a hold of his mother's typewriter? Or were they phantoms thrown out by dope-induced paranoia, shadows from a Chinese lantern? One at least was flesh and blood, though the chinless character with the waterfall moustache scarcely inspired dread.

One way or another, it had the heart skipping about inside him. He wondered what his father would have made of it all. Made of how he was rising to the challenge.

Puffing and blowing, Br Aodhán was bustling up and down the sideline like a man possessed. 'Moran, you eejit! ní mór seilbh a choimeád air. Carry it! Carry it! brostaigh ort! Anois, buail é. Now! muise ní raibh sé sin ch. m. moladh beirce. Devlin, ná bí ag faire ar nós cuma liom. That's it. Tosha fir. Now! Chr an crasnán leis! Take your point, O'Reilly! Take your point, you óinseach!' He'd been aware for some minutes of the well-dressed couple who were standing by the gate. Damn it all, couldn't they come back when the match was over?

While the players went to retrieve the *sliotar*, which had yet again been driven left and wide, he shuffled across to them, red-faced and panting.

'Pardon,' said the lady. 'I'm so sorry to interrupt your game. Would there be a boy here named Tommy Kinkaid?'

'KINKAID!' the great lungs bellowed out.

A boy who was togged out, but sitting on a bench by the changing room, rose and began to trot clumsily toward them.

'Out of sorts,' grumbled the formidable Christian Brother. 'I don't know what's got into the dúradán lately. Can't keep his mind on anything for longer than two minutes together.' As the boy drew level, the coach headlocked him and knuckled his hair. 'Now. This lady would like a word with you. éist liom anois. Don't let yourself down, and don't let the school down. An dtuigeann tú?' One eye was already back on the players, at their incipient horseplay.

'That'll be fine,' smiled the woman, releasing the lay-brother back before his game got out of hand entirely.

Tommy Kinkaid scarcely looked at the pallid man in coat and homburg. All his attention was on the woman. She was elegantly dressed and very beautiful. Something in her face made him wonder had he seen her before some place. 'Your mother told us we might find you here,' she said. She appeared to be waiting for him to answer.

'Yih?' It sounded stupid. It was all he could manage.

'She said there's someone you might be in a position to help me find.'

This time, even 'yih' stuck in his throat. He could feel his face burning. He focussed on a patch of scutch grass between her boots. One of them had picked up a smear of mud. He fought an urge to wipe it clean.

'This individual called out to your home some weeks ago. Dressed like a rag and bone man, your mother described him. With some sort of scarf tied around his head.'

The flush deepened. This time it wasn't only on account of the woman's beauty.

'Well, boy,' interjected the man. 'Have you seen him or have you not?'

'Please. Reg.' A finger in a glove touched his chin and raised his face. 'Tommy?'

'Yih?'

'This man I'm looking for is my brother.'

Instantly, he knew why she looked familiar. It was those same eyes, though there was nothing haunted about the ones now humorously examining him.

'Yeah,' he said. 'Yeah, I know he is.'

They were sitting in the bay window of a Tea Rooms. What came out of the teapot when she poured was scented like a flowerbed. Nothing like the tea back in Dorset St. But the burn he felt inside him had nothing to do with the tea. It was a burn the like of which he'd experienced only that time they'd fecked the altar wine out of the Jesuit church across in Gardiner St.

She'd removed her hat. Her hair was cut short as a boy's.

'Would you manage another custard?' she squinted, as though assessing him. He shook his head. There was a lump in his throat, a spitball of guilt that was making it difficult to swallow. At least by this point she'd sent the man outside on an errand.

As he'd been talking, she'd executed a deft portrait of the vagrant, her brother, in pencil and paper she'd taken out of her handbag. It was as though she were seeing him there before her. She'd absolutely caught the cheekbones, the haunted gaze, the very bandana he'd described, the buccaneer's moustache. Seeing his astonishment, she'd remarked, 'I must have sketched him, oh, a dozen times when he wasn't much older than you are now.'

'Go on with your story, Tommy,' she now invited. 'Then what happened?'

Images flickered about his mind. A confusion of images he needed to rapidly scan so as to filter them. His instinct was to keep the worst of the account from her. In what he'd told her thus far, though he'd mentioned the ague from which he periodically suffered, he'd omitted any mention of the substance he'd seen the vagrant smoke. The pinpricks for pupils. He'd kept to himself the name 'Judd', and the terror it had instantly inspired. Also, any hint of what the manuscript actually contained—he'd dismissed it to her as, 'Just something Jimmy asked me to type up for him'.

'Jimmy?' she'd echoed, with something close on amusement. 'You call him *Jimmy*?'

'That's what he calls himself.'

She nodded, a smile definitely flickering around her lips. 'When he used to do magic tricks, Freddy'd always call himself Jimmy. Jimmy the Genie.'

There was nothing in the remainder of the account he could filter. 'By the time I got it done—' he resumed. 'You see, I had to wait for the Ma to be out. She works in a hat shop in Henry St, she does. Only, this was a Saturday. So the next day was Sunday. I bunked off school on Monday, and that's when I got that thing typed up for him.'

'Monday just gone?'

'Yih. But when I went down to the place, there was no sign of Ji...' He flushed. 'Of your brother.' He stirred the tea. Any time he lifted the cup, he either took too much of it or too little. If the matter weren't so serious, her eyes would be making fun of him. Of his exquisite discomfort. 'It was later on again I got to go down to him a second time. The Ma was out at one of her meetings. She's forever going to meetings, she is. It was bucketing down. A real stinker of a night. There's this alleyway, immediately before you get to the place he's been kipping. A dead end.'

He breathed. The breath snagged. His eyeballs felt hot.

'Go on.'

He swallowed. It hurt to swallow.

'There was something going on in that alleyway and I

passing it. Some commotion. I couldn't see clearly, on account of the rain. It was coming down that heavy it was bouncing back up off of the street. So I edged in. To get a better look, you know?' There was an appeal in his look. She said nothing, but he knew she'd noticed it. Accepted it. It gave him the courage to own up. He'd wanted to paint her brother in lighter colours, to protect her. He would paint himself warts and all. 'Three of them, there was. Two were standing over this figure on the ground. Laying into him, they were. Punches. Putting in the boot. One of them had a cosh. The other, the third one, he was the man who'd come to the house, with the big moustache and all. The fella the other two were laying into was curled up, one arm covering his face and the other held out to ward off the blows. In between these dustbins, he was. Then the fella with the cosh seen me, and he let out this almighty yell.' Tommy swallowed. It was the moment. He had scarcely slept this last couple of nights. 'So I ran for it.'

She was still waiting. She'd sensed the story wasn't quite finished.

He'd done it, owned up to his cowardice. Now, he might continue more calmly. 'Maybe I could find a peeler. You know? Even if I had to run as far as the station in Marlborough St because the streets were empty. On account of it was raining, you know? But I'd no sooner ran out of that alleyway than I ran slap bang into one, standing there with this cape on him. I tried telling him what was going on. There's a fella down there, I said, getting the shi… getting the guts kicked out of him. But do you know what he done? He grabbed me by the scruff of the neck, and he put his face right up to mine. "Run along home, sonny." That's what he said, real mean. "Run along home, sonny. Get the hell away home before I make you sorry you didn't." He knew well what was going on. Must have been in cahoots.' He pulled in a painful breath. 'So that's what I done.' He stared at the teapot. He was afraid to look at her.

'And what makes you sure it was him being beaten?'

'That it was your brother?' He glanced up. The eyes were intense. Formidable. 'I seen his hand, the one he was holding out. It has this spasm.' He saw her wince. Why hadn't he told her that, earlier? A trapped nerve. Nothing to do with. 'The next morning,' he picked up the story, 'yesterday morning, I dropped by the place on the way to school. The cellar. I had a gut feeling I wouldn't find him there. And the place was empty right enough. Only it had been torn asunder. Everything, wrecked. The kitbag tipped out and the contents kicked around. The mattress cut into tatters, like they were searching for something hid inside it.' He swallowed. He could feel how large and dry his eyeballs were. 'Then on the way out, in the yard, thrown in among the weeds, I seen the body of the dog. Soaking wet, hair all matted. Like a rat out of the canal it was.'

She nodded. She was taking all this in. 'And do you think, Tommy, you could take us there?'

'To the cellar?' There was no reason he couldn't. Though it was a bad part of town. Tenements with gaping doorways, thronged by day with layabouts and street Arabs. He wondered if she realised. 'Fair filthy, it is. It's kind of a shed, really, or maybe a coalhole. Filled with dust, it is. Cobwebs.'

'Even so.'

'Now, you mean?' Her face told him, yes, now she meant. He all but sprang up from the table.

'We'll just wait for Reginald to come back.' She signalled for the waitress to come over. She took out her purse. She paid, leaving silver as well as coppers for a tip.

As they waited, he felt emboldened to ask a direct question. 'And what'll you do after seeing the cellar?' He was on the pop of saying 'yous', but he had no wish to include the man in the query.

She considered. That meant she was treating him as an adult. 'We'll visit the hospitals, I expect.'

And if that yields nothing, he thought, but kept the thought to himself, will yous try the City Morgue?

CHAPTER TEN

After he had shown them inside the cellar where the few possessions were still strewn about—on their way through the yard, he'd managed to shield from the lady's view the corpse of the mongrel—the man with the pencil moustache and unsmiling lips hailed down a hackney. Tommy resisted brushing a cobweb from the lady's shoulder. Before she'd climbed up into the cab, she squeezed his forearm, 'You've been very helpful. Thank you.' He watched the cabby recede until they turned onto Talbot St. Then he sat down on his hunkers and considered what to do next.

He was glad she hadn't enquired as to the contents of the script he'd typed up for Jimmy Cade. Or Freddy. It was curious to think of him as Freddy; curious to think of the kind of childhood he'd had, growing up with her as a sister. The account the manuscript contained could only have added to her distress. To her fears for her missing brother—if not for his safety, for his sanity. The question was, what should he do with the two fair copies he'd typed—though the one beneath the carbon paper was dusty and difficult to read.

As he'd been about to take his leave of him those several nights back, the vagrant had detained him. 'If anything happens to me,' he said, 'if for any reason I've disappeared from here, hold on to them for a couple of days. You understand. A couple of days. If by the third day there's still no sign of me, here's what I want you to do. First off, I want you to add the names it says on this piece of paper.' He handed him half a torn page, upon which were spelled out two names. 'One goes at the opening, where it says 'the true account of Lt 'H'', the other at the finish, 'Councillor 'M'. Are you with me?'

'I can do that.'

'Good. Good man. Now. One of the copies I want you to send in to John Edward Healy. Will you remember the name? John. Edward. Healy. He's editor there at *The Irish Times*. A staunch unionist. So that means he's squarely behind our friend the Councillor. It's highly unlikely he'll publish. But I want him to know what kind of a bad bastard his paper is supporting. Now, that copy you may send by post. There's very little chance you'd get to speak directly to a man of the calibre and standing of John Edward Healy. Have you stamps?'

'I can get them.'

'Good. Now. The other copy, and this is vital.' The fugitive's eyes glittered. 'Come over here.' He followed him over to the recess containing the miniature window and watched him incline the candle, illuminating the ochre newsprint as though it were some sort of shrine. 'What do you see?'

Tommy shrugged. 'Old newspaper?' The torn pages had been plastered there for months, probably since last winter.

'There!' insisted the other. With dirty fingernail he poked at a torn article, pasted obliquely. 'You see it?'

Tommy shook his head. No, he didn't see. What delirium was this?

'I hadn't seen, either. Not until tonight. This night. By day, you see, light filters through. But darkness makes it opaque. Tonight, while I waited, something drew my eye to this piece. In the corner. You see it? "A.T."' The dirty finger tapped on the initials. 'Right there. You *do* see it?' In the candlelight, the eyeballs were feverish. 'I was *meant* to find this. Tonight. Just as I was *set* here on this shore.'

'*Meant* to?' echoed the boy, dubious.

'Atonement. Fate. Call it what you like. Giving me this one chance.'

'I don't understand.'

'Listen to me now. This is what it means. The second copy. You have to give that to this man. Into his hands. And along with it the original scribbled version, yes? Because that bears my signature, and without that, he'll not publish.' He set down the candle, gripped Tommy confidently by either shoulder. 'Give them only into the hands of the man goes by the name of "Ay Tee". Have you got that? "Ay. Tee." His real name is Wall, but that's what he goes by. Freelancer. That's how he's always signed his columns.' He released the grip on Tommy, looked beyond him, trawling memory. 'A little fella. Head on him like a cockatoo, or at least he had when I knew him. This article. You see? There? Torn out of the *Freeman's Journal*. Go there. Though you mightn't find him in there, I don't know.' The mad eyes were back on Tommy's. 'But you have to find him. Ask them in the *Journal* have they an address for him. You've to give it to him into his hands.'

'Into his hands. Got it.'

'Wait! Hold on a second. Now, if anything has happened to me. I mean, you know. *Happened.* He has to know that what you're giving him is genuine. That it's the real deal, not some old wives' tale. Tell him... Tell him he knew the author in the Cape the time he was attached to 'B' Company. The 'Dublins'. Tell him.' He took a triumphant breath. 'Tell him, "...*and none for Wall*". Will you remember that?'

Tommy's head was in a spin. '...and none for Wall,' he repeated, doubtfully, before marching back out into the night.

Posting off the article to John Edward Healy was simply accomplished from the GPO. In that envelope he'd placed the dustier carbon copy, the fainter words it contained overwritten in pencil. After all, Jimmy had said he was very unlikely to publish.

Then, filled with an odd mixture of purpose and apprehension, Tommy Kinkaid made for the headquarters of the *Freeman's Journal* on Prince's St North. Inside an envelope bearing the initials A.T. was the top copy, which only needed a couple of corrections, together with the messy original.

He dawdled outside the offices, composing in his head sentences he might use. He'd finally hit on a formulation and was about to cross the street to enter when he saw the very man emerge!

At least, he assumed... No, it had to be! He was a full head taller than the individual, the ends of whose raincoat swept along the pavement in the wake of his energetic walk. What's more, hair like a hen's cockscomb stood up on his head. Under one oxter was a portfolio.

He ran after him, hesitated to touch his shoulder, then tapped at it clumsily. 'Mister,' he tried. The man halted, wire-framed lenses flashing as he turned.

'Would you be *Ay Tee*, mister?'

'What do you want?'

Faced with a ferocious gaze, words failed the youth. Dumb, face scalded with mortification, he thrust the envelope forward.

'What's this?'

'I've to tell you,' stuttered Tommy.

'What? Speak!'

'I've to tell you,' he repeated, inhaling, looking skyward, '...*and none for Wall*.'

The next Saturday, the first Saturday of December with the election fast approaching, the *Freeman's Journal* ran the following in a supplement:

A DESERTER SPEAKS OUT
being the true account of Lt Frederick Hart of the Irish Imperial Yeomanry pertaining to the events that led to his turning deserter on September 11th, 1900.

'POLICE ACTION'
After the last of the sieges was lifted and the army entered victorious into the rebel capitals, Bloemfontein and Pretoria,

there was a general feeling that the war had been won. Field Marshal 'Bobs' Roberts, a popular figure among the 'Tommies', would return to Britain within the year to a hero's welcome. To Horatio Kitchener of Khartoum would be entrusted the task of putting order on the restive republics— mere 'police action', as he termed it. That, as we know, is not how things panned out. The Boer kommandos *were far from defeated. This is not the place to rehearse the arguments and controversies that surrounded Kitchener's 'scorched earth' policies, nor the terrible conditions that obtained in the infamous 'concentration camps'. This is a personal testimony.*

A NEW OFFICER

Our Company, 'the Dublin's', having been decimated by dysentery and enteric through April, had been rotated out until it could be brought back up to strength. Without having seen any action, we left behind, interred in Bloemfontein in hasty graves, one officer and sixteen men. That officer was 2nd Lt 'K', a personal friend and very fine horseman. Our Captain, who suffered from migraine and bouts of depression, had to be invalided out. A number of other troopers were too weak to continue in the service, and had to be shipped back to Cape Town. It was on account of this 'rotation' that our Company was not present during the action at Lindley toward the end of May, when our Lieutenant-Colonel surrendered almost the entirety of the 13th Battalion of the Imperial Yeomanry, after the Boer set fire to the veldt and smoked them out.

It was in the wake of that inglorious surrender that we first made the acquaintance of our new acting C.O., Major 'H', a no-nonsense Ulsterman who'd fought at Colenso with the 1st

Inniskillings. There they had endured, he told us, the withering fire brought to bear on a Brigade exposed and unready. He brought with him on his secondment several other veterans of the battle, all of them from Fitzroy Hart's 5th Irish Brigade, though not all from the Inniskillings. They were there to harden us "fox hunters" who had no idea of regimental history and honour, to make us battle-ready. As he put it, looking at each man in turn with his lifeless stare, against a merciless foe they might never actually see, they must needs be equally merciless.

SCORCHED EARTH

Farmsteads had been looted and burned, families turned out and livestock slaughtered before ever the army got to Bloemfontein. I myself had witnessed families of refugees driven from the veldt. And not everyone was aghast at the policy of cutting the civilian support from under the Boer kommandos. *'Bobs' himself had ordered the destruction of Christiaan de Wet's farm. Our own Company was divided on the issue. For some, it was a chance to gad about the country, a welcome break from rations of biscuits and bully beef. I recall having long and heated discussions with Lt. 'N', with whom I'd sailed to the Cape Colony. To my mind it smacked too much of the forced evictions at the time of the Land War. He argued that we were viewed by all Afrikaners as an army of occupation; that their farms and families were the chief source of food, logistics and intelligence to the guerrilla fighters. His vehemence surprised me. He'd taken to heart the untimely death of 2nd Lt 'K'; was acting as though in some way the farmer families might be to blame for poisoning the Modder river.*

One way or another it was a dismal business. Is there anything less soldierly than enduring the derision and hatred of women and children as you watch your men slaughter their cattle, pigs and hens and put to the torch the barns and homes they've worked all their lives to build? The country is nothing like ours. The areas and distances are vast. It might be half a day's ride between one farmstead and the next. For this reason, Major 'H' had got into the routine of dividing our Company into its three platoons or troops, each consisting of around two dozen men, so that we might cover three times the farmsteads in each outing. He'd ride out with each of the platoons by turn, whichever had the remotest farms. We might be away for a week or ten days at a time on these medieval chevauchées, *to rid an entire area of the farms it contained and to drive the civilians from them. We lived off the land.*

BURNING OF A FARMSTEAD

This brings us to the morning of September 11th, to an isolated farmstead somewhere along the valley between the Magaliesberg and Witwatersberg mountains in the Transvaal. The family name was Esterhuizen. Strange, that what was etched in the memory that day remains, ten years on. Now, it so happened that a number of days previously, the troop under Lt 'N' had discovered an ammunition cache hidden in a barn. This happened occasionally, and both he and the Major used such instances as justification for our general policy. Because the ordnance tended to be of German origin and so of no practical use to us, it was routine to make a register of the contents and then destroy it in situ. *While he was engaged in this, something detonated prematurely. Two men were killed outright; the Lieutenant took shrapnel to the face. That incident already had Major 'H' and the hardliners in my troop fired up.*

We arrived about noon at the farmstead, where the men made great sport of chasing the pigs and hacking them in two. Others ran about, hens flapping ludicrously from their hands. From the rafters already came the cackle of flames, the acrid smoke smell we'd grown so accustomed to. I and Lce Cpl 'O' stood with the horses, to keep them pacified. Major 'H' had just dismounted and was standing beside his white charger when a shot rang out and whistled past him. There was a horrible scream, a horse's scream. As though scythed, the charger went down on its forelegs. The bullet had struck it somewhere about the shoulder.

In a trice it was over. Two of the troopers dragged a youngster out of an outhouse, a third carrying the fowling piece that had evidently been used. The youth can have been no more than ten or eleven, scarcely more than a kid in fact. There was a great wail and cry from the mother, in that barbarous language of theirs. If she thought it might move the Major she was sadly mistaken. Coldly, he asked me to take out my revolver and dispatch his horse. While I was attending to that, he gave the Lance Corporal his instructions. I didn't hear what was said, but I saw Lce Cpl 'O' shake his head. Remonstrate. In the interim, the youth's hat had got knocked off. It became apparent that not only was it a child. This was a girl.

The Major was unmoved. I saw him strike Lce Cpl 'O' across the face. He informed me he was placing him under arrest and to set two men to watch him. I looked away, and so

113

he ordered them himself, and dispatched others to find a rope. When she saw them emerge with a hawser and fashion a crude noose, the woman, the mother, fell to her knees and threw her arms around the Major's legs. He pushed her away. Among the children and kaffirs there was great distress and wailing. To my shame, to my undying shame, I did nothing to intervene as that girl was strung up from a tree. There was no fall to break her neck. For fully five minutes that child danced and kicked as she tugged at the noose that strangled her.

MASSACRE

Even that is not the worst. After we'd ridden for perhaps a half mile, the Major evidently reconsidered what needed to be done. He had us halt. He assessed me with those cold eyes, came to the conclusion that I wasn't fit for purpose. In my place, he dispatched a section back to the farm led by Sgt 'J', the worst of the desperados who had seen action at Colenso. I think we all knew what dark business they were about. There followed distant shouts, shots, screams. Through my field glasses, I watched a kaffir carrying a white child fall beneath the hooves of a horse and the trooper return to trample them. The Major did not want any living witness to what had transpired.

That night we made our base in a ruined farmstead. I couldn't sleep. It was a cloudless night, starry under the strange constellations of the southern sky. I couldn't stop my mind returning to that tree, to that girl's legs kicking wildly. To the acrid smoke and the cackle of flames. It became more and more clear to me that a man who had ordered a massacre of an entire family would not stop short at anything or anyone that might compromise him. Lce Cpl 'O' had stood up to him.

But some inkling told me it would never get as far as a court-marshal. He would never get to testify as to why he had failed to obey an order. Some accident would happen while we were out here, on the veldt. I knew, too, that the Major no longer trusted me. How long would it be before I found myself in the Lance Corporal's position?

All was quiet. It may have been about three in the morning. I rose, walked the perimeter. At a picket I came upon Sgt 'J', huddled under a blanket, his back to me. I dealt him a blow with the butt of my revolver. I then called by the toolshed where the prisoner was held. I relieved the sentry, told him I'd take over. I know, as the prisoner and I crouched along as far as the horses, that we'd been seen by at least one of my own men. But he failed to call out. I imagine he knew well enough what we were about.

That is the night I deserted the army. Myself and Lce Cpl 'O' took leave of one another several nights later. He had decided he'd stay to fight on in one of the Boer kommandos. *I made my tortuous way into Portuguese East Africa. I never saw him again. I hope he lives.*

THE MAJOR NAMED

For many years I wandered from port to port, a labourer or water clerk or longshoreman, on my slow journey back— Mombasa, Aden, Alexandria, Gibraltar. I worked passage on merchant ships. I bought the papers of a deceased Able Seaman. For several years more, I did likewise in waters nearer to home—Bristol, Liverpool, Glasgow, Belfast.

Chance brought me to Dublin in September, a port that, as a deserter, I'd heretofore avoided. I was amazed to discover that Major 'H' had made a name for himself here, a bailiff and rising politician. I tried to call him out at a meeting in Liberty Hall, but was shouted down by a faction of his henchmen before the meeting was broken up by the DMP.

I hereby name Major 'H', and call him out for his crime. He is Councillor Cecil Havelock-Saunders DSO, who is to stand in the College Green constituency in the forthcoming Westminster election.

Is this the sort of individual that Irishmen would want to represent them as MP?

CHAPTER ELEVEN

The company gathered in the front room of the terraced house in Ranelagh was growing restive. A 'Council of War', Cpt Jack Montagu had dubbed it. Today he was dressed in 'civvies', a tweed herringbone jacket with a chrysanthemum for a buttonhole over a mustard waistcoat. Dapper as ever, she thought. The nutty smell that emanated from his pipe was pleasant.

It was a quarter past, and still the barrister didn't show. Really, what could be keeping him?

It was already Monday. Her brother had not been seen in a week. After the city hospitals, they'd tried the police stations: Marlborough St; Sackville Place; Henry St; Frederick Lane. No, ma'am, there'd been no report of an assault or any disturbance on the night in question. Nobody had been taken into their cells matching the description. With trepidation they'd called by the City Morgue. There was one corpse that had lately been pulled from the Liffey. But the drowned sailor was filthy with tattoos and might have been anywhere in his fifties.

On the Thursday, Reginald had to go back to Boyle. The Hart family wasn't the only concern of the legal practice, far from it. Needs must! Before he set off, he delegated a junior barrister named Foley to take his place. And it was this man, Foley, they were now awaiting.

After Reg's departure, they'd tried the Salvation Army and the various Seaman's Institutes, she and Cressida Fitzsimons. They'd called by Liberty Hall, where he'd been scheduled to speak, thence to the Association for the Suppression of Mendacity, down in Moira House. In the Pembroke St atelier, they'd run off mimeographs of the sketch of Freddy as the Kinkaid boy had described him, to which they'd appended her own name, Katherine Hart, c/o Cressida Fitzsimons' address as a point of contact. '*Have You Seen This Man, Jim Cade?*' These fliers they'd distributed as they went.

She'd hesitated before Cressie convinced her, in her muted vowels and fluent hands, that it was too early to mention a reward. A reward might attract the wrong kind of informant. A.T. Wall must have seen one of the fliers, because when they arrived back out to Ranelagh on Saturday evening, they'd found his card in the letter-box. She was eager now to distribute the surplus fliers to the various Carnegie Libraries, because Freddy had always been a great one for the books. In short, Kate wasn't the person to sit still and play a waiting game.

Because she knew he was still alive. As a sister, she knew.

She felt it, deep in her water. Though Cressida was an only child, she'd understood this when she'd told her. Such a pity she was mute, Cress. She expressed her soul through stained glass: primal and primitive, no time at all for decorative Victoriana.

Hands that danced like butterflies, she'd told her.

But there was no point in Kate saying any of this to the men. Intuition! Men frown patronisingly upon such things. She was bothered by a line, though. A line from one of Freddy's letters. Down the years she'd read them so often she could all but recite them. "*The light we see from stars which have died thousands of years ago.*" Could her intuition be affected by a like illusion?

Cpt Jack looked up from his copy of *The Irish Times*. 'Carson is crying foul, of course.'

'Is he?' Her eyes were still on the street outside.

'Says it's patent election interference.'

The statement appeared to deflate the journalist, who, in a red waistcoat under a brown corduroy suit, was perched like a robin on the sofa.

'Well. I mean to say,' the Captain continued. 'Can't do Nannetti any harm, now, can it?' His question, which smacked of being rhetorical, aroused no response. If A.T. Wall had been notable for anything that morning, it had been for his reticence. He was a preoccupied individual.

'Not that I'm saying old J.P. needs the help, mind. Still, in politics, one never can be sure. Now you take, for instance, the events that took place in their infamous Committee Room Fifteen that black day Tim Healy played Brutus to the Chief's Caesar. Now, then. At the time, don't you know, I said to…'

Abruptly, from the hall door, erupted a thunderous rat-at-tat. 'At last!' muttered Kate Hart, following Cressida as she went out to answer. What it was that the Captain had said and to whom he had said it would have to wait a more opportune moment.

The gaze of the ruddy man who stood at the door lingered on her. Over her. She was used to being admired. But this wasn't admiration. This was more how she imagined a racehorse is assessed to see whether it was a goer. And it disquieted her.

Dominic Foley was not a man to beat about the bush. He strode into the front room, taking command of it as he did so. He bowed curtly to A.T. as though they were old acquaintances. Toward the retired Captain he fired an 'Ah, we meet again' expression. This had the instantaneous effect of springing the latter to his feet. 'Now, then. I have an item here for you, sir.' Already the old man's hand was reaching for the inside pocket of his jacket.

'Oh yes? And what might that be?'

For a few seconds the item appeared to have been mislaid. Befuddled, the Captain momentarily looked his age. Then he pulled from his pocket in triumph a letter, which he held aloft. 'This, sir! The last time we met, you practically accused me of having mislaid it.'

Foley's eyebrows rose. If he had done so, he had no memory of it. He held out a hand and accepted the exhibit. 'Ah yes,' he said, perusing. 'The infamous letter.' He nodded. 'Very timely, I might add.'

For the first time that morning, the journalist's interest was piqued.

'You'll notice,' said the Captain, who'd recovered his

youthful mien, 'that it has been PPd. I think I told you that before.'

'*Per procurationem*,' Foley examined the signature. 'Caleb Judd, Sergeant.'

'Freddy's article mentioned a Sergeant,' put in Kate.

'Sgt 'J',' confirmed A.T. Wall, '"*the worst of the desperados.*"'

Foley looked to the retired officer, 'What are we to make of that, do you think?'

'Search me,' shrugged Cpt Jack. 'The whole business of a letter strikes me as peculiar. One doesn't write to offer family advice when a soldier deserts, even if that soldier happens to be an officer. It's simply not done.' He frowned. 'I should never have let Edmond talk me into securing him that commission. Freddy never was officer material.'

'May I see it?' said Kate Hart. Neither her father nor Edmond had ever let her see that particular letter's contents. Frowning, she read through the paper in silence. '*To desert in time of war*,' she then read aloud, '*is a capital offence. If your son should ever get in contact with a view to returning to Ireland, tell him in no uncertain terms his life would be forfeit.*' Then she looked to Foley, to whom she returned the letter.

'It's simply not done,' the latter declaimed, as though he were on a stage, 'and in particular it's not done *when there never was a desertion in the first place.*' If he had hoped by his words to arouse consternation, he was not disappointed.

'I had my man Hendrick, in the Castle, go through the records. Medal lists, so on and so forth. It seems there's no record of his having deserted on September 11th, nor on any other date for that matter. What the entry beside your brother's name indicates is that on the 13th of September, (note the date, please), Lieutenant Frederick J Hart is reported "missing in action". It appears there was an ambush, during the course of which…'

'But I don't understand,' cried Kate. 'The article.' She frowned. 'His own testimony!'

'Well that's just the point, isn't it?' Then, as though ceding the floor, 'Captain?' he invited.

'Well damn it all!' exclaimed the latter, flustered. 'Are you saying Freddy's article was just a pack of damned lies? How do you explain that letter then, eh? The man deserted. It says so, plain as the nose on your face.'

'And yet,' replied the barrister, 'the records don't speak of a desertion. I had Hendrick locate the report on the ambush. Now that *did* take place. There can be no doubt about that. Small river called Ouhondspruit. Three troopers killed. A number of injuries.' He turned to Wall. 'Perhaps you yourself covered it?'

Nibbling his thumb, the reporter shook his cockatoo crest. 'After Bloemfontein I was no longer with the 'Dublins'. By that time… let me think. September? Why, the whole of London had gone absolutely mad for news of the Boer commanders, the game of hide-and-seek they were playing with the entire British army. Botha, de la Rey, de Wet. Romantic heroes, man! It's a tricky ole game, journalism. Second guessing the whim of the public is like betting on which way a frog might jump. Now the Boer generals were Dick Turpin, Captain Moonlight, Robin Hood. But then! Mark this. When news came out about the horror in the concentration camps, well, it was the Boer women the public turned on! Twenty-six thousand dead? An unhygienic people! Neglecting their own kids.'

'In any case,' resumed Foley, as though the interjection had been no more than a heckle from the gallery, 'in the course of the mêlée, it appears the Lieutenant got separated. While they were still under fire, a Lance Corporal O'Byrne set out to find him.' He turned to Wall. 'There's your Lce Cpl 'O' for you. Beside his name, too, is the identical entry; "M.I.A.". Missing in action. Now, Captain, what are we to make of all that?'

'Blamed if I know.' He squinted at the other as though he were an opponent in a chess game. 'What do you suggest?'

'Well now you see, I'm no military man. But I've been thinking it over. Here's what springs to mind.' Even while her attention was on what was being said, the thought came to Katherine that the man was practising for the day he might be Senior Counsel. He turned briefly to the miniature journalist. 'Let us suppose for a moment that what was written in the article were true.' Smartly, he pivoted. 'What would happen, Captain, if a Major were to report that two of his officers had deserted?'

'What?' Like knitting needles, Cpt Jack's eyebrows puzzled it out. 'It'd be most unusual, I can tell you that. Men desert. Can't be helped. But officers? I expect there'd have to be a Court of Inquiry.'

'Precisely my thought.'

Wall teetered forward. 'Like what happened with Handcock and Morant.'

123

'What's that?'

'Handcock and Morant. Lieutenants, I think. Colonials. On foot of a Court of Inquiry they were executed by firing squad for killing Boer prisoners. Kicked up a hell of a brouhaha at the time.'

'Precisely! Almost set off an international incident, as I recall. Now, your account...'

'Fred Hart's account,' corrected the reporter.

'Quite so.' The barrister's appreciative mien declared he wasn't above a correction. '*Fred Hart's* account suggests that there was already division in the camp as far as the scorched earth policy is concerned. The burning of farms and what have you. One can only imagine the effect the dreadful events he describes would have on those who were already uneasy. If a Court of Inquiry were to be held, at the very least the whole dismal affair would be dragged out into the light.' He wagged a knowledgeable finger. 'Far safer mark the absconders "missing in action" and have done with it.'

'And the letter?'

'Well, now. It simply wouldn't do to have young Frederick show up back in Ireland to spread rumours of a massacre. Would it?'

'And to cover his tracks,' put in the Captain, eyes animated, 'if ever the letter were to come to light, the Major never signed it. Had his Sergeant PP it in his place. Why, there's no evidence of his having a hand in it in the first place.'

'The policy of deniability.'

'But hold on! Wait!' Kate Hart's eyes were shut as she teased out her thought. 'You're saying there's no record of Freddy's having deserted. Officially, Freddy went missing in action. Is that what you're saying?'

'During an action neither he nor the Lance Corporal took the least part in.'

'But that's marvellous!' She laughed. She looked wildly from one of those present to another. 'Don't you see?'

They didn't see, apparently.

'If Freddy's not a deserter, then they're not looking for him.' Around the room, the significance began to dawn. 'We have to get word to him!'

They looked from one to another. It fell to the barrister to speak. 'How might we go about doing that, do you think?'

'Personal message?' tried the Captain, doubtful. 'In a newspaper?' All eyes turned to Wall. He was biting his thumb as though it were a worm he had unearthed.

'Don't you see?' Kate appealed to Cressida Fitzsimons for support. 'As far as Freddy is concerned, he *is* a deserter. How could he not be?' She shook her head, amazed at their slowness. 'He won't have heard about any ambush. For the last ten years, he's been a fugitive, running from port to port. He only wound up in Dublin by chance, and he's been in hiding ever since. But if the military police have never been looking for him…'

'If the military police have never been looking for him,' took up the barrister, who appeared to hold the floor, 'they well might begin to, in the very near future. It seems to me, Mr Wall, that your article constitutes a *prima facie* case for considering him a deserter.'

'Fred Hart's article.'

'Fred Hart's article. On the other hand, there is this business of the dates. How can they put their faith in a declaration that confesses he deserted on September 11th, if their own records show he was present at an action on September 13th? That'll be a circle any Court of Inquiry would have to square. Though I might add, someone's being declared missing in action doesn't preclude the subsequent discovery that they had in fact deserted. In the meantime, what the article does achieve is to buy us time.'

Kate Hart wasn't so sure. 'But he *was* being pursued. The Kinkaid boy told me how Freddy talked constantly about shadows circling, getting ever closer.'

'Ah yes, the boy.' Behind his back, Foley's hands clutched one another. 'I should very much like to talk to the boy.'

'As would I!' interjected Wall, looking entirely ferocious. 'Why?'

'Why?' echoed the barrister. 'Because, my dear, he's the only eyewitness we have. There's every chance he knows more than he's been saying. It may well be,' he concluded as though building toward an axiom, 'he knows more than he thinks he knows.'

Some half hour later, the War Council began to wind up. As the company made to leave, Katherine Hart was astonished to hear the barrister imitate a bugle, then harrumph, as though they were in a Gilbert and Sullivan operetta:

"*Oh where's the slave so lowly, condemned to chain unholy,*

Who, could he burst his bonds at first, would pine beneath them slowly?"

Had he taken a drop? It was too early in the day, surely.

"*We tread the land that bore us, the green flag flutters o'er us,*

The friends we've tried are by our side, the foe we hate before us."

CHAPTER TWELVE

'Where was it he was sent, Collins?'
'To Van Diemen's land, sir.'

'To Van Diemen's land, sir. And tell us. Did they keep him long in Van Diemen's land, sir?'

'No, Brother.'

'They did not. And why was that?' Deftly, a stick of chalk was flicked by the teacher at a boy to the back of the room. 'Kinsella, you bıchıúnach! Coımeáo oo chláb oúnca.'

Tommy Kinkaid stifled a yawn. From the clár oubh—the blackboard upon which was scrawled "Young Irelanders", twice underlined, and under it, in a line that subsided as it advanced, Meaghar, Mitchel, Smith O'Brien—his attention moved to the window. Lunchbreak was approaching. Already, he could feel dregs of low-grade dread weighing down his gut. If only they'd leave him alone, pick on somebody else for once.

Fat chance of that!

His eye followed a flight of pigeons. From this high up you had a fine view of Findlater's Spire, and beyond it, down as far as the Pillar from the top of which Nelson looked out over the second city of Empire. Though you wouldn't want to let Brother Aodhán hear you call it that. Somewhere out there, if he lived, his fugitive had gone to ground.

'Mr Collins?'

'He was dressed up as a priest, Brother.'

'He was. ᵯaɪċh an ɼeaɼ. And sure the authorities, God love them...' The general lethargy of the history lesson was interrupted by a promising rap at the door. With a scowl, Br Aodhán bustled across to answer it. All ears strained to catch the low exchange outside in the corridor.

The Brother re-entered. 'You seem to be fierce popular this weather, Kinkaid. bɼoscaɪʃh oɼc, ċá an pɼíomhoɪᵭe aꞅ ɼanaċc leaċ. I wouldn't have him wait if I were you.'

Outside stood Br Colman. He waited until the schoolboy had shut the door behind him. 'You have a visitor,' he remarked, nodding his head as though considering this. Then he added, mock horror on his ancient features, 'Principal's Office!'

A visitor. The word dispelled any dread occasioned by the term Principal's Office; conjured in its place a vision of the elegant lady. Miss Katherine Hart. Why had she come to see him, here? Was there news of her brother? As he walked along the corridor behind the librarian and down the four flights of stairs, he was paying scant attention to the words of the Brother. Something about 'bygones' and 'forgotten' and 'penance done'. He gathered the old man was lonely aloft in the book room. Many an afternoon he'd been the only pupil there. At first it had been his refuge, a safe place where he'd hide out until Soot Kelleher and his gang got bored hanging around the streets outside the school. Why was it Soot Kelleher was accepted, and he wasn't? Kelleher was half-caste. His mother was meant to be some Bengali Memsahib his Da brought back with him from India. Titch Brennan said she was black as a chimney sweep and wore colourful robes made of silk. But Soot was born and raised in the tenements, and that made him one of them. Whereas he…

Briefly, he recalled those featureless afternoons in the library, before his adventure had begun. Because it was precisely as though a real-life adventurer had stepped from the pages of one of the novels. It must be how young Davie had felt in the presence of Allan Breck Stewart. Though Allan Breck had no sister. Whereas this sister had heard about his lowest deed, his cowardice in the face of danger, and she hadn't thought less of him for it.

But it was not the pretty lady, with her boy's haircut and her ironic brow, who was standing beside the desk. It was a middle-aged man with a large head and high complexion. A head on him like a boiled ham, his Ma would have said.

'Young Kinkaid. Yes. Good. This, ahm. This is a Mr *Foley*.' Negligently shuffling papers atop his desk, the headmaster executed an awkward half bow aimed toward the visitor. 'I'll leave you two to it,' he declared, brightly. He added by way of a postscript, as he navigated a hesitant passage between them, 'Mr Foley is a barrister.'

Tommy had only the vaguest idea of what a barrister was. But it had something to do with the law. He shifted from foot to foot. He could sense his palms already sweating. When they were alone, the barrister assessed him from under hooded eyes. He motioned to a chair, 'Take a pew.' He waited for the boy's tentative compliance, then turned his back to him and examined minutely the portrait of Edmund Rice that dominated the room. 'The Congregation of Christian Brothers,' he mused, aloud. 'They're remarkable men. A breed apart. They're not ordained, you know. Can't say mass nor minister the sacraments. And yet. And yet.' He turned onto the schoolboy a merry look. 'Public vows of poverty. Of obedience. Of chastity.' Had he just winced? Winked? 'Now what do you think of that, young Tom Kinkaid? I can't say I'd be up for a life of poverty and obedience. And *chastity*.'

'No, sir.'

'No, sir. You're… fourteen, is it?'

What was this? Was he trying to win him over? 'Fourteen next week,' he answered, guardedly.

'Very good. Fourteen. Which is to say, you're already older than Juliet was when she married her Romeo. Did you realise that?'

Tommy Kinkaid shook his head. The man was playing with him, merely. He was looking intensely at him, merriment still dancing about his eyes. Suddenly resolute, the schoolboy said, 'You didn't go to the Christian Brothers.'

'Me? God no!' Tommy watched the man come to the decision to elaborate. 'Went hereabouts, though. Belvedere College, for my sins. Where you get Cú Chulainn battling Ferdia in the ford, we got Caesar's *De Bello Gallico*. Rugby, cricket. Foreign games. No such thing as '*cooplah fucal Gaelick*' for us. Oh no. Church Latin, boy. *Introibo ad altare Dei*. "The

Jays".' His head wobbled comically as he pronounced this last. 'Same three vows, mind. Only along with theirs, they at least get to do the hocus pocus with the bread and wine. You're not an altar boy? Just as well.' Then he added, 'It's beside you there, on Denmark St.'

'I know where it is.' The retort came out too aggressive. The barrister raised his hands in token surrender. He scratched at the corner of his mouth, examined the fingernail. All a game. It was transparently a game. A performance. He wasn't even trying to conceal the fact. 'You're Padraic Kinkaid's boy.'

'You knew my father?'

'No. No, I didn't have that honour.' The merriment was ceding to seriousness. They had apparently approached the matter that had brought him to the school. 'I know *of* your father.'

There followed a silence. Was he waiting for something? 'I don't remember him.'

'No. So I understand. You were, (what?), three when he died?' He acknowledged the curt nod which corroborated the figure. 'This man that you've been seeing, this vagrant. Now he knew your father. He was there, in South Africa, when he was taken ill.'

Tommy watched him, wary. What side was this man on? What was he angling for?

'I daresay that was part of what attracted you to him. Where did you two meet?'

'At my mother's.'

'He came to your mother's?'

'Yih.'

'How did he come to have the address?'

132

The youth shrugged. It wasn't a question that had occurred to him.

'Of course it's quite possible he got the address from your father. You haven't moved since he...? No. But then, a decade. That's a long time to remember an address. Don't you think?'

Another shrug.

'Tom. Can I call you Tom?' The barrister sat jauntily at the corner of the desk. He looked down at a trouser leg. He straightened a crease. 'Tom. I'm not the enemy here.'

'Why *are* you here?'

The barrister laughed. He actually laughed. 'Why indeed? Very good. I'm here because, no more than yourself I expect, I want to find this man. Fred Hart. The man you know as Jimmy Cade.' Now, the barrister's eyes remained firmly fixed on the crease in his trouser leg. 'I want to find him because I want to help his sister find him. His sister Katherine. You've met her. I want to find him because we're very much afraid his life may be in danger.' He glanced up from his leg. 'Tell me, did your friend ever mention a man named Judd?'

He turned the question over. Weighed it. 'Yih.'

'Oh come on, Tommy. This isn't a game. Judd. Caleb Judd.' The boy looked directly at the barrister, hostile. It was an instinctive hostility. He himself couldn't have explained it. 'He's mentioned in that article you passed on to your friend Mr Wall. The journalist? Yes? He's mentioned in it as Sergeant 'J'.' He waited. 'Yes?'

'He sometimes said it. When he was unconscious.'

'Said what?'

'Judd. The name, Judd.' All at once, and again he couldn't have explained why, Tom Kinkaid took the decision to trust this man. 'I once asked him. Who is Judd? And he said. He's the Devil. It was the way he said it. You know?'

'Go on.'

'I think he seen him here in Dublin.'

'Did he say so?'

'He didn't have to.'

'I see. And what else?'

'There's nothing else.' This wasn't quite true. 'I got the idea it was him, Judd, as gave him the scar.'

'Scar?' He shook his impressive head. 'What scar?'

'He has a scar, here. Under his headscarf. Where he's missing the top of his ear.'

'And you didn't think to tell any of this to his sister? Tom? You didn't think it might help her track him down, this information? She was drawing a portrait for God's sake!'

Was the man's outrage real? So much of him smacked of pretence. 'I was trying to protect her.'

'You were trying to protect her. She was visiting the hospitals. The police cells. The morgue, for goodness sake. She was looking for a man she hadn't seen in ten years. Not since he was a teenager.' He opened his hands, palms upward. 'And you were trying to protect her?'

The schoolboy shrugged. 'I told her how his hand is banjaxed. With the shakes and all.' He could feel the scald in his cheeks.

'You did. You told her he always contrived to keep that "banjaxed" hand out of sight. Now. Is there anything else you didn't tell her, to protect her?'

'I never told her...' he began, then stopped.

'What? You never told her what?'

'That he takes dope. Opium. Laudanum.'

'Laudanum, or raw opium? Which?'

'Both. I think. I seen him once firing up this little marble made of tar in his pipe. And another time, I seen him dropping these little drops into water. Out of a tiny little vial it was.'

'Ok. Good.'

'I remember him holding up this little ruby bottle up to the light and saying, by rights it should be sweet as cherry wine. Instead of which it was bitter as ashes.'

'I see. And did he do this often?'

'I only seen him maybe two, three times. Another time, though, he was shaking and sweating for days under a blanket with a fever.'

'Malaria?'

'I think.'

'Ok. Good. This is all helpful, Tom. Do you see?'

'Yih.' He rocked back and forth, building to the question. Finally it came. 'Is he still alive?'

'There's no reason to believe he isn't. Those men you saw setting upon him. Can you describe them for me?'

Tommy did so. As he did so, the sense of being in an adventure began to stir in him again.

'Ok. Good. Your friend with no chin and the walrus moustache. I've crossed paths with that gentleman before. Mr George Weadick. Crops up on the witness stand in divorce cases. A nose for hire. Sniffs out errant spouses to gather evidence, that sort of thing. That's all the more reason to believe Fred Hart is alive. Our chinless friend may be a lowlife, but he's not the man to involve himself in a murder. Wouldn't have the balls for it.'

Tommy stifled a guffaw. Not that it was funny. It was the relief. For the last week, he'd been more bottled up than he realised.

'Tom. Did your friend ever mention someone named Nuzum?'

'Bertie Nuzum?'

'That's him! What did he say about him?'

'He didn't. I mean, I never heard Jimmy... heard Fred Hart mention the name. My mother knows Bertie Nuzum. He was in the army with Da.'

'Yes! I forgot that your mother knew him. Even before her wedding. Is that correct?'

'Da knew him then, too. They grew up together. The three of them.' He was scouring his memory to think if the vagabond, the fugitive, had ever mentioned Bertie Nuzum. 'He came back from the war with his face all messed up. Like a jigsaw puzzle, Ma describes it. She uses him as a kind of a bogeyman any time she thinks I might be thinking about joining the army. There'd be fat chance of that, with my bad chest and all.'

'Very good. Excellent. And he's staying out in Delgany, is that correct?'

'I think.'

The barrister rose, flicked down the trouser leg. 'Well, then.' He extended to Tom a meaty hand, which the latter tentatively accepted. The shake was firm, just a little too firm, as though he were making a point. 'You've been helpful.'

'Where will you and the others go, now?'

'Onwards! To Delgany, I expect.'

CHAPTER THIRTEEN

She saw, in the corner of the looking-glass, that his dark eyes were fixed on her. Gypsy eyes. Aware that she had seen, but in no way abashed by the knowledge, they were wolfishly stalking her naked shoulder. Beneath her skin, her unblemished complexion that had been so admired earlier at the ball, she experienced a rush, as of a grass fire, blown to life as it seemed by that brazen gaze. It was all she could do not to

Rapidly, she rolled the typewriter drum. She pulled the sheet from it with impatience, then angled it momentarily toward the dying light. A breath of dusk, entering where the sash window was ajar, rippled it. It bore on it the scent of soot. It was high time Tommy was home and in out of the dirty dusk. She ran once more a critical eye over what was typed, just to make certain. Then she balled it up and, testily, dispatched it into a wastepaper basket that had been filling all afternoon with rejects.

'Read *The Nunnery Tales*,' she'd been told. 'Read *The Autobiography of a Flea*. Read von Sacher-Masoch, because that's what sells.' Which after five novels smacked just a little bit of teaching granny to suck eggs. And, yes, sales of the last two had disappointed. 'It's just not racy enough, dear.' Not *racy* enough, if you don't mind! Well, 'read *The Nunnery Tales*' was all very well. All very well, that is, if you were writing for one of those shifty, watery characters with collars turned up on their dirty mackintoshes, sneaking around backstreet bookshops, seeking the squirming thrill of the mouse. Young girls getting the birch, or strict mistresses giving it. But what did Mr "M.N.R."—and it had to be a man, churning out that kind of drivel—what did he know about a woman's pleasure? About what women themselves desire?

Because, when the authoress who'd published five novels under the *nom-de-plume* Lydia de Lacy imagined a reader of her (what they coyly termed) 'top-shelf' fiction, she imagined a woman reader. A solitary woman, perhaps a schoolgirl or a debutante, discovering with a thrill that she wasn't alone in her erotic fantasies.

She took a clean sheet from the ream to her right and rolled it into the drum. For a long time she stared at its unbroken whiteness, letters and words and even entire phrases bowing and cavorting like uncertain dancers trying for a polonaise.

She heard a noise outside. A creak on the stairs.

'Tommy, that you?'

She turned back to the page's blankness. She blew upward at a mutinous lock of hair. This rewrite was getting her nowhere.

'Tommy? I'll be right in to you, love.'

The doorknob of the bedroom shook, then revolved. She pivoted about, alarmed. Tommy would never walk right in on her in her boudoir. Not when he knew she was at her writing.

The door pushed open, and in the doorway was outlined against the dusky landing a man's shape. A coat. A bowler hat. She slammed the draw of the bureau. 'Not so fast, my lady,' growled the intruder, advancing rapidly. But she was too fast for him. In a trice she'd slipped the key from the lock, stood up and gripped it tight in her fist.

Then he was upon her. Invading her bedroom. Her personal space. She held her arm aloft. He gripped it and pulled it down. The face was so close to hers that it took a moment to come into focus. She recognised the huge moustache. The absence of a chin. 'Not so fast, my lady,' he hissed, again, his fingers trying to prise open her fist.

She turned, stamped a heel backward into his shin. There was a bark of surprise, and as he reeled, she twisted her hand from his grip. In the next instant she was on tiptoe, and had slid the key out through the gap at the top of the window. She waited for the tinkle as it hit the cobbled yard. Then, fierce and defiant, she turned to face the intruder.

He rattled the drawer, testing the lock. Then he pushed his face right up to hers. His breath was wet with a waft of porter. His voice petulant. 'Now that was a stupid thing to do, miss.' For some reason, despite his eruption into her boudoir, the man did not inspire the least bit of fear in her. Indignation, rather.

'What are you doing here? What do you want? How dare you!'

The man slid a hand inside his ulster. 'What do we have here?' In answer to his own question, he withdrew a furled up newspaper. He tossed it onto the bed. 'Know nothing about this, I suppose?'

She gave the paper only the most cursory of glances.

'Nor nothing about a supplement? A little piece concerning a war, perhaps?'

She didn't. She never bothered with newspapers. She snatched it up and pushed it against his chest. 'Get out of here! This instant.' Then she became aware of another presence.

She turned. At the threshold stood a figure, watching them.

He was tall, far taller than the other. Bareheaded, dressed in an unbuttoned army greatcoat and, as he strode inside, the knee-high boots of a horseman. Although his hair was thinning at the top, it was long enough for him to wear it drawn back into a ponytail. She felt a chill from the street enter the room along with the stranger. Perhaps it was that the man beside her had stiffened.

'You'll have to make allowances for George,' said the tall man. 'George isn't the brightest so he isn't.' His voice was calm. Preternaturally calm. The accent, close to that of Moira who used to sit across from her in the workshop behind the milliner's. Moira Diver, from Letterkenny.

'She only went and locked the drawer,' said George, looking like someone who wasn't the brightest.

'She only went and locked the drawer,' repeated the other, in a tone devoid of passion. Though his eyes were restless, his face was so entirely immobile it gave the disquieting sensation that the eyes were looking out from behind a mask. They seemed to blink far less frequently than other men's eyes.

'She threw the key out of the window,' continued George, mortified as a scolded boy.

'Now, why did you do that?' he shook his head, one hand holding open the greatcoat. Stuck into his belt she saw the head of a long cudgel. But it was something concealed in a sheath inside the coat that he reached for. A hunting knife, notched with use, the blade perhaps eight inches long. With his free hand he pushed her and, unbalanced, she sprawled awkwardly onto the bed. 'Hold her there.'

Peeping around the ulster of the man named George, she watched the tall figure step to the bureau and work the point of the knife. In a matter of seconds there followed a grind and snap of wood splintering. 'What else have you been up to?' he wondered aloud, but the question wasn't aimed at her. He lifted from the drawer a sheaf of papers, all of them typed.

'Put those down.'

'Keep her quiet.'

'Put. Those. Down.'

The back of his hand shot past George and crashed into her face, bringing hot tears. First came the shock. Then an intense wave of pain, then a hot dribble into her mouth tasting of copper coins. She cupped her nose with her hands and drew them away, bloodied. 'Keep her quiet, Georgie. I won't say it again.'

Hands back about her nose, she watched him skim through the papers in his hand. He looked at her. 'What is all this? Heiress makes love to stableboy, is it? I daresay you'd know all about that, hey?' He reached the end of the sheaf. 'Your wee lad know you write this muck, does he?' She watched him, silent, furious.

141

He lifted a sheet of carbon paper, looked at it, looked at her. Tut-tutted. Then he looked to where the newspaper had fallen and poked it with the toe of his boot. 'You've not been preparing any other wee surprises for us, then?'

What was he talking about? She would have shaken her head to intimate she had no idea, but deep resentment held her mute. Then a sound was heard from outside, a rattle at the front door. 'Hold her. Keep her quiet.' George's damp hand clamped her mouth while the tall man backed until he was concealed behind the bedroom door.

The front door opened, shut. She wriggled. She bit. There was a yelp.

'Tommy! Run! Get away!' The hand gagged her, pushed her roughly back onto the bed. There was a cumbersome clamber of footsteps and Tommy Kinkaid charged into the bedroom. At once he was swept off his feet. Kicking wildly, he was thrown against the dresser as though he weighed no more than a scarecrow. He sprang back instantaneously. But the man was too strong for him and Tommy was again lifted and thrown to the wall. This time he lay where he fell until the man stood him upright by the scruff of his neck.

'Bring her into the kitchen, hey.'

They sat them both unceremoniously at the table. 'Don't try anything stupid. Either one of you.' The man with the mannequin face drew the cudgel, a long blackthorn, from his belt and laid it on the table. He then lifted a pale of water that was sitting beside the crockery and set it too on the table. He reached up and pulled down a towel from a laundry line that was suspended from the ceiling by block and tackle, and this he slowly wetted. He tilted back Tommy's mother's head, and he dabbed at her chin and to either side of her nose. All the while the other man stood guard by the entrance.

When he was finished, he dipped the towel once more into the pale, lifted it, and wrung it out. Pink water dribbled down his wrists. He then turned to Tommy Kinkaid and, with a dart of a hand, gripped him around the throat. 'Is this your handiwork?' He pulled from a pocket and thrust up to the boy's nose the carbon copy of the typescript, replete with pencilled-in words.

'Where did you get that?' rasped the latter.

'Never mind where I got that. What I want to know is, what else did our friend have you type up for him?'

'Tommy?' called Cissie Kinkaid, alarmed.

The man at the door made a move toward her, but the other put up a hand to stay him. 'I told you, Georgie there isn't too bright. In fact, he's a bungler. You see George there actually had him at his mercy so he did. The man you know as Jimmy Cade. That's right. But then George let him go. Isn't that right, Georgie boy?'

'I…' the other began, but a tiny movement of the man's hand stopped the sentence.

'I've a wee job for you, Georgie boy. Take down that line they have, strung up there with the clothes on it. Do you think you can manage that much?' The smaller man busied himself about the task. Without relinquishing the grip about Tommy's throat, he put out his other hand to accept the rope. He laid it on the table, then drew out the hunting knife, which he passed to his confederate. 'Cut it into two lengths. Then bind each of them where they're sat.'

The man did so. Then the other rose, selected two

handkerchiefs from the linen that had been drying on the line. One he balled, and, squeezing on her jaw and forcing it open, he pushed it into the woman's mouth. He then used the second to secure it there. When this job was accomplished, he laid the knife alongside the cudgel. Unhurriedly, he examined Tom Kinkaid, whose throat still bore the mark of his grip.

'When I was about the same age you are now, I used to love hunting. Hunting was my passion, you might say. I might be gone from dawn to dusk. Always on my own. I tell a lie. I always took my dog for company. A German shepherd bitch she was, only her pelt was pure white. Ghost, I called her. A beautiful animal. Now, the thing was, like any royal family, my folks had their heir and a spare. And I was the second son. Now, I had no intention of hanging around to play the part of bailiff on my own land when the big brother came into it. Are you with me, Tommy? So that's how I took it into my head to enlist. I set off for Enniskillen one fine morning. I lied about my age. And I must've been good at the soldiering, too. I got a field commission so I did. Then I blew it.

'But that's not the point of my story. The point of my story is, before I left, I went out with Ghost for one last time. Dawn to dusk. And then I sat her down, and I cradled her, and I stuck that wee knife there into her heart. And I wept like a girl so I did. But if I couldn't take her with me, my brother wasn't going to get her, along with everything else. Now. If I could harm the creature that was dearest to me in the world, do you imagine I'd think twice when it comes to someone who means nothing to me?'

For a while, the only sound in the kitchen besides the ticking of the clock was the laboured breathing of the two bound figures. 'Have you ever heard the shrieks of a man who's being tortured, Tommy? I have.' He briefly paused, as though considering. 'It's not a sound you're likely to forget.'

Cissie Kinkaid teetered in her seat, agitatedly groaning, but once more the man's raised palm, as though it held a magnetic charge, stayed the sound. He lifted the hunting knife and toyed at the table's varnish with the point. 'Have you ever seen a mutilation, Tommy? I have. Places I've been, they're carried out in public squares. For public instruction, but at the same time, for public entertainment. Or... a blinding, maybe? I haven't seen it *done*. I can't claim that. I've seen the result, mind.'

'There's nothing I know.' The sentence smacked as much of defeat as of fear.

Leaving the knife, he stood straight. He circled behind the boy. 'All that amputation business, it's so crude. Clumsy, you might say. Because one thing you have to admire about the oriental. He's a refined gentleman. Voluptuous. Yes, I think that's the word I'd use. It sounds the class of word you might use, ma'am. In one of your dirty books. Do you know about those, Tommy? Have you read any of your mammy's books?

'It's the right word all the same. Your oriental is voluptuous. Think of his love for ornamentation. Think of the spices, man. Think of the dark-eyed women with their faces veiled. And he's *voluptuous*, too, when it comes to inflicting pain. He dreams up the most exquisite tortures imaginable. And if they don't leave a trace on the body, that's the real trick.

'And do you know where I learned all this, Tommy. Will I tell you? I learned all this the time I was holed up in a stinking pit of a gaol in Tyre, in the Levant. Two years I spent in that wee circle of hell. Two.' He grabbed the boy's hair, jerked his head back. 'Now. Do you know who it was landed me there? Can you guess?'

He pushed the head away. Leisurely, he paced around to the table. From the side of the pail he lifted the wet towel, snapped it open, sending spray in the direction of his accomplice. 'Were you ever drowned, Tommy?' He paced slowly back around behind him. 'I was. It was in the Red Sea. Though, as you see, here I stand. They say it's a pleasant death, drowning. They're wrong. There's nothing pleasant about it.' Abruptly he stooped, plunged a forearm past Tommy's throat and angled the head back. Over his mouth and nose he clamped the wet towel. At once the boy began to struggle, to kick, eyes huge. The woman too struggled, moaned wildly, tried to rise again and again until her chair crashed to the floor, sideways.

'Beg pardon?' He released the head. Then he turned to the man who'd resumed his vigil by the door. 'Let her speak.' And when he hesitated, 'Undo the gag, George.'

The instant the first handkerchief was loosened, she spat out the second. 'Please,' she rasped, mouth bone dry.

'I'm sorry, I didn't catch that?'

'Please!' Her voice dropped. 'He's tubercular.'

'He's…?'

'He has consumption. Please. What is it you want?'

'Well,' the man straightened to his full height, 'I thought no one was ever going to ask me that. What is it I want? Georgie, what is it I want?' His accomplice shuffled uneasily between two uncertainties. Whether to answer. What to answer. 'I'll tell you. Firstly, there had better be no more unpleasant surprises appearing in the press. Not one more lying word. Is that understood? That's number one. Number two. If you see the man. *When* you see the man. You know who I mean. Tell him, if I find him anywhere on these isles, it's not just him I'll go after. It's his father. It's his brother. It's his sister. And after that, I'll come for your mother, Tommy. And only then, you. Can you remember all that, Tommy? Anywhere at all on these islands, tell him. Tell him to go on away back to sea for himself. And you may add that my fervent hope is that he drowns there.'

The boy swallowed. 'Who will I say…?'

The tall man left the unfinished question dangle. Then he approximated a wink. 'He'll know.'

'What if I can't find him?'

'That's your lookout, isn't it?' He lifted the hunting knife, replaced it in the sheath concealed inside his coat. Then he picked up the cudgel, and slid it into his belt. He stooped to the woman whose chair was still on its side. 'To stop the nose from bleeding, ma'am, I'd say a cold compress would be the man.'

He tugged briefly to try the two ropes, then flicked a forehead to the bungler standing at the door. 'Come on away. We'll leave them to figure out how to untie your oul granny-knots.'

And as abruptly as they had entered, they were gone into the night.

CHAPTER FOURTEEN

Once the train had rounded Killiney Head, the panorama out over a sea of tarnished silver was all at once spectacular. Out of the carriage window, she followed the sweep from Sorrento Point down as far as Bray Head and the Little Sugarloaf. A sullen light, would you call it? Metallic. Wintry, but lovely for all that. Was it comparable to the Bay of Naples, as Auntie Vickie Bowman always insisted? She'd yet to visit the south of Italy, so the jury was still out on that one.

'You know Nuzum through your brother, is it?' The journalist sitting across from her had boarded at Dalkey Station.

'Actually, I never met the man. I feel as though I know him, though. Freddy wrote such wonderfully descriptive letters.' Briefly, she fought a smirk. *A little hop-o'-my-thumb with wire-framed glasses and hair like the* Last of the Mohicans; *round as a turkey-cock and every bit as ferocious!* She had no memory of Freddy having mentioned the stubby fingers and wispy beard of straw. 'You knew him, in South Africa?'

'I was attached to their unit for a stint. Nuzum, Kinkaid, your brother. The Three Musketeers. All for one and none for Wall!' He winked. 'Little joke we had. Can't remember the Captain's name. Melancholy type, long face on him like a sorrowful mystery. Suffered from epic headaches. He had to be shipped out in the end I believe.' He tossed his head, faintly amused. 'I do remember thinking Nuzum was tall for a horseman. Not a pick of meat on him. Gangly, I suppose is the word. All knees and elbows, like a collapsible music stand.'

A music stand, bedad! 'Freddy wrote how there was always a toe poking up out of his sock.' Also, that they'd quarrelled over the policy of laying waste the farms. That much was clear from the article. 'I do hope your note got there in time. I should hate to arrive unannounced.'

'From what I understand, Miss Hart, he seldom leaves the place.'

'That wasn't what I meant. He mightn't wish to see us.'

'Why wouldn't he?'

'He mightn't wish to see anybody.'

'You mean on account of…?' A.T. Wall sprawled a stubby hand over one half of his face.

'Well, would you?'

'Thing is, *'e weren't exactly no oil painting to begin wiff.*'

Kate looked away. She was never sure when the man was joking. And his accent wandered all over the place, as though to wrong-foot whomever he was talking to. He was like someone in a fancy-dress shop with costumes strewn about the place. One never knew which he would don next, nor why.

Perhaps he didn't, either.

Had it been a mistake to invite him along? But then, would Albert Nuzum be likely to agree to talk to her, if she were to show up alone? Particularly if he was sensitive about his appearance. Dominic Foley was otherwise engaged. Devilling, whatever that might be, though the verb chimed with his fiery complexion.

The train began to slow into Bray Station. 'Where are you from?' she asked. 'Originally.'

'Me? Liberties.'

That seemed to pose more questions than it answered. 'Do you really think Havelock-Saunders will sue your paper for defamation?'

'He's already threatening it. Denied the whole thing of course. So much balderdash! A fabrication pure and simple, timed to scuttle his chances in the election. Front page article in yesterday's *Irish Times*, courtesy of Mr John Healy esquire.'

'I didn't think he had any chances in the election.'

'That's beside the point, it would seem. The Major had his confrère Ned Carson send in a strongly worded solicitor's letter. Brayden, our glorious editor, is having kittens over it. Told yours sincerely in no uncertain terms,' here he adopted a piercing Armagh brogue, '*if thas wee curate's egg of yourn avver comes to a laybel trayl, my frond you had batter be in a position to produce your source so you had*.' She watched the little man climb onto the seat to reach down her travel bag, which rather defeated the chivalry of the gesture. 'By which he means, your brother,' he added, unnecessarily. 'What's in the case?'

'Just a few bits and bobs. If Freddy is out here, I might be invited to stay over. Cpt Jack has a useful maxim: better to be looking at it than looking for it.'

'Nice. I must remember that. A testy old codger, your uncle. I liked him.'

'My great-uncle.'

'I stand corrected.'

On their way to the Nuzum estate a mist began to fall, fine as gossamer, and the jarvey paused to pull up the hood of the hackney. Kate Hart lit up a cigarette. She took in the measuring glance of her companion. 'You don't approve?'

'Of your smoking?'

'Of a woman smoking.'

'Dunt bother me.' He shrugged. 'Should it?'

'You'd be surprised. A lot of men tut-tut.'

He looked at her shrewdly. 'That why you do it, is it?'

She tossed back her head, exhaled luxuriously. 'I smoke because I enjoy the taste.'

'Very daring, I'm sure.'

'If I were daring, I should smoke cigars.'

His shrewd eye was still on her. 'You're not a bit like him, you know. What I remember of him. Don't get me wrong, you look the spit. But you're very different people.'

'Oh?'

'There was always something nervous about Second Lieutenant Hart, however hard he'd try to hide it. One glorious night, we'd had a bit too much of the ole rum ration, he told me straight. He hadn't the foggiest what he was doing there, dressed in khaki. Not a notion! His men picked it up of course, the indecision. They always do. He was forever looking to take his cue from the other two. From Nuzum and Kinkaid.'

'Whereas I?' she prompted.

'You? Now you're what I'd call a thoroughly modern woman.'

She laughed, blowing out a trail of smoke. 'And what's that, I wonder?'

'Confident.' He narrowed an eye. 'Brash.'

'And you don't approve.'

'Dunt matter whether I approve or not, my dear. It's the future.'

'Well I'm glad we agree on that much, at least.'

'Your friend, now. She dunt say much, does she?'

'Cress? No. Very smart, though.'

'I don't doubt it.' After a half-mile of country road, he sighed, 'She's a nice looking Judy.'

'I'll be sure to tell her you said so.' They turned in through castellated pillars onto a gloomy avenue crowded by yews. On the steps beneath the portico of the big house, a tall, birdlike woman was awaiting them, a bottle-green cashmere shawl drawn about her shoulders. The fine mist had silvered her hair, which was drawn up into a top-knot.

Instinctively, she picked up the balance of deference within the hackney. 'You must be Katherine Hart,' she smiled, a gaunt smile in keeping with her gaunt figure. Kate climbed down onto the gravelled semi-circle, leaving her companion to take care of the fare and the travel bag.

'I'm Albert's sister,' the woman continued, looking disconcertingly past her. 'He's out in his workshop.'

'Oh?'

'He is expecting you.' When the new arrivals failed to move, she specified, 'It's around at the back of the south wing.

Some years back, Albert converted one of the old stables. I'd gladly take you there,' the head flicked, a peculiar, birdlike motion, 'except I can hardly see, you know. Shadows. Shapes.'

'Oh, I'm...' Kate was unsure what word was required. Briefly she glanced to Wall, whose grimace indicated he'd be no help. It came to her the woman hadn't told them her name. '...*sorry* to hear that.'

'I'm getting used to it. It's progressive, I'm afraid. Still. Nothing to be done.'

They were rounding the south wing when a single resonant bark brought them to a halt. 'Trajan! Heel!' From the door of one of the stables, a trapezium of butter-coloured light spread over the wet cobbles. A figure, tall and lean, stood in silhouette, a huge dog to one side. 'He doesn't bite.' There was something muffled in the words, as though the figure was chewing.

Tentatively, they approached. No matter where she put her gaze, it was impossible not to take in the man's left cheek. It was as though someone or something had taken out a great bite, then set it clumsily back and stitched it there, askew. The skin gleamed as though waxed and polished. A half inch higher and he would have lost the eye. Hair was missing, also, as though the scalp to that side had been scalded. The jaw, too, beneath a half-moon cleft, looked as if it had taken a hit, and had not set back in a continuous line.

Kate reached the back of her hand toward the mastiff's muzzle. 'Hey, Trajan.'

A.T. Wall arrived alongside. 'It's been a long time, sir.'

The figure tossed his head and stood to one side, an invitation to step in out of the fine drizzle. The interior was set up like a miniature factory, a pedal-driven lathe in the centre, benches with vices about the walls, from which hung a multitude of tools. There was the sharp scent of burnt sawdust.

Kate advanced to a corner in which were stacked wooden bowls. She lifted one, the grain of which was stained with contour lines in a fabulous geography.

'Beech.'

'Is it? It's beautiful.' She estimated there were maybe a dozen bowls in all. 'Were you always interested in carpentry?'

'Woodturning.'

'Oh. Yes. Joining is a different skill. I remember now. What will you do with so many bowls? Do you sell them?'

'Charity.' The man was patently uncomfortable. The dog, gazing up at its master, knew it.

'Yes?' She had to work to keep the pleasantness on her features. 'Christmas bazaar, is it?'

'Dotty.' He looked quite fierce, but somehow the impatience was aimed at himself.

'Dotty's your sister?'

He corrected, 'Dorothy.'

'We met her.' The awkwardness was catching. 'Around the front.'

'I'm sorry,' he declared, advancing into the workroom. 'One gets out of the habit of talking.' The left side of his face dragged as though it were numb or paralysed, but there was nothing wrong with his fluency. 'Living out here as we do.'

'Must be rather isolated, I expect.'

'What did you wish me to tell you about your brother?'

'Actually, I was rather hoping he might be here.'

154

'Here?' The surprise was genuine. 'Why should he be here?'

'You do know he's returned? You saw his article?'

'Your letter drew my attention to it.'

'My letter, Bertie,' put in A.T. Wall. He'd been looking for a point of entry.

'Albert. Please. No one's called me Bertie in years.'

'As you wish.' With both hands the reporter tousled his shock of hair. 'Thing is, Albert, he's gone on the run. Disappeared. He has powerful enemies.'

'I don't doubt it. The article names names.'

'Even before the article. A week ago he was set upon. Took a bit of a beating.'

'I'm wondering,' put in Kate, 'what you can tell us about a man named Judd.'

'Judd?'

'Caleb Judd. We think he might be the Sergeant 'J' mentioned in the article.'

'Yes. Yes, I remember Judd.' Nuzum scoured the rafters for the memory. 'He was one of several who were brought in to stiffen us up. It was after the Lindley affair. The entire Thirteenth along with most of the brass and Basil Spragge himself had simply surrendered. There was a general feeling the yeomanry hadn't put up a good show. The Ascendancy, in particular. Let the side down. Most of Spragge's units were Anglo-Irish, you know.

'We weren't there. Quite fortuitously. We were still being brought up to strength after so many had been laid low at Bloemfontein. Dysentery. Enteric. And we were rudderless without Cpt Plunkett.' Now that he'd begun, all his former

155

loquacity was coming back to him. 'The measure was to be temporary, Havelock-Saunders taking the helm. Brought with him a few veterans of Colenso. A couple of Royal Dublins. A Connacht Ranger, I recall. Regular soldiers. With the exception of Sgt Judd, these were assigned the rank of acting Corporal. The idea was, they'd give us a bit of backbone. Teach us gentry to fight. Rightly so, we were a bunch of amateurs. Even the militiamen amongst us.

'At the Tugela river they'd been caught in a murderous crossfire. They felt they had a score to settle. But by September, Havelock-Saunders was more than fired up, he was absolutely bulling that he'd not been with his own Royal Inniskillings at the action that came to be called the Battle of Belfast.

'After the events of September, they were all returned to their former units. I wouldn't read too much into that. We had them on secondment, you understand. It was always intended to be a temporary measure. I can't really say what happened after…' A hand hovered suggestively over the damaged cheek.

'And Freddy?' she prompted

'I recall there was one skirmish, well actually there was scarcely a shot fired in anger, during which your brother distinguished himself. A section he'd taken out on recon had come across a trio of Boer scouts, hidden up in rocky outcrop. Spotted the sun reflecting from their field glasses, clear as a heliograph. Didn't let on. While the rest of the section was engaged in keeping their attention, your brother did an Ali Baba, sneaked around behind. Came galloping away with their three horses. Well, ponies really. That's what the Boer used. Left the scouting party stranded high and dry.

'We shouldn't have been surprised. It wasn't ever courage

he lacked, just years. There was even talk of a medal, though it didn't come to anything. A citation. And he was made a full Lieutenant on foot of it. That Judd fellow you were asking about, now he wasn't one bit happy about that citation. If Hart had the jump on them, why hadn't he plugged them in the back when he had the chance? They were the enemy. There was no love lost between him and Lt Hart, who was after all his senior officer. He didn't take kindly to being ordered about by a kid still smelling of his mother's milk.

'*Caleb* Judd. Yes, that was it. Sharpshooter. A bare-knuckle boxer, had represented his regiment, won medals. From a town called Ramelton. I remember because that's where my mother's people hail from. Had he come across from the Inniskillings, along with the Major? I believe so. He'd been a subaltern before being reduced to the ranks. We never found out why. All sorts of rumours followed him about. He'd struck a fellow officer. Funds had gone missing. A horse. You can imagine the sort of thing. A desperate character. I've an idea he was Presbyterian. Or if not, then he was a Jansenist. You never heard him swear. Never once raised his voice that I recall.

'I was all for the regulars giving us a bit of grit. The Boer were quite ruthless, you know. Never fought fair. I disagreed fundamentally with your brother's naivety—in a scrap like that, there are no such thing as civilians. The wives and families were giving the guerrillas every kind of assistance. Not just food and shelter. Ammunition caches. You could say,' he winced, 'I had first-hand experience of that fact. I'm not saying I condone what your brother maintains happened on that farm. But you have to put it in context. Atrocities did happen. On both sides. It's the nature of war, I'm afraid.

'I have to say, though, I wasn't at all sorry when Judd wasn't assigned to my squadron. There was something about him, you could tell instinctively. A born gambler. Dicer with death. Which is all very well, they're qualities you might look for in a soldier. After all, whatever feat of derring-do he'd pulled off at Colenso had regained him his Sergeant's stripes, on his rise back up through the ranks.

'But there was something grudging in him. A pettiness. He could never bear a slight.'

'Had you heard about the massacre? The girl they hanged?'

'Nothing. First I heard was your brother's article. Of course, I was stretched out in a field hospital at the time, getting my face stitched back together.' If he felt self-pity, he was proficient at concealing it. 'No. So far as I was aware, and this is what the reports concluded, there was an ambush.' He tapped at his forehead. 'Can't remember the place. A Boer *kommando*, lying in wait for your brother's squadron.' For the first time, he looked directly at her. 'I'd always assumed that's where he'd died.'

'Now therein hangs a tale,' remarked A.T. Wall.

From the damp air outside, a gong was heard to sound. 'That'll be Dotty,' said the former officer. 'Tea and sandwiches, and her famous Dundee cake.'

As they took their leave about an hour later—they'd told the hackney to return for four o'clock—Albert Nuzum called after them, 'All for one…'

Standing up in the cab and pivoting back to face him, the journalist executed a brisk salute, '…and none for Wall!'

CHAPTER FIFTEEN

The figure hiding behind the rhododendrons and tree ferns was on edge. There might be dogs on the estate. Racked with a shiver he glanced to the west, where the sunset had sharply dimmed as though coal slack were being shovelled over embers. Soon it would be dark. The previous night he'd watched a gibbous moon, yellow and misshapen, rise up over the Shannon near Jamestown. An hour later each night.

On the veranda in front of the French windows, he could make out the figure of a white-haired man in a bath chair. Wasn't he cold, sitting out on a winter evening? The cold in his own body, honed by a sharp easterly, had seeped all the way to the bone. The fatigue. The cramps, smarts, aches. The nettle scalds. The bramble-torn skin. The cavernous hunger that craved food, yes, but craved more than food.

He shifted, winced as a spasm gripped his wrist. Now a

figure inside, dressed in black and white, was lighting lamps with a taper. None of the bedrooms was lit, nor the mansard windows above them. The conservatory was in darkness. The music room. If it weren't for a thin trail of smoke from the chimneystack above the scullery, you might think the whole place abandoned.

The figure—a maid?—left the dining room. But why had she left the old man sitting outside?

Stiffly, he rose, levered himself upright. His limbs smarted as life entered back into them. It wasn't that he had come to a decision. To leave the hide; to set out across the open lawn. His body had made a decision, and his mind was too punch drunk to resist. When he was about halfway across the wet grass, the head of the figure in the bath-chair turned. A face haloed with white hair. He continued, stepped out of the darkness to where lamplight fell on him, and stood. He saw the old man's eyes narrow, to bring him into focus.

'Freddy?'

His eyes were shut now, the scald of the hot tub hurting him back to life. The burn from the brandy. In his father's medicine cabinet, he'd found a bottle of Tincture of Opium, half full. Adult dose, twenty drops. Forty took the edge off his nerves.

How many days had it taken him to get here? Eight? Nine? How many vision-tormented nights, skirting the towns, clenched against the cold? When he'd come to after the beating, the downpour had stopped. His one thought was to get the hell out of the city. His assailants had warned him to do so. He knew from the jabs of agony, any time he moved it, that his left wrist was fractured. His ribs too, that sent darts through him every time he breathed. One eye had closed up, and the swell about it felt taut as a duck's egg.

Gradually, in fits and starts, he'd crawled and stumbled down as far as the canal. Before dawn he'd found a coal barge, had crawled under the tarpaulin and onto the rough black boulders of lignite.

They were beyond Maynooth before he was discovered. Had a day passed? Two? Despite the coarse oaths and jutting blue jaw, the bargeman turned out to be a Good Samaritan. He'd shared sweetened tea with him. Half an oatcake. Later, around Enfield, a lock-keeper the bargeman knew by name had taken him in. Allowed him to sleep on a bench by the stove. It was the lock-keeper's wife who'd washed the wounds on his face. Who'd bound his ribcage. Who'd found a splint for his arm and fashioned a sling out of her kerchief. In a mirror he'd seen how battered and misshapen his face was.

Three nights he'd spent with them, too bruised to help with the lock. People could be kind.

Later again, a sheepdog had chased him out of a barn. Caught him by the calf and ripped the leg of his pants. That was as he skirted Kinnegad. Near Mullingar a farmer had discharged a shotgun that whistled past his ear, to chase him from a chicken coop where he'd fed on raw eggs. He'd vomited up the mess into nettles.

What was it his father had said, after he'd wheeled him through the French windows into the familiar interior? '*Though thy tackle's torn, thou show'st a noble vessel.*' Shakespeare, though he couldn't swear to the play. The old man was looking storm-worn himself. So much older. More uncertain, though he was covering it with bluff. Far more frail. The white hair's abundance and encroaching sideburns gave the effect of having shrunken the face. 'Tell Cook there'll be one more for dinner,' he'd said to the maid, without asking him was he staying. When she'd left, he'd inquired as to where Wilson was. Had to be let go. Money problems. Always, money problems, despite Edmond's Trojan efforts. He feared the age of the Great House was over. Hart had noticed there was no fire in the grate to take the chill from the room. And Nana? Nana died some years back. In summer of oh two.

'Go up to my room,' his father told him. 'Anna will draw you a hot tub. You can go through my clothes in the wardrobe. Edmond's would be several sizes too big, I'm afraid.'

'You still dress for dinner?'

'Have you seen what you're wearing?'

And his damp rags really were a disgrace. Sweat-heavy, mud-stained, in tatters.

Would Edward be joining them? 'He's gone to Dublin. Didn't you know?' No. How would he know? 'Because my dear boy, he went there to find you!'

When he arrived down after his bath, a fire had been lit in the hearth and his father was seated at the head of the table, looking almost jaunty. The decanter had been filled with claret. After soup, Anna brought in a silver platter on which sat a small roast pullet. 'Not quite the fatted calf, I'm afraid! Anna, Freddy can stay in Edmond's room for the time being. Tomorrow, you might see if we can't make up his old room. Have a look what's up in the loft. If it wouldn't be too much trouble.'

He waited for her to leave the room. 'Father, you know I can't stay.'

'I know nothing of the sort.' He'd stood out of the bath-chair to carve the fowl. How the years had shrunken him. At least the tremor had got no worse. 'I saw your article, of course. Edmond showed it to me. But...'

'Then, it has been published!'

The old man nodded his mane of white hair.

'Well then? How could I possibly stay here?'

'Then you don't know! A letter came for Ed.' A scrawny thigh was suspended on the prongs of a fork as he retrieved a memory. 'I think, yes. I'm pretty sure it's in the music room. Try on top of the piano.'

Fred Hart all but sprang up, seized a candelabrum from his end of the table, rushed from the room. On the lid of the baby grand sat an open letter.

Edmond

It is Freddy alright. There can no longer be any doubt. He's in hiding. But I've every hope that we'll find him.

Even that's not the 'best' *news. It's the strangest thing! Freddy's* 'not' *a deserter! I know it must sound as if I've been biting on the insane root. According to military files, he's listed as Missing in Action.*

Come as soon as you can. I'm still staying with Cressida Fitz. Will explain all then.

Much love,

K

He marched back into the dining room, letter in hand. 'Then Kit is in Dublin too?'

'Where did you imagine she was?'

'I don't know. I'd assumed she must be… *married* or something by now.'

'Phwah! If you think that, you don't know your sister.'

He again pored over the letter. He flopped across his chair. He stared intensely at the figure at the head of the table as though he were having the greatest difficulty bringing him into focus. 'But this changes nothing,' he declared at length.

'How can you say that?'

'Because it comes too late!' he cried. His palm slapped the table. 'Because I've done things. Terrible things.'

'Freddy. no one thinks…'

'No. Wait. Listen to me, Father. What I described in the article. The girl. What happened afterwards. That was no more than the straw that broke the camel's back. That sort of business, ransacking, burning. Slaughtering livestock. Destroying everything we chanced upon and leaving families with nothing. That had been going on for months. I did nothing to stop it. Not a blasted thing. I'd seen that man, Judd, drag a woman into a building. Two of my men followed him in. And I did nothing.

'I could see the men were growing drunk on it. It was a form of delirium. And I stood by. That day I saw them pull that young girl from the shed, when I saw them throw the rope over the tree, I stood by, mute as a post. I made no protest. Yes, the Major rode with us that day. It was his direct order. But I was the platoon's commanding officer, the men still looked to me for leadership. And I did nothing. Said nothing.'

'You didn't stand for it.' The frail face. The white hair. 'Fred? In the end. You left, in the end. That took courage of a kind.'

'I sneaked away like a thief in the night.'

'You brought that Lance Corporal with you. They might have killed him.'

'We don't know that. Maybe I just took him along because I was afraid to face the veldt on my own.'

'Freddy. You're tired. Kate's letter…'

'No. Wait, Father.' He snatched up a wine glass. Drained it. 'Even if it were true, this letter comes too late I tell you. I've done things *since* then. I've run guns. Worse. In Valetta…' He drew a thorny breath. 'In Valetta I killed a sailor. I left him for dead, my knife still stuck in him. Some row in a dockside tavern. But do you know the worst part? I have no idea what that row was over, my mind was that fugged with fumes.' He drew another ragged breath, deeper than the last. He shut his eyes. 'Father, listen to me. Do you know why I came here?' his eyes opened, wildly. 'Do you know what brought me here, tonight?'

'It's your home.'

'I came here because I needed money.' He slapped down the wine glass. 'Money!'

'Well, you know Fred, as far as I'm concerned, all my children…'

'Wait!' His voice had coarsened. He had no wish to mitigate what he had to say. 'I was prowling out there, under the rhododendrons. I watched you. You were sitting out under your rug on the veranda. I needed to find out who was here, you see. Whether Edmond was at home. Wilson. Then, I was waiting for you to go to bed. Do you understand? I was going to wait until you were all in bed. There's a window over the pantry. The latch has never been secure.'

'It's where you and Kit used to sneak out at night.'

'You knew?' The old man looked ancient in the firelight. To avoid seeing him, he picked instead at a stain on the tablecloth. 'I was going to climb up. Try that window. One way or another, I was going to get into the study. Your safe. It's behind the etching of the wrecked Spanish galleon.' He knew that all blood had drained from his face. 'The combination. Is it still Mother's birthday?'

'Eleven, six, fifty-four.'

'I knew it would be. I knew you wouldn't have changed it.'

The old man's voice was quiet. 'What made you change your mind?'

A wave rose up, of sorrow, of disgust. A huge wave, top-blown by weeks of fatigue and solitude and disgrace but driven by a surge ten years in the making. Though his eyeballs were dry and hot, it whelmed over in great sobs. It rocked his body so hard it was agony.

'Father,' he whimpered, biting so hard unto his knuckle that blood was drawn.

CHAPTER SIXTEEN

F irst light woke him. Disoriented him. He was in a bed. What bed? A bed with linen sheets. He was in a room. What room? He tried to sit up. A spasm racked from wrist to shoulder. He fell back among the feather pillows. His eye wandered from the stucco on the ceiling to the dresser to the sash window. Not his room.

Edmond's room.

The talk from the night before came back to him. His father, so old now. Though what was he? Sixty-one? Sixty-two. No more than that.

They'd gone to Dublin to find him. Edmond. Kit. Did he dare wait, here, for their return?

Kit. She'd be a young woman, now. In her middle twenties. He'd dearly love to meet her. To get to know her, again. *If you think that, you don't know your sister.* Had she gone in for music? Or art? How many times, in the early years, had he been on the cusp of writing to her. How many times had he actually begun a letter? But in the end, it was shame as much as the spasms that always stayed his hand.

He was warm here. It was good to be warm. He felt the balm of the soft bed massaging his body. He shut his eyes and felt his whole frame drift.

One night, in one of the dope dens down the docks in Dublin, he'd seen the face of the Devil.

When he opened his eyes the light had altered. It was more defined. Brighter. Edmond's room must be east facing. Of course it was. He made up his mind to rise. If he stayed where he was, he'd drift back into unconsciousness.

At the window he pushed aside the net curtain. From here there was a view over the orchard. It had an air of long neglect. Boughs still laden, stooped under shrivelled fruit. Windfalls, thick on the ground, blackening in dew-heavy, frowzy grass. Everything in the garden overgrown, yellowed, tumbledown. A vision came to him. It can't have been a memory, because it was as though he could see them from this window, the girl of five in a pinafore, the boy eight or nine, both dangling from a branch. What game were they inventing? It was autumn. From a rusted drum, leaf piles were giving up scarves of tow-coloured smoke.

After last night's breakdown, after the hysterics, he'd sat inert by the grate, exhausted as a drowning man thrown up by the sea. With eyes shut he'd listened to the old man's account. How Anna was both maid and housekeeper. How a char came out twice a week to do the laundry and help keep the place in order. Edmond had taken over entirely the running of the estate. He'd taken a second mortgage on "the Elms" itself. He'd wanted to employ a live-in nurse, but by God the old man had put his foot down at that one, no nurse. Pat the gardener no longer came, though Maguire still acted as bailiff over the three farms that remained.

How was it he hadn't asked about Kit? He hadn't asked anything. Had just allowed the old man's words wash about him.

He was still damnably hungry. What time was it, anyway? Out of the window, he watched a tomcat advance crouching through the grass along the base of a hedgerow. What prey was it stalking? He opened the wardrobe, found and put on Edmond's dressing gown. It really was several sizes too big. So too the slippers which sat under the night table.

The house was still as a grave as he made his way downstairs. The grandfather clock had not been wound; declared an unfeasible eight minutes past three. The breakfast room had a musty smell, that odour of stale spices peculiar to a dining space no longer used. Nothing had been set out on the buffet. The little spirit lamps were unlit; the silver service empty.

He really was devilishly hungry. Would there be any pickings left on that chicken carcass? Probably. The maid, Anna, had taken it away for Cook to make stock the next time she was out. It would likely be in the pantry. From across the hallway he heard a shuffling. Perhaps it was Anna, up and about? He crossed the hall, slippers slapping the parquet floor, and entered the study.

Foostering with papers on the desk, his back to him, stood an individual of middle build. Wearing gloves, like a common burglar. 'Who the deuce are you?'

Disturbed, the man pivoted, lifted a pince-nez. 'Frederick!' he declared. 'Frederick Hart.'

'I asked you. Who are you? What are you doing in my father's study?'

The man tugged down the ends of a silver-threaded waistcoat, advanced, extended a gloved hand. 'The name's Orr. I'm the family lawyer.'

'Where's Father?'

'Charles hasn't got up, as yet.'

'Hasn't he?' This pallid character, with his thin smile and thin moustache and pinstripe suit and oiled hair parted in the centre, was making an altogether unpleasant impression on him.

'I understand Anna is attending to him. I'm sure he'll be down directly.'

'Orr, you said?' He considered. 'The land surveyor's son?'

'Precisely so. Reginald Orr.'

'What business can you have here, with Edmond away?'

The solicitor hoisted his eyebrows, an attempt to be agreeable. He was choosing to ignore the suspicion, the ill-disguised hostility, in the questioner's tone. 'I just need his signature on a few items.'

'Oh? Because I understood Edmond had the running of the place.'

'Indeed. But not power of attorney. In certain matters, Charles…'

'In certain matters, I should very much like to see those papers you'd have my father sign when Edmond isn't here.'

'With the greatest respect…' smiled the lawyer professionally, then his gaze lifted beyond. Turning, Hart saw that his father was being helped down the stairs. Two steps below him and with her back to them came Anna.

'Ah!' cried the old man. 'Reginald. You see! Freddy's come home.'

'Indeed.'

'What do you think of that, eh?'

'What's this man doing here, Father?'

A second time, the solicitor ignored the tone of the question; the intent behind it. 'Perhaps I might call back at a more convenient time? I hadn't expected to find company.'

'No, I daresay you hadn't.'

'Come, sir. Let's not get off on the wrong foot.' Once more, he extended the hand of friendship.

'What did you say to me?' Had he been pressed, Fred Hart could not have explained why he'd taken such a turn against this fellow. It can't have only been down to the jitters in his gut. There was something amiss in the house. He'd sensed it, the moment he'd stepped in through the French windows. He'd sensed it even before, while he was lurking in the rhododendrons, a fugitive. Some poison was at work. 'Who exactly are you?'

The lawyer stood an inch straighter. 'I have the honour to be Katherine's intended.'

'The devil you are!' He turned wide open eyes to his father. The old man, disconcerted, shrugged his shoulders. Shook his mane of hair in bewilderment.

Reginald Orr cleared his throat. 'Yes. We hadn't intended saying anything. As yet. It was, you know. Well it was intended to be a surprise, you see.' His eyebrows hoisted. 'Christmas.'

'Don't be absurd!'

'I beg your pardon.'

'Kit would never marry the likes of you.'

'With respect, sir, you don't speak for her. You don't know your sister's mind.'

'With respect, I know she'd never consent to marry a whey-faced pettifogger.'

'I won't stand to be insulted.'

'Then don't.' Hart took a menacing step forward. 'Get out. Go! Get out of here, before I throw you out.'

He watched as, with comic haste, the lawyer snatched up hat and coat from a chair in the hall, then hurried out the front door to where his horse and cart were still standing. In previous times, they'd have been taken around to the stables. This place really had gone to the dogs.

Once the family solicitor had made his hasty departure, he turned to face his father, who was shuffling away toward the breakfast room. The housekeeper's eyes were superbly on his, daring him to stop her charge's egress. 'What did he mean?'

The old man raised a hand over his shoulder and quivered it equivocally.

'What did he mean about Kit?' He took a step toward him, touched him on the shoulder. 'Father? What did he mean?'

'How would I know!' The old man's face was furious. 'How the hell would I know? Hmmm? Nobody tells me anything!' Anna was staring at him in a way that encompassed both a warning and a plea.

'What else don't I know?' he called after the man's retreat into the breakfast room. 'Edmond. Is *he* married?'

The figure shuffling away in the care of the housekeeper

hesitated. 'Edmond,' he echoed. 'Now that I do know. Edmond is engaged. He's been engaged to the same woman for years.'

'Oh? And who's that?'

'That,' said his father, turning, and raising his unkempt eyebrows with a little of the jauntiness of the night before, 'is Miss Dora Golden.'

'The banker's daughter?'

A trill of the eyebrows replied in the affirmative.

'But aren't they Jewish?'

'Assimilated,' his father observed. 'The grandfather converted,' then, as though it might explain, he specified, 'the time he married the Pollexfen woman.'

Mr Reginald Orr whipped at the horse's flanks with the reins until the dogcart was jouncing along the road at a velocity far in excess of what he was accustomed to. He really was worked up. That damned impudent pup. What the devil did he mean, pouring such disdain on him? How dare he! He knew nothing. Nothing! To be met with suspicion, and that by a scoundrel who'd been on the run for nigh on ten years.

The implication, that he was trying to pull a fast one on Charles Hart. When nothing could be farther from the truth! Why, he'd been conscientious, more than conscientious in his dealings with that family. Ever since McSharry had entrusted him with the Hart portfolio, he'd handled it with the utmost prudence. Of course, Consols mightn't be everyone's idea of a high return investment. But they were safe as houses. And they yielded three per cent per annum. That wasn't to be sniffed at.

When he'd started as junior partner, Pierce McSharry had sat him down and gone through the terms of the will with a fine comb. It was ironclad. Copper-fastened under the provisions of the Married Women's Property Act of 1882. She'd made it quite clear, the late Frances Montagu. The capital itself could not be touched. In the first instance, the intention was to keep the legacy out of the hands of her husband. He was honourable in his own way, Charles Hart, but a hopeless case. Why, the entire sum would have been squandered on farm machinery that it would take Jethro Tull himself to figure out how to operate. So that instead, the Montagu inheritance was to be equally divided between her three children. Once they came of age, naturally, and she'd fixed that age at twenty-one. But even then, they weren't free to touch the capital. Only the interest. And a good thing too. How much good money had Edmond thrown away on that doomed estate down the years. Well. He'd always told him it was an albatross round his neck.

But Frances Montagu Hart been cannier than that. The three weren't even to know of the provision she'd made for them until such time as they achieved their majority. This was so that they wouldn't sit idle, in expectation of their annuity. So that if that damned scoundrel hadn't cast his aspersions of fiscal impropriety, he'd have been in a position to inform young Frederick that he'd come into a pretty penny. At three per cent per annum, ever since he'd turned twenty-one. And at compound interest, too, since he himself had taken the greatest care to reinvest the sums accruing to the client's advantage. He hadn't done the calculation, but it must amount to not much shy of three thousand pounds!

Well, there was irony for you. They bounced wildly over a hump-backed bridge. He had to grab at his hat to stop it from flying off.

Why, the mother's uncle, Cpt Jack Montagu himself, had stood guarantor over the arrangement. And he was a shrewd old fox. Three per cent per annum. It meant he was in a position to make out to Katherine Hart a quarterly payment of fifty pounds. Once or twice, he'd even topped up the sum from his own pocket! It wasn't a fortune. Far from it. Nobody could accuse him of being a gold digger, nor of taking advantage of a fiduciary relationship for his personal gain. Still, it was a solid return. The only thing that could drive Consols down would be some sort of national calamity. A war, for instance. And there was little fear of that.

Edmond received his payments in two moieties, but with Katherine they'd agreed upon quarterly returns. It had become something of a ritual. And a most pleasant one. They'd take tea and cakes in the Bridge Arms Hotel. And she'd always tease him for being so punctilious. As though being punctilious were a fault. She was quite the tease, Katherine. At times, it was more than teasing. She positively flirted! Tapping his nose roguishly with that fan of hers. 'Clever Reggie!'

But what devil had got into him, to say that she was his intended! When what he'd meant to say, what he'd intended to say when he'd opened his mouth, was that there was an understanding between them. Nothing more. And even that would have been saying too much. The Christmas payment, on December twenty-first, in the Bridge Arms Hotel. That was the time they'd agreed upon. When she'd give him her answer.

But then the word had slipped out. *Intended*! Of its own accord, like some sort of impish fairy. It was all he could do not to flush purple as a beetroot. And once it was spoken, there, in front of Charles Hart and other witnesses—and it was an axiom of his profession never to make an affirmation that one couldn't back up, and even then, sparingly—he couldn't very well take it back, now, could he?

God. It was a mess.

First things first. He'd have to go to Boyle Post Office. He'd have to send a wire off. Care of Cressida Fitzsimons. What was the address? Damn it, it was back in that blasted house. He couldn't very well return, tail between his legs. Not while that scamp was there.

Pembroke Street! That's where the atelier was. The stained-glass foundry. Now, what's this it was called? Something Gaelic. Something Gaelic.

Should he try to arrange a phone call? Arrange for her to be at such-and-such a place at such-and-such a time? He had to speak to her, that much was certain. And before she became aware of where her brother was, to hear the account from his lips.

He couldn't very well chase off to Dublin on the morning train. What would he say to McSharry? The last foray had used up the balance of his annual leave.

Katherine. Katherine. Well, he'd made a right blooming hames of that one. His hand touched his waistcoat pocket. The box was still there, at least.

He'd simply have to get word to her before Frederick could. That was the essential thing. But what could he possibly say, in his defence? He'd laugh it off as a joke. A misunderstanding. No. She'd never believe that. And of course, the irony was—oh how the gods must be laughing—to seal the deal with Katherine, to win her admiration and secure her consent, he'd set off to Dublin on that fool's quest to actually find that damned impudent pup!

And the subterfuge! The subterfuge he'd gone to. First, there was his ascertaining what her favourite stones were. He'd pulled that one off at Eastertime without her suspecting a thing. And all under cover of talking about Consols and investments. Which bored her terribly. *I daresay if it were up to you, you'd invest the lot in jewellery? Sapphires, I expect.* And that's when she'd said, no, rubies. And if not rubies, emeralds. Now, the time they'd gone to Carrick to see the exhibition, she'd gone into ecstasies over one of Vickie Bowman's self-fashioned rings. Two tiny spiral arms, tipped with jet and onyx.

And then that tomfoolery, at Halloween. Out in "the Elms". His horsing around with the ring from the barmbrack. And would it fit her finger, or wouldn't it. What if she tried it on the ring finger? Well, McDowell's of Sackville Street had certainly pulled it off. She couldn't but be impressed when she saw the delicacy, the care that had gone into the ring, the attention he'd paid to her whims.

And he'd determined that she should have it, even if her answer were no. That was settled.

Once again, his fingers touched the miniature box in his waistcoat pocket. And was all the good to be snatched away, because that scoundrel had made him lose his composure? A rack of wind took him. Acid stomach. Bicarbonate of Soda, must get. Damn the fellow.

Not that he'd been counting his chickens. Far from it. But was he such a bad match? After all, he was on a decent salary. And with every hope of being, one day, senior partner. It was more than a hope. It was an expectation. What's more, he was an only child. And as his father's solicitor, he had a very good idea of what he stood to inherit, one day. These considerations weren't by the by.

And it's not as if he were old. He was eighteen months younger than Edmond Hart, and *he* hadn't as yet put his head in the noose. Though shilly-shallying over it for years, what was the fellow at? If he was going to marry the Golden woman, he had better marry her and be done with it. They were neither of them getting any younger.

There was no rival, so far as he was aware. And Katherine did like him. That much was certain. 'Clever Reggie.' She laughed at him, but that was a sign of affection, surely? Of course he'd shilly-shallied himself. It had taken him months to finally pluck up the courage. September in the Bridge Arms Hotel, where else? He'd made it abundantly clear. She'd be absolutely free to go on with her painting. With her piano. With her amateur theatrics. He had no interest in tying a woman down to the house. And as if to test his sincerity, she'd lit up a cigarette, there and then. Blew the smoke towards him!

Well, then. If she found the prospect disagreeable, surely she would have come out and said so. Why ask for three months' grace, in which to weigh up the advantages of the proposal, unless she were prepared to give it serious consideration? After all, she was no longer the young girl he'd been introduced to, when first he'd gone through the terms of the will with her.

But now! That damned scamp. How on earth might he…

Turning a dog-leg, he had scarcely time to take in the waggon, inching out of McDaid's quarry. Three huge granite slabs. A cart horse, stalling.

He had scarcely time to pull on the reins. Scarcely time to

reach for the brake. To feel the dogcart swerve, and the wheel depart the verge of the road.

CHAPTER SEVENTEEN

The tiny Church of Ireland cemetery dedicated to St James the Less in the Diocese of Kilmore, Elphin and Ardagh that lies about halfway between Boyle and Lough Key is not particularly easy to find or, if found, to access. But for more than a century, it had been the final resting place for the Orr family.

Once the Reverend Eugene Daly DD had finished incanting his words and the old widower had dribbled a handful of dumb clay onto the coffin-lid, the latter made his slow way over to Katherine Hart and took both her hands. 'Rain held off, anyway.'

She looked at the ash-grey sky. 'Yes.' What else was there to say? So much had happened, and so rapidly, over the last number of days. It had her dizzy. Quite numb.

The morning the telegram arrived was set to be one of

Sarah Purser's famous second Tuesdays. She'd been very much looking forward to that. They both had. A chance to catch up with some of the old gang she hadn't seen in months. And who knew who else might be there. Those evenings in Mespil House really were a free-for-all, one simply never knew who one might be introduced to. Just that it was sure to be someone active in the arts with something original to say for themselves. After all, it was at a second Tuesday that she'd first made Cressida Fitzsimon's acquaintance. And really, Cress had assured her, it was such a pleasant walk out along the canal this time of year.

Well, the telegram really had turned all that on its head. *fred here come home* Cressida had suggested that she still might go to the soirée, after all what possible difference could one more day make after an absence of ten years? She was doubtful. Still, she might just have allowed herself to be persuaded. Then they'd run into young Tom Kinkaid.

Or he'd run into them. He'd been looking all over, he panted. Breathless, wide-eyed. Altogether in a flap. He coughed long and wretchedly into a hanky, and when he took it away, there was blood on it. It was hard to make out what the lad was saying. Far easier to interpret Cressida when she was excited and wove words rapidly on the loom of her fingers. But there was no gainsaying he was more than just excited. Something had terrified the boy half out of his wits.

In fits and starts they'd got it out of him. The visitor. The menace. The threats.

So that was that. Not a minute to lose! They'd marched straight back to Ranelagh, she'd gathered her things, then made directly for Amiens St Station. She assumed that Edmond, who was staying at the Imperial, had received the self-same telegram.

Freddy was no longer there by the time she got to "the Elms" late that Tuesday evening. But she'd scarcely walked in the door and found that much out from Charles when she received a piece of news even more shocking. There'd been a dreadful accident, that very morning. Reginald Orr, taken to Sligo Hospital. In a critical condition.

And then next morning, when she'd called out to see the poor fellow in the private ward—and he really was in a terrible state, the doctor's tone had been most grave as he'd listed the injuries—the lawyer actually flinched upon seeing her, had shrunk down under the bedcovers as though he were mortified.

Her mind was returned abruptly to the graveside as the old widower squeezed her gloves. He really was most reluctant to let them go. 'It was so good of you,' he cleared the phlegm in his throat and for a moment she was worried he might, finally, break down, after so much stoicism. 'So thoughtful of you, to brighten up his end. Calling to see him, every single day. I know how much that meant to him.'

'It was the very least I could do.'

'I really do wish you'd take this, you know.' She felt him press the little box into her palm. 'I know he wanted you to have it.' She felt her fingers being folded over it. 'He told me. On the day he…'

'I can't. I'm sorry. I wouldn't feel right.' And she wouldn't. How could she?

Such an exquisite creation, she'd told him as he lay there, bruised and bandaged and abashed. Such fine craftsmanship. Dear Reg, you really were a fool. Fancy his telling everyone, just like that! That's what she couldn't understand. When he was always the very soul of discretion. Then blurting out to her family what simply wasn't the case.

And the irony was, she *was* giving his offer serious consideration. After all, she couldn't very well stay in "the Elms" all her life; become the eccentric spinster aunt if and when Edmond and Dora Golden finally tied the knot. But just try setting up elsewhere on four pounds a week—or even six, if she could supplement the legacy through giving private piano lessons. Had it not been for the generosity of Auntie Vickie Bowman, whose views really were commendably liberal, not to say modern, she and Cressida would never have seen Paris, much less the splendidly quaint Pont-Aven in Brittany.

How much did Reginald know? How much had he guessed?

Her father had guessed, she was pretty sure. He was a shrewd old bird, Charlie, despite how absolutely Edmond had written the old man off. He could be foolish, yes, but that was no reason to sideline him entirely. Would never say a word to her, of course. But she had a gut feeling. He knew all right.

But Reginald? Oh, he was shrewd enough where it came to matters financial. But had he ever really understood her? That it would have had to be a loveless marriage? What the novelists she'd always had a predilection for referred to as 'a lavender marriage'. He had no interest in tying a woman down, he'd said. She'd be absolutely free to go on with her painting, her piano, her amateur theatrics.

Which was all very well. Commendable, even. But what about her companion? Had he really expected she'd be prepared to give up Cressie? That would have had to have been made perfectly clear in advance. And that would simply have been a step too far. She wasn't prepared to put into words for Reginald Orr, or for anyone else for that matter, what it was that she and Cressida Fitzsimons had together.

And then, of course, the opportunity simply hadn't arisen to go through the ins and outs of the proposal with Cress herself. It wouldn't have been entirely out of the blue; after all, they'd joked about that sort of set up. But she could scarcely have raised the issue seriously. Not with Freddy still missing.

'You'll come back to the reception?'

'Of course,' she smiled at the old land surveyor. She really did feel so terribly sorry for him. A widower, and now to be left without his only son. 'We all will.'

As they were leaving the cemetery, Edmond came alongside her. Now that Freddy had said it, he really had grown stout of late. Of course, when one hasn't seen someone in ten years…

'I see our friend has followed us out,' he growled out of the side of his mouth. She followed his gaze to a drumlin about a quarter mile off, on the crest of which stood the barkless skeleton of a tree. Under it stood a solitary figure holding by its rein a piebald stallion. The same tall figure had been loitering across from the church, earlier.

'He wanted to see if Freddy would put in an appearance at the burial.'

Edmond grunted his agreement. 'Just as well for Fred he didn't.'

It was passing strange to be back in the Bridge Arms Hotel and not be in the company of the family solicitor. For their ritual, that appeared to afford him such pleasure as he doled out her quarterly allowance. Such a private individual. So buttoned up. It really had come quite out of the blue, that little speech of his.

But she didn't want to think about that, now. About any of it.

When she'd got back from the hospital that first day, Fred had left word for her to meet him down at the old boathouse an hour after the sun went down. As children it had been one of their favourite hideouts.

It had been years since she'd been down there. She'd been surprised at the state of decay. Boards gave as soon as they took any weight. Another winter would surely see the end of the shack. There was the carcass of a boat rotting in the reedy water.

She watched the last tawny glimmer fade in the west, then sat on a hassock in the half-light. She had a storm lamp with her, but it would be unwise to light it. A moorhen erupted across the quicksilver lake. About the eave a bat began its polygonal flight.

Then he emerged.

Even had she not been expecting him, she'd have known it was Freddy. Every nerve in her body told her so. He was dressed in a short jacket she recognised as having been their father's, until it had grown too loose across the old man's shoulders. One of their father's peaked caps. The pale breeches, too. 'Kit,' he whispered.

'God, nobody's called me that in years!'

'You're still Kit,' he said, advancing, taking her into a clumsy embrace. 'I've been watching you this last quarter of an hour.'

'Oh Freddy.' Her body yielded and it became a proper hug, long and comforting. 'Let me look at you!' she pushed him back. They laughed. 'Christ, it's good to see you.' She paused, searching for the words. 'I thought…' There was no need to spell it out. They'd both thought it. For years they'd thought it.

'Light that lamp for God's sake. I want to see what Miss Katherine Hart looks like in the bright. I love the hair, by the way.' A finger touched it. 'Why are we whispering?'

'We're the *whispering alibis*!'

'The what?'

'Don't you remember, Freddy? It was Cpt Jack's name for us.'

'Was it?'

'Because we were always whispering together! Surely you remember those notes in invisible ink you used to send?'

'Did I?'

'Lemon juice! Oh, Fred! I had to hold them near a candle to read them.'

'Light the lamp, Kit.'

'Do you think we should? Is it safe?' She hadn't told him. Of course she hadn't. 'That young lad.' She took a breath. 'That Tommy Kinkaid that used look in on you. He said someone was coming after you.' It sounded so lame, out here, beside the wind-rippled waters. 'He was scared half to death.'

'Did he say who it was? A name?'

'He described him. Tall. Hair in a ponytail. His voice was strange. Lifeless, he said.'

'Did he say he had the eyes of a jackal?'

'He said he looked starved. And there was something uncanny about the face. It was like seeing a wax dummy talk, he said.'

'Judd.'

'The Sergeant? But who is he, Fred? What does he want?'

He lifted the cap, angled his head toward her. 'You see that?' Taking her hand, he brought it as far as the scar, let her fingers trace it. The hair was cropped, soft. 'And the ear.' She touched that, too. 'That was Judd. He came at me one night. With a cutlass in one hand, an ugly knife in the other. We were off Belfast Lough. A brown sea mist had come on suddenly. We'd dropped anchor. Too dangerous to navigate blind. That night, I was on anchor watch. I was supposed to wake the Captain if and when the mist dispersed.

'I didn't hear him approach. There wasn't a sound, I'd swear to that. Not a sound. At the last minute, something made me turn. He was coming straight at me, out of the mist. A lucky thing I was standing by the side of the sloop. I stumbled backward. Just as the blade caught my skull I tumbled overboard, otherwise it would've sliced it clean open.

'He didn't jump in after me. He must have assumed I was dead, or would drown soon enough.'

'He was one of the crew?'

'That's just the thing. I hadn't seen him in years. Not since Tyre. I have no idea how he came to be there. How he found out I was on that sloop. How he came to be on board. We were a good mile from shore. Had he really swum that mile, in the blind fog, carrying a sword? Or had he been in hiding on board all the time, ever since we'd left Liverpool? Waiting his chance.'

'But why does he want to kill you?' He appeared frozen. Inanimate. 'Freddy?'

'Some other time I'll tell you. I promise. What did the boy say he said, can you remember?'

'Oh Fred. You can't stay here. If you stay here, he'll kill you. The message he gave is you've got to go back out to sea.' Still, it sounded lame. Across the lake, a curlew was calling a shrill lament. 'He knows about Father, and Edmond, and me.'

'Then he knows where you all live.' Their attention was drawn to a yelp, echoing across the twilight. A dog fox? 'I won't stay in the house, to put you in danger.'

'Where will you stay?'

'For tonight?' He indicated the decaying shed. 'Don't worry. I've a blanket and a change of linen hidden out there in my kitbag.' Seeing her grimace, he grinned, 'I've stopped in far worse, believe me.'

'Freddy.'

'I say, Kit. You aren't really engaged to that lawyer fellow?'

'To Reg?' She examined him. 'What on earth made you think that?'

Her attention was drawn abruptly back to the present. The Bridge Arms. Sweet smell of whiskey. Beside her loomed Dominic Foley, sandwich in hand with which he was pointing to the company. 'A decent turnout.'

'It's his father I feel sorry for,' she responded. A reflex. It was her third time saying it. 'To lose an only son.'

'Indeed. Can't be easy on him.'

She looked about the room. Who were these people? Professional acquaintances, she supposed. Clients from the legal practice. William Orr was seated in a corner, McSharry, the senior partner, next to him. And her father, Charlie. All three silent. She was piqued to see Cpt Jack's nose was stuck in a newspaper. Couldn't he for one day forsake that compulsion of his? Over by the bar, the Reverend Eugene Daly DD was nibbling on a drumstick, a glass of sherry in his free hand. Edmond and Dora Golden were conversing with the Musgroves.

She felt irritated, and couldn't quite have said why. Cressida had inquired should she come down from Dublin. No. After all she'd scarcely met Reginald. But that wasn't it. In some way she couldn't quite nail down, it would have been disrespectful if she were here. To his memory.

Foley leaned in. Waft of malt, sweet as cut grass. 'You saw of course who trailed us out to the graveyard?'

'There was no reason for Freddy to be there. Reg only became the family solicitor after Freddy'd left. So far as I'm aware, they only ever met that one time. And poor Reg was mortified by it, said he'd made a right show of himself.'

'Sergeant Judd mightn't be aware of that.' He took a bite of the sandwich, wet his lips with the whiskey tumbler. 'Where did you say you'd packed him off to?'

'Achill. There's no reason for Judd to go there.'

'What's in Achill?'

'Just a circle of huts. Some of us stay out there sometimes. Artists' refuge. Fred will be doing well not to perish with the cold, this time of year.'

They watched Cpt Jack return the newspaper to the front desk and gravitate toward them. Katherine had been piqued the night before when, at the removal, he'd confided in her ear,

'I never warmed to him, you know. Cold fish.' Waft of stale tobacco. Stained teeth.

'I see our friend Nannetti held onto his seat,' he now said, brightly.

Foley shrugged. 'There was scarcely any danger of his losing it.'

'I daresay not. Just try telling that to Mr Havelock-Saunders.' He grimaced toward his grand-niece. 'Your pocket journalist will be expecting another solicitor's letter, I shouldn't wonder.'

Foley picked up that ball to run with. 'One more reason for young Fred to be *persona non grata*. They're neither of them of the forgiving nature, the bold Sergeant and his former Commanding Officer. Is it a coincidence, I wonder, that Havelock-Saunders' henchman should resurface in this country precisely now?'

'Freddy never named Judd,' she frowned. 'In his article.'

'But he very well might, if push comes to shove. If it comes to a libel trial, for instance.'

She made her excuses. She was feeling vexed. She couldn't have said why, precisely. Except that Dominic Foley had been his confidant. The closest thing Reginald Orr had had to a friend. And here, at his funeral reception, it was as though he were quite forgotten.

CHAPTER EIGHTEEN

The light was dying over the Atlantic. A sullen light. On a leaden ocean.

He sat huddled against the hut's undressed stone, in the most leeward of the cluster of what were scarcely more than beehive cells. A wind got as far as it all the same, blowing in off the sea, rattling door and window. Howling about the place, the night before, like a demented banshee. Small wonder that, as his sister had told him, the fishermen about these parts told tales of sea-hags.

Floors of packed clay. Rough-hewn furniture. A solitary, smoky oil lamp. Hard to picture Kit, Kate, Katherine as she now was, staying here, even in summer. Part of the game, he supposed. Artists playing at how the peasantry lived.

Careful of the cast encasing his left wrist—in Castlebar a doctor had poured plaster of Paris into a wooden frame—he laid a couple more cakes of turf on the meagre fire. He blew on it and was blinded by acrid tears each time the smoke billowed. He drew the cloak closer about him. One thing to be said for this godforsaken refuge. It'd finally get the poison out of his bloodstream. The craving. At first it had been forgetfulness he'd sought in the opium pipe. Then it became a weakness. Then a demon. He'd taken handouts from anyone that would offer them. When that failed, he'd stolen. Too long he'd been brother to the bowsey who can't get through the day without a bottle for a crutch.

He'd put Kinkaid's youngster in the way of danger. That was unforgiveable. Had he known beforehand that A.T. Wall was in the country, there'd have been no need to involve the boy. But the addiction sapped all initiative.

He'd sort it out. This would sort it out. This purgatory.

He was famished. But it felt clean; an honest hunger after the body has been purged. He'd roasted the last of the potatoes the evening before. Tomorrow he'd have to make another trip into the fishing village to stock up on provisions. Praties; smoked fish; buttermilk; a quid of tobacco. A drop of poteen, against the chill. Gaelic speakers, all, and he hadn't a word of the blessed lingo. Last time they'd managed by pointing. It was beyond ironic; he'd spent ten years wandering amongst people who babbled in barbaric tongues and had largely got by on a handful of Turkish phrases he'd picked up; on a smattering of Arabic; on school French. Now here he was, not a hundred miles from his home, and unable to understand a word. Except from the few who, when they chose, had a facility in English.

It would be a chance to catch up on the news. Though

the single newspaper that sometimes came in from Dublin and even the copy of the *Connaught Telegraph* would be a week old. It was in the latter that he'd learned of the death of Reginald Orr, Solicitor, late of Boyle, Co. Roscommon. Kit had mentioned an accident. That he'd been taken to Sligo Hospital that same morning. Had it been on account of their altercation that his dogcart had left the road? He arriving like the thirteenth guest to dinner, the bringer of calamity. A cursed figure, a Jonah or a Cain, doomed to wander the earth.

There was irony too in the fact that here he was, quite literally, starving, and in his jacket for the first time in months sat a pocketbook with just shy of thirty pounds remaining. It was all the ready cash his father had had to hand.

How was all this going to end? This ten-year Odyssey without wife or palace or son to come home to. Because he was weary of it. Weary to the bone. If his calculations were correct, today was Thursday. Sunday would be Christmas Day. Another Christmas spent in lonely exile.

That night by the boathouse, Kit had explained the brief message she'd sent Edmond. So far as the army was concerned, he wasn't a deserter. Never had been! If it were true, the irony was perfect when, with his own hand, he'd told the world how he'd deserted.

When it had been discovered that the collier was taking on water and they'd have to make for the port of Dublin, he'd fully expected there would be two men with carbines across their shoulders waiting for him as he disembarked. A form of hubris, surely. As if, after ten years! Then, when he'd discovered by chance that Cecil Havelock-Saunders was to stand for parliament, he'd actually imagined that Fate had contrived to spring that leak in the collier's bulkhead so as to bring him to Dublin, like some sort of Nemesis. Hubris again. And was it not Fate that had directed his gaze to chance upon those initials, A.T., that last night the boy had come to him. And then, to sign his own death warrant with his own hand, declaring himself a deserter! Not Aeschylus, nor Sophocles himself, could have contrived a finer trap for him to have walked himself into.

But then, why had Edmond told him, all those years ago, that they had him down for a deserter? The time he'd wired home from Alexandria. The return wire had warned in no uncertain terms: Ireland would be a death sentence. Perhaps he should have stayed on another day at "the Elms", to clear that one up. He'd watched his brother through a window, earlier that evening. How stout he'd grown. Where, now, the sportsman?

And another point. Cecil Havelock-Saunders was by the by, when it came down to it. A killer, yes, and a ruthless son of a bitch. But none of this would end, this crazy pursuit, until the day he came face to face with Judd. Kit had said what the message he'd sent him through the boy was: go back to sea. Don't be found anywhere in home waters. But that was Havelock-Saunders, speaking through him. Because he'd never rest, Caleb Judd. Not until he'd made that sea into a watery grave. He'd sworn as much as he was being dragged from the dock, in Tyre. How the devil had he escaped from that incarceration?

How long would he have to spend here, at the very edge of the world, before Caleb Judd believed he had gone back to sea?

The New Year was several days old when he saw it.

He was seated, as was his custom on his bi-weekly visit, by the window of the shebeen that served as meeting house, bar and general store. Solitude had driven him to pick up some phrases of the Gaelic, but the locals remained closed. Private. As though he might be an excise man. Solitude might drive him back to sea yet, if Judd didn't. On one of his days wandering the island, he'd come across a whaling station. Closed for the winter, but perhaps when the weather picked up they'd be taking on crew.

He sat at the window so as to keep half an eye on the brambled path that led down to the shebeen, while slowly going through last week's newspapers. And sipping, more slowly yet, at the glass of scalding poteen.

He sputtered. He was so surprised by what he'd just read that he had to check it twice. Three times. Then he checked the date on the front page of the paper. He stared at the old woman who was nodding by the fire where the counter was, as though she might throw light on the obituary. But she was a Gaelic speaker and besides, was illiterate. Like most of them hereabouts. Or so they would have you believe.

The death has occurred of Charles Stewart Hart of 'the Elms', Boyle, Co. Roscommon. Predeceased by his wife, Frances 'Fanny' née Montagu, brother John and sister Margaret. Deeply regretted by his son, Edmond and daughter, Katherine.
May He Rest In Peace.

*The remains will arrive at the Church of Ireland,
Boyle, at 7pm on Thursday 29th of December to
repose overnight. Funeral Mass will be held at 2pm
on Friday 30th, followed by burial in the
adjoining graveyard.*

How could it be that no one had told him? How could Kit have failed to send word?

They hadn't even included his name amongst the children who deeply regretted the passing of their father!

He passed the dozing woman, slapped down a silver coin on the counter. He indicated for her not to wrap his customary bundle of provisions. Instead he set off in the direction of Achill Sound, though it was already past three o'clock. If he walked all night he could be in Castlebar by morning; in Boyle by the following night.

He wasn't wrong, though it was long past midnight when he stood in the grounds. In the moonlight the mansion looked artificial, an oversized doll's house. He hadn't eaten in a day and a half, his march driven by indignation. The absolute injustice of it.

Should he rap at the door? Rouse them all? Sound the alarm? He had half a mind to.

But instead, though it cost considerable discomfort on account of his damaged wrist, he shimmied up the drainpipe and onto the pantry roof. He approached on all fours the familiar window, rattled at the casement, tugged with right hand only. The latch slipped. In ten years, they hadn't seen their way to repairing it. He slid up the sash, climbed inside.

The house was in darkness. But navigating its corridors and stairwells in the dark was familiar. How often had he and Kit done it in years gone by? He crept along the half-landing that led to her bedroom. He hesitated outside her door. Listened. Then he rapped, softly.

He heard a movement inside. 'Edmond?' came a voice.

He opened the door, just a crack. 'Kit?'

'Freddy!' A match ignited. 'Freddy, is that you?' The bedside candle illumined her. She was sitting up, a bed-jacket about her nightdress. He fought a wave of tenderness. 'Where's Father?'

'Fred.'

'Where's my father?'

She shook her head, her eyes huge and liquid in the candlelight. 'He's dead. He died, Fred.'

'I know he died.' The words came out in a hiss. It was an effort to keep his voice down. 'I *read* that he had died. In a newspaper.'

'Fred. Listen.'

'You didn't see fit to send word?'

She angled her forehead down.

'You didn't even see fit to include my name in the obituary? *Deeply regretted by son Edmond and daughter Katherine*?' He advanced, grabbed her shoulders, shook her. 'For Christ's sake, Kit, he was my father too!'

'Freddy…'

There was a pounding of footsteps along the half-landing and a large frame filled the doorway, a lamp in hand up-lighting his brother's frown into that of a gargoyle. 'What are you doing in here?'

'Edmond! I want a talk with you, sir.'

Edmond bit on his little finger, puzzled. 'How did you get in?'

'My father. Why wasn't I told?'

'How did you get in here, Fred?'

'I…' Edmond's insistence wrong-footed him. It was a trivial detail. 'The window over the pantry. If you jimmy it, the latch comes free.' Edmond continued to nibble on his little finger as though he were worrying something out. 'Dad. How did he die?'

Edmond nodded toward Katherine, giving her permission to tell. 'He took a fall. He broke his neck. Oh Freddy. We found him at the foot of the stairs.'

'He fell down the stairs.'

'It was in the morning we found him. The body was cold. He must have got up during the night to get a glass of water or something. Or perhaps he'd heard a noise. You saw how unsteady on his feet he'd become.'

'Why didn't he ring for Anna?'

'It was her night off.'

'Her night off.' Hart sat at the edge of her bed. All this was too abrupt. He looked at the figure filling the doorway. A paisley dressing gown, a nightcap. The face, bloated. The chin, that had once been chiselled, was the corner of a crate subsiding into quicksand. This was ludicrous.

'You couldn't send word?' he turned back to his sister. 'Kit? You couldn't send word?'

The voice from the doorway was still that of the big brother of old. Throaty. Authoritative. 'That was my idea.'

'Oh?'

'I was suspicious. The whole damned business was doubtful.'

'How?'

'Our father was many things. But he was never one to go wandering in the night. And then, if he had fallen down the stairs, how was it that neither of us had heard a sound?'

'What are you saying? That he was pushed?'

'Pushed, or placed there.'

'Phhh!'

'But even if he wasn't. Even if it was a coincidence. A pure accident. Your friend Judd threw quite a shadow over Reginald Orr's funeral. There to spy out if you'd put in an appearance. How much more certain, that you'd be at Charles Hart's funeral. So long as you were still in the country, that is.'

Fred breathed heavily. Weighed this. 'So did he?'

'Did he what?'

'Shadow Dad's funeral?'

'We didn't see him there, no. But just because we didn't see him doesn't mean he wasn't there. Think about it, Fred. Even if he hadn't arranged the death in order to flush you out, you may be damned sure he'd take advantage of it.'

'With respect, you could have allowed me to decide for myself whether to attend my own father's funeral.'

His sister's fingers touched his. 'And what would you have decided, Freddy?' He pulled the hand away. He stood. 'You didn't even include my name in the obituary. *Deeply regretted by son Edmond and daughter Katherine*. As though I didn't exist. Or care.'

There was a creak as Edmond took a further step into the room. 'If we'd included your name, it might have given the impression that we were in contact with you.'

'No. This is…'

'Until you spoke just now, I couldn't imagine how he could've got in here. There was no sign of a forced entry. That's one reason the RIC wouldn't entertain my doubts. But if that window can be opened by simply jigging it about…'

'And how would he have known that! No, this is all too fantastic. There's something else going on, here.'

'What do you mean?'

'Why did you tell me the army had me down for a deserter?'

'I don't follow.'

'When I was in Alexandria. You told me. To return meant death.'

'Yes. A letter came.'

'What letter?'

'There'd been a letter, Freddy,' said Katherine. Tired. Conciliatory. 'From the army. It spelt it out; you'd be facing the death penalty.'

'Show me the letter.'

'Captain Jack has it.'

'Convenient.'

Edmond loomed forward. 'What are you trying to say? I made it up, is it?'

'All I know is that my father is dead and buried and no one saw fit to tell me.'

'Yes. For your own good.' Edmond was unruffled. That much hadn't changed. 'For your own good, Fred.'

'And what else don't I know, for my own good?'

'Actually, now that you ask, there is more.'

As though he didn't trust his older brother, Fred Hart turned to Kate a look of cautious inquiry.

'There is, Freddy. I was so desperate to get you away from here, it quite slipped my mind when we spoke. You'll have to talk to McSharry to get the details. To sign the relevant forms and so forth. But there's a legacy you're entitled to.'

'A legacy. From father?'

'No, not Charlie. From our mother. Fanny.'

Edmond picked up the explanation. 'Quite a considerable sum, in point of fact. What it comes down to is an annuity. But as you haven't been here to collect yours, Reginald Orr was looking after it for you. Investing it. Quite a sum has accrued, as I understand it. He wouldn't reveal the figure. But certainly in excess of two thousand pounds.'

'Two thousand pounds.' He sat back onto the bed, weak.

'There are formalities you'll need to sort out. I'll be happy to arrange a rendezvous somewhere safe with Pierce McSharry.'

'Hold on! If this comes from mother, how comes I never knew about it?'

'None of us did. You'll have to talk to McSharry. He can explain the ins and outs of the will.'

Fred Hart frowned. 'And what do you suggest I do with this two thousand pounds?'

'You might go abroad.'

'So it's to buy me off? Buy my silence?'

'Quite the opposite! Really, you've developed into quite the suspicious character, you know. We're all on your side here, Fred.'

'Oh yes?'

'It's certain, now. Havelock-Saunders is to sue the *Freeman's Journal* for libel. Also your acquaintance, A.T. Wall. Defamation of character. There's talk of his seeking quite an outrageous sum. There are powerful backers behind the lawsuit. Keen to bring the *Freeman's Journal* down a peg or two. Put a gag on Brayden. Let's not forget, when Carson brought down Oscar Wilde, that began life as a libel trial.'

'Carson is taking it on?'

'It hasn't been settled. But the salient point is, if it does come to trial, Mr A.T. Wall had better be in a position to produce you. To defend that article you wrote. So in the meantime...'

This was all too fantastic. He stood, peered at Kate. 'I was sorry to read about your friend the lawyer. Truly I was.' He circumnavigated his brother, made to leave the room.

'Where are you going?'

'Downstairs. I'm absolutely famished.'

He felt a meaty palm squeeze his shoulder. 'It's good to see you, Fred.'

CHAPTER NINETEEN

After Pierce McSharry had assured him that it was all above board and that there were no conditions attaching to the annuity, Hart signed the papers. They were seated in a brougham about three miles out on the Sligo Road. Once these formalities were completed, the old lawyer examined the young man. Must be awkward, managing those bags with one hand in a cast. 'Where can I drop you, sir?'

'Aye, there's the rub.'

He'd told the lawyer as little as he could, except in so far as it related to the matter of accessing the legacy. He'd be travelling abroad; that much the solicitor needed to know. But he was still in two minds. Make for Enniskillen and thence to Belfast and on to Scotland and maybe the Isles; or take care of a few loose ends in Dublin before catching the mail boat to Holyhead, to lose himself in the Welsh valleys.

Either way, he wanted to leave some sort of trail.

At the boathouse, Kit had been scared. There was something she wasn't telling him, he felt it instinctively. He'd picked it up again, the night in "the Elms". There was a sense of threat hanging over the place. Edmond himself, unmoveable as a rock, suspected foul play. Would Judd really have lain hands on their father, to smoke him out? If so, what else might he do? It wasn't a chance he was prepared to take. No. He'd leave just enough of a trail for Judd to pick it up. Draw him abroad. Then strike, end this purgatory for once and for all.

Belfast had been a nest of suspicion and sectarianism. It wasn't sufficient that the Harts were of good Protestant stock. The accent wasn't right. Around the docks he'd been treated as an outsider. A pariah. Perhaps that was how Judd had tracked him to the sloop, before. He at least had the tribal accent. Ulster Presbyterian. If Fate decreed he should go via Dublin, so much the better. It would be easy to lay a trail there.

'Kilfree Junction is as good as anywhere,' he decided, on the spur. 'If it isn't too far out of your way.' He would leave it to chance. Whichever train came first would carry him either northwest from Kilfree or southeast.

Chance brought him to Dublin on the Midland Great Western. Collar turned up, he stood in the great foyer of the GPO. Could he take the chance of calling round to the *Freeman's Journal* on Prince's St North? Would they be watching for that? Probably. But how else to contact A.T. Wall? There was no listing for any Wall, A.T. in Thom's Directory, nor for an Aloysius Terence. It had been a mistake not to have secured that address before boarding the train. He could now send a wire to the paper suggesting a rendezvous, but who was to say whether or when the reporter would get it.

He'd never thanked the man, not merely for publishing, but for taking the article on trust. At a time when he'd been the least trustworthy of men. A mendicant; a down-and-out. At times a thief, in thrall to the demon of forgetfulness. Well, that was all done now. He'd exorcised that demon from his body. That craving. He wanted not only to thank A.T. Wall in person, but to assure him. He'd stand by that article. If called upon, he'd come out of exile. Even if it meant facing up to a court-martial.

Then there was Patch Kinkaid's wife. The wife he'd never written to, at the time of the soldier's miserable end. They'd hit it off on the wrong note. He'd taken money from her. A handout, like the lowliest of beggars. Then he'd abused the trust of her son. Patch's son. He'd needlessly led him into harm's way. But no, he thought. Calling out to her to make his peace was a balm only for his own soul. What benefit would she derive from it? Or the boy? No, better leave well enough alone. They were safer, to be well shot of him.

He toyed with the idea of dropping out to Delgany. His sister had described Bertie Nuzum's injuries. A carved up face. Of course, Nuzum hadn't been around at the time of the incident itself. There was no reason to think anyone would be watching the Nuzum estate. Also, there was no sense in which his visit could be construed as having an ulterior motif. And then, they'd always differed, at times quite heatedly, on Kitchener's policy of scorched earth. Nuzum's vehemence on the subject had taken him quite by surprise. No, he wouldn't go. What was such a visit for, if not to assuage some vestige of guilt he felt deep inside him?

That left Cpt Jack. After all, he hadn't seen the old codger in years. Kit assured him he'd scarcely changed one iota. It would be a pleasure to drop out to the Royal Hospital, Kilmainham. Bring him a quid of tobacco for his famous briar. Too late, this evening. But on the morrow. For the present he'd find lodgings; compose a letter to A.T. Wall which he'd charge his great-uncle with delivering. Then he'd take the boat.

But as he left the GPO, indecision once more took hold of him. He felt a craving for company. Or it was a fear of solitude. Of the pangs of anxiety that his nervous system was prone to. He made his way across the river to Westland Row Station, and boarded the next train bound for Bray. Damn it all, he'd drop out to Bertie Nuzum. Unannounced. Kit had told him he rarely left the workshop he'd built himself out there.

So many months, so many years, he'd been in exile from anyone who had known him. Who'd known where he'd been; whither he came. His tongue, bound. It'd be good to talk freely to someone who'd actually been there.

The sum being sought in damages set tongues wagging the length and breadth of the country. Ten thousand pounds. It was generally understood that what was already being dubbed the 'trial of the year' would take place in June or July, certainly to this side of the summer recess.

In late February, what Cpt Jack dubbed the "Second Council of War" was gathered in the Bridge Arms Hotel, in the very room that had played host to Reginald Orr's funeral reception three months before, and to Charles Stewart Hart's so indecently on its heels. For the moment, the party gave the impression of a collection of individuals treading water.

'Cressie tells me there's one of Grace Gifford's lampoons doing the rounds,' commented Katherine Hart, to no one in particular. 'Wicked. Absolutely delicious.'

'All of which is grist to the mill for Havelock-Saunders,' commented Dominic Foley.

'Bah!' squinted Cpt Jack. 'How so?'

'It's a trial for defamation of character. Damages might well be assessed in terms of how much damage has been done to the man's public image.'

'Really,' Edmond exuded an air of impatience. Whether it was occasioned by the unnecessary delay in getting things started or by the earlier mention of Cressida Fitzsimons was unclear. He turned his attention to Foley. 'What's the word in Kings Inns on what judge might preside?'

'Your guess is as good as mine, or anyone else's for that matter. I have heard Justice Stanley Nuzum's name bandied about.'

Kate was surprised. 'Bertie Nuzum's father?'

'You've met him?' glowered Edmond, dismissive.

'Bertie? Oh yes. Same company as Fred. Picked up a dreadful injury to the face. He was in a field hospital at the time described in Freddy's article.'

'But if Stanley Nuzum is his old man, he'd have to recuse himself, surely.' Edmond nodded methodically. 'Skin in the game.' The unfortunate expression had an unsavoury effect on the party, and a shiftless silence followed until they saw Mr A.T. Wall's mustard corduroy three-piece approaching them from the direction of the men's room.

'It's set, then?' asked Foley, looking faintly amused. 'You're actually going to chase off to Africa.'

By way of answer, the journalist executed a smart salute.

'Bit of a wild goose chase, wouldn't you say?' suggested Cpt Jack.

'You have to remember, gentlemen. And lady,' he bowed. 'I was nigh on three years down below.' He stood a half-inch taller as he specified, 'War correspondent. Sending home my weekly report, right up to the surrender at Vereeniging. I even picked up some of the lingo.'

Kate hoisted a sceptical eyebrow. 'Oh yes?'

He stood ramrod straight, clicked his heels. '*Staan op jou lui swart baster*!'

'Sounds positively formidable! What does it mean?'

'Oh, something along the lines of, "Stand up there, please, I've had just about enough of you." So you see, at one level, it'll be a homecoming. I know the terrain.'

The junior barrister didn't look convinced. 'You've been to the location Fred's article mentioned?'

'Valley that runs between Magaliesberg and Witwatersberg? Certainly I have. I know the Transvaal like the proverbial back-of-the-paw. Been all over it. They were four days out from camp, which was itself about forty miles west of Jo'burg. Fred says the farmstead itself is etched like a lithograph into his memory. The precise configuration of the hills. The low stone bridge over a culvert on a dog-leg at the approach. The outhouse the bullet came from standing at right angles to the main buildings.' His voice dropped. 'The tamarind tree they hanged the girl from.

'And then, we have a family name to be going along with. Esterhuizen. Ok, you'll tell me it's not exactly unique. But then, it's not as common a beast as your Bothas or de Klerks, who wander the veldt in great herds. Also, I've been thinking about it.'

'I'm glad to hear it!' Kate smirked.

'That ambush, now. That happened two days after the massacre. Yes? September 11th. September 13th. And the ambush *actually* took place, that's not in dispute. It wasn't some fiction dreamed up by Havelock-Saunders. *Ouhondspruit.* Which is something along the lines Old Hound Creek. So that our farmstead can't be more than two days' ride from Ouhondspruit, and likely back from it in the direction of the military encampment, if we can only track down the old hound.'

'Not so fast,' interjected Cpt Jack. 'A creek could be many miles long, surely.'

'But not the site of an ambush,' the reporter crowed, as though playing the five of trumps.

'Well, it's something, I suppose.' Katherine was frowning. 'But after ten years, what do you hope to find? The shell of a house? What can you possibly learn from that? Fred told me by the end of Kitchener's campaign, there were in excess of thirty thousand farms put to the torch. How will yours be any different?'

'We're ten years on, yes. But it doesn't exactly make it an archaeological dig, either. I might be inclined to agree with you, except there's this. Those dates: September 11th; September 13th. I'd lay even money the reason for that ambush was to take revenge on your brother's squadron for that very massacre.'

'That *alleged* massacre,' corrected Foley.

'Quite so. And if I'm right, it'll be more than a mere folk

memory. Are you with me? General Hendrik Schoeman will have had a hand in the affair, for all that the *bittereinders* came to revile him. It's his stomping ground. Some of the *kommando* involved will have survived. Stands to reason. And them boys'll have an interesting tale to tell, you may be sure.'

'At least,' concluded Cpt Jack, 'you'll be in a position to establish the massacre itself took place. That'll take some of the wind out of the sails of Havelock-Saunders' lawsuit.'

'Precisely. No smoke without fire.'

'The question would remain, though. Who set the fire.'

'The ambush site mightn't prove they were the arsonists, but it should place the squadron in the vicinity. Motive, means, opportunity.' Wall counted out three stubby fingers. He then abruptly ruffled his crest with both fists. 'Here's something for yous will make yous laugh. Shows how military logic works. I've been out to General Schoeman's place. Interviewed the old boy, though he was far more interested in talking about irrigation schemes than the state of the war. Had a fine old plantation house he called 'Schoemansrus'. Told me how the month previous, he'd watched the Boers routing the Tommies up at Silkaatsnek from the very terrace we were sitting on. Pretoria had fallen, and now he was of the faction pressing for peace. Want to know something rich? For that most grievous sin, he was tried three times for treason in the space of six months. Three times, just fancy! Coetzee and Botha both had it in for him. Escaped the firing squad by a whisker on each occasion.

'About the time Fred's massacre was *allegedly* taking place, he returned from acquittal at the first treason trial to find that 'Schoemansrus' had been burned to the ground. But here's the punchline. Ladies and gentlemen, drumroll, please! It wasn't the *bittereinders* who'd done it, oh no. It was the British Army, in all its wisdom. For all we know, it may even have been Havelock-Saunders' boys, and Freddy among them.'

'You'll ask this General about it, then. The ambush? The girl?'

'I'd love to, my darling. Only I don't think that'd be altogether feasible. He was blown to smithereens the following year in a living room, in what Scotland Yard would describe as highly dubious circumstances.'

Edmond had been watching the reporter as he performed as though he'd been assessing an unlikely candidate for a position. 'Brayden going to finance this little safari, is he?'

'If only! I tried to make the case. Public interest. Ten years on and all that; the press has a weakness for anniversaries. That cock wouldn't crow. It was ten years, he declared dryly, last September that's gone. But Willie, says I, it'd be your neck we'd be saving! Your newspaper, man! No go. I'm afraid your humble servant is still very much *persona non grata* when it comes to Mr W.H. Brayden. No. Freddy's putting up the readies.'

'And when do you sail?'

'Personally, I leave Kingstown tomorrow on the night boat. Holyhead. London. Southampton. Fred will meet me in Southampton. Then we set sail Tuesday evening.' He grimaced comically. 'Steerage.'

CHAPTER TWENTY

Friday, March 24th
Johannesburg

*D**ear Miss Hart,*
*   I wanted to begin the letter 'Dear 'art', as any self-respecting cockney might have done, but Frederick simply wouldn't have it. You'll have gathered that I've been assigned the role of scribe. Any time he tries to concentrate on something dextrous, your brother's right hand seizes, or shakes like a dancing dervish.*

*   Fred insists I put in a little of the local colour on his behalf, so here goes. What struck him the moment he stepped off the steamer and onto dry land was the scent, apparently. The aroma of a continent, he called it, as if he wanted to set up as a perfumer; though if you discount brief stopovers in the fleapits of Mombasa and Alexandria, he's*

never got further north than Lourenço Marques. Africa's aroma is hot, dry, spicy. Tinged with the musk of a cat, maybe just a hint of human sweat. Unmistakable, he says, as though the first lungful had abolished in an instant the ten years he'd been away.

We didn't dilly-dally more than a couple of days around Cape Town, and that chiefly to recover from the foul fare and still fouler air of steerage. After all, what could we possibly find out, there? I was all for leaving the first morning, but Fred said he had a few loose ends to take care of—I can't imagine what these might have been. I took the opportunity to pick up one of Kodak's box cameras, replete with tripod and several rolls of film.

Fred says the train up to Jo'burg came as a pleasant surprise. Back in his campaigning days, they were as like as not to be shunted about on the kind of open-goods wagons that railroads traditionally use for transporting cattle. Me, I wouldn't know. I travelled up to Bloemfontein in a regular carriage. 2nd class, if memory can be trusted. Incidentally he had us stop off in Bloemfontein, to pay our respects at the grave of Padraic Kinkaid. A white cross, one of perhaps a hundred drawn up in rows. It was a chance to develop my skills as a photographer. He'd like a photographic record for Kinkaid's widow and boy, he told me.

I've heard it said by the begrudgers that the Boers may have lost the war, but they won the peace. After all, Jan Smuts is Prime Minister of the Unie van Zuid-Afrika, not Sir Alfred Milner. But I have to say, I can't see it myself. They're a bitterly divided people, it seems to me. Far *more entrenched than James Craig's naysayers versus the rest of us islanders—though we'll see how that pans out when Asquith finally shoves the Home Rule Bill down the gullets of the indignant Lords. Fred noticed it too, though he doesn't speak the lingo. He told me I should write: you have to think of Swift—the Big-Enders versus the Little-Enders? Only down here, it's the* Joiners *against the* Bitter Enders. *Hate each other far more sedulously than they hate any mere Anglophone, I can tell you.*

So tomorrow we go in search of horses and a mule for hire. A good ordnance survey map, a portable tent, mess tins, lamps, lentils, beans, pots, pans, sundry accoutrements (hence the mule). They're well used to provisioning pioneers and gold prospectors in this corner of the world. Why, I'm almost tempted to try my hand at it myself. Dip a pan into any pebbled creek we stumble upon.

After that it's out unto the dry ocean of the open veldt. Expect the next Letter of St Paul to the Hibernians on our return to civilisation.

In the interim, I beg to remain
Your most 'umble,
A.T.

Cressida Fitzsimons had the most eloquent of smiles.

'I know,' grimaced Kate. 'I fear Freddy's fallen into the hands of a lunatic.'

Looking at Cressie, she was reminded once again of Cpt Jack's tall tale about his time on a tiger hunt in Bengal. 'We were a day's elephant ride into the jungle when I heard a roar,' he'd said. '"Was that a tiger?" I asked the dragoman. "If you have to ask," he replied, "then it was not." And just as night fell, right on cue, a bone-shaking roar erupted out of the darkness, as if conjured by the dragoman himself to illustrate his point.'

Well, she had no such doubt where Cressida was concerned. Never had.

The second letter followed three weeks after the first. The third, hot on the heels of the second.

Dear Miss Hart,

You find us sleeping out under the great expanse of the southern sky with its strange constellations. Though 'sleeping' is a shameless euphemism. On the one hand, the earth is stony and unyielding as sailors' hard-tack; on the other, we brought with us no mosquito nets. Nightly, as we sweat and stifle under the canvas, the little bastards (apologies) blighters sound their victory whines in the amphitheatre of our ears. By morning our faces are bumpy as spotty adolescents.

We weren't too long, a matter of three days, in finding the ruined farmstead, which Fred assures me he remembers right down to the distribution of the aloe plants on the approach. He pointed out the bough of the tamarind from which the girl had been strung up; the trajectory of the bullet that felled the Major's steed. Like any tourist worth his salt, I made a faithful record of all the above with the help of Mr Kodak. We then rode out to the spot where they halted their egress, and from which he witnessed the massacre of the innocents that followed through field glasses. The occasion of another photograph. After all, his eyewitness testimony is sure to be challenged when the case comes to trial.

You astutely suggested, back in the Bridge Arms Hotel in fairest Boyle, that it might be difficult at ten years' remove to have the stones yield up their secrets. The overall sense one gets out here is indeed one of silence, and not merely the yawning silence of an open plain depopulated by war and its ravages. If they were a reticent people before, the Afrikaner is so suspicious, not only of us uitlanders *but of his own neighbours, that it's difficult to get much beyond* 'hoe gaan dit?' *As yet we haven't even established how many were in the Esterhuizen family, much less their names or where they might be buried or remembered.*

Then there are the natives. The conflict was said at the time to be a white man's war, despite the numbers of 'kaffirs' enlisted on both sides, many of whom bore arms they were pretty loath to give up afterwards. Now, in the peace settlement, these have been entirely forgotten, and have no rights. So one can well understand their reticence. And then of course there's the small matter of language. Those 'kaffirs' that Freddy saw trying to protect the Boer children were presumably from the Bophuthatswana people, which is just a little outside yours sincerely's linguistic province. So that, yes, for the present, the testimony we're here to glean has eluded us. But nil desperandum, *as our legal eagle friend might say.*

Tomorrow we ride north, to the area around Hartbeespoort where, as I think I told you, I once interviewed the Boer General Schoeman. A man of peace, and so I reported him. I'm hoping his descendants might give me credit for that, and that it might provide the key to unlocking the collective memory. After all, if there was a massacre hereabouts perpetrated on the part of the Tommies, it would hardly serve their interests to hush it up.

That's all for the present. Freddy of course sends his best.

A.T.

A mere four days later, on Friday, April 28th, the third letter arrived. In the company of Cpt Jack Montagu, Kate Hart called in to Kings Inns to show it to Dominic Foley.

Dear Miss Hart,

The most extraordinary stroke of good fortune!

At the time I was interviewing Hendrik Schoeman a decade ago, I was impressed by the fact that he was far more motivated to talk about his schemes for the irrigation of the veldt hereabouts than the present state of the conflict, and the terms of peace that might be offered or demanded by the warring parties. His place, 'Schoemansrus', which the Brits in their wisdom razed to the ground, lies on the concourse of the Crocodile and Magalies rivers. He'd already built a small scale dam, but his planned irrigation scheme was far more ambitious.

Now, ten years on, though sadly he didn't survive the war to see it, Pretoria has embraced the grand plan. Work is scheduled to begin on the epic project within the year. For the present, engineers, land surveyors and geologists are to be found like migrating impala all about the hinterland, estimating the catchment area of the basin and digging test holes in the riverbeds and what have you. You won't guess who one of the chief geological experts charged with this endeavour turns out to be? Freddy absolutely swears that Providence has taken a hand—as clear as anything you might find in the Greek drama.

So you remember, when Fred stole away from camp on the night after the outrage, he brought with him a Lance Corporal 'O' whom they were holding in custody? O'Byrne. Cathal O'Byrne, to be precise about it. Fred says you might recall he was one of two Privates (!), the one with ears on him like jug handles? He it was who'd refused to carry out the Major's orders in relation to the girl. After they'd stolen away from camp and made their way north, they'd parted company. Fred made for the border, and the relative safety of Portuguese East Africa, if he survived the gauntlet of tribes that stood between him and the coast. O'Byrne on the other hand determined to stay on, to try his luck joining a Boer kommando. *How he fared, how he got from that decision to this, a position of authority on a capital project for the* Unie van Zuid-Afrika, *and how he now has gone entirely native and speaks Afrikaans by default, is a tale of wonder worthy of a Scheherazade, but one which would use up a deal more than the remaining stocks of my writing paper.*

The salient point, dear lady, is that we have our first witness for the defence. Please to inform Mr Foley. A first-hand account, and one moreover that supports everything that Fred's article claims. At the very least, Lce Cpl

O'Byrne should be able to furnish a signed affidavit to the effect. In addition, tomorrow being Sunday, a Sabbath strictly observed down here even during the sieges of Mafeking and Ladysmith, he promises to lead us to a cross that commemorates the Esterhuizen victims— useful not merely in furnishing their names and ages, but as evidence the massacre itself took place and on what date. Incidentally, Esterhuizen père *survived the war, but emigrated soon after, part of a wider exodus. To the Argentine, in his case.*

Frederick James (as ever) wishes to be fondly remembered to you and your brother, while I beg to remain Your most diligent servant,
A.T.

'Quite the stylist, your little friend,' said Foley, dryly. 'I wonder who he models himself on.'

There was a postscript, written in a jerky hand, presumably Fred Hart's own.

PS If Foley still has a contact in the Castle, tell him he might do worse than have them track down other survivors from my troop of 'B' Company who witnessed the atrocity—Havelock-Saunders is certain to suborn witnesses sympathetic to his side.

'Tell me, Miss Hart,' continued the same Foley, 'do you write your brother?'

'I haven't. As yet.'

'Might you, by return?'

'The only address we have for Freddy is *poste restante,* Johannesburg.'

'I see. Hardly ideal. Still. Could you write him that a signed affidavit is all very well. But ask him to see if he can't persuade this O'Byrne fellow to sail back with them. We really do need him as a witness who'll take the stand. Counsel for the prosecution will be looking to cross-examine. Which is as it should be. Oh, and you might add that the course of action he suggests in regard to other troopers is already well under way.'

Cpt Jack sucked air through his empty briar, then used its stem to point toward Foley's chest. 'Chap in the *Daily Express* has it that Brayden has made an offer to settle out of court. Any truth in it?'

'I've heard the rumour echoing down these dusty corridors. A cool five hundred is the general consensus on the offer. Guineas, it's a nice touch. Though you'd have to concede is considerably less than the ten thousand they're suing for.'

'He won't accept?'

'If it were down to the Major, perhaps he might be tempted. Honour saved, reputation restored. Why invite the whole shameful episode to be dragged into the daylight and drooled over by the salacious public?'

'I'm inclined to agree with you.'

'But that's figuring without *cui bono*. The salient issue being, five hundred sterling would scarcely put a dent in the finances of the nationalist press. And that's the real target his backers have been after all along.'

CHAPTER TWENTY-ONE

They'd left camp before dawn, were trekking steadily southwest along the valley as the sun rose behind them. Three horses and a mule, lonely in the vast landscape. The Esterhuizen place was a good half-day's ride, and by noon, the sun would be merciless. They would put up in some shady spot, wait for the zenith to pass.

Hart was out front on a gelding, the journalist to the rear, the utensil-laden mule tethered to his mount. In between the two rode O'Byrne, the geological engineer. He was much changed from the not-fully-formed student that Fred Hart remembered, soft-spoken, hesitant, but with a quiet authority when the subject turned to the earth sciences. His face was craggier, now. Weathered, unsmiling. No trace of Westmeath in the accent. In fact, one would be hard-pressed to identify the Irish brogue still trickling beneath the harsher rocks of

Afrikaans and the clipped flint of Cape English.

His outlook, too, had hardened under the southern sun. Hart had been surprised, dismayed even, to hear him talk now of 'the kaffir'. How he was lazy; resentful; not to be trusted. But what about the injustice, he'd protested, the lack of rights? Rights! Had he never read Galton? You needed to treat these people like children. Besides, the kaffirs were treated far better here than under the Portuguese, or in German South West Africa.

Toward eleven they came upon a blockhouse, one of thousands that Kitchener had had built in an attempt to fence in the Boer. Hart rode ahead to scout it, found it deserted, rode on. Once more, he looked through his binoculars to the twin ranges, the Witwatersberg, the Magaliesberg. At this point along the valley perhaps ten miles separated them. The geologist's mare drew up alongside. 'What is it you're looking for? You're constantly scanning the landscape as though you feared an ambush. War's been over a long time, you know.'

'What do you remember about Sgt Judd?'

'Judd? I remember his eyes.' From beneath the rim of his hat, the engineer gazed at the sun, whitening to a disc of molten metal. 'I remember, on the occasion of one of our raids. It may have been the first. He took a kid goat, held it on his lap, fondled it, stroked its soft hair, and drew a knife across its throat. And all the time he never took his eyes from mine. Those unblinking eyes. It was a challenge of sorts.' He looked from one side of the valley to the other. 'You can't imagine he's here?'

'Why not?'

'What in God's name would draw him to this wilderness?'

'The same thing that drew us, I imagine. Tell me. You say you went back to the Esterhuizen place several times. What was it made you go?'

O'Byrne took off his hat, mopped his brow. One thing you'd have to give him, he took matters seriously. Gave any question serious consideration. 'The first time was by chance,' he said. 'It must have been toward the end of the second year of the war. I was riding with a section. You can't really call it that. They were individuals, always. Rebels. They'd come and go as the mood took them. Dissolve. Coalesce. Though by this time we were a ragged bunch, quite literally. Starving. Kinfolk burned out and rounded up into their infernal camps. In any case, there were about five of us. Something about the landscape was suddenly familiar. We scarcely stopped, but I vowed to return one day. When things… you know.

'The second occasion was after the surrender. It was in the company of Jani Esterhuizen himself. He'd fought with Christiaan de Wet's *kommando*. Had been with him on any number of his scrapes and miraculous escapes. Somewhere, he'd got wind of the fact that I'd witnessed the massacre of his family. We rode out to the *plaasopstal* together. I described for him what I'd seen. He was silent as granite. I'll always remember that. But he could no longer bear to stay in the new South Africa. Before he left for the New World, he decreed that the family should be remembered not at the *plaasopstal*, where the atrocity had taken place. About a mile from the site is a *kopje* with a serene view. That's where the memorial was to be placed.

'I promised him I'd oversee the erection of the memorial. Maybe six-seven years ago? That was the third and final occasion I visited the Esterhuizen place.' They were approaching the elephantine trunk of a prehistoric baobab. Enough dappled shade to break up the heat of midday. Beneath it they halted, listened to the clop and clatter of the mule as it approached.

'Either of you ladies want to take over leading the donkey?'

The woman in the cloche hat and fox-fur paused outside the window of the milliner's. But she'd scarcely the chance to appreciate the elegance of the display before the doorbell jangled and the floor manager's head popped out. 'I've a half hour. Is there somewhere we can go?'

'Maybe Bachelor's Walk? It's pleasant enough out.'

By way of acquiescence, the floor manager nodded to a member of staff inside, then led the way in the direction of the river. 'Good of you to make the time. I realise it's… Did your deaf friend tell you what this is about?'

'Cressida? Cressie's not deaf.'

'Isn't she? I assumed…' Ciss Kinkaid let the silence complete what she'd assumed.

'Most people do.' Katherine Hart decided to be expansive. She didn't want them to get off on the wrong foot for a second time. 'When she was sixteen, she had to get a growth removed.' She tapped her throat. 'Here.'

'Poor thing.'

'Yeah. Unfortunately, it entailed taking the larynx. It's funny. When they see she can't talk, people assume she can't hear, either. They begin to speak loudly. And in monosyllables, as though being mute meant you were somehow in your dotage.'

'She could be a symbol. Irish womanhood.'

'Cressida's no symbol.'

'No, I only meant,' Cissie Kinkaid was ill-concealing her agitation. 'She's denied a voice. I realise of course she must have her own life.'

'How did you know where to find her?'

Rooting briefly in her bag, the woman pulled out a flier and flattened it on her sleeve. With the horseshoe moustache and bandana, Freddy really did look every bit the corsair.

'Tommy had it hoarded away, like it was some class of religious icon. My son.'

'Yes, I've met Tommy.' Beneath the arched back of the Ha'penny Bridge, a couple of gulls were scrapping over a crust. 'Cress tells me you've been receiving postcards?'

'Two. That is, they're addressed to Tommy.'

'Are they?'

'The first one came maybe... a couple of months back? From Southampton in England.' She removed from her bag a picture postcard. The writing on it was sparse and spasmodic. '*Return to the scene of the crime*!' she read aloud. '*We sail tomorrow, J.*'

'Jay?'

'Jimmy Cade. Your brother went by that name. The second one arrived there just last week. Also addressed to Tommy. Who knows nothing about them. I made sure of that.'

'May I see?'

Cissie Kinkaid passed her the two postcards. The second had been sent from Bloemfontein, the handwriting in pencil and scarcely legible. 'Bloemfontein. That's where your husband Padraic is buried, isn't it?'

'Look it. Here's the thing. I don't know what this man wants. What he's writing to Tommy for. And frankly, I'm sorry, but I don't care. He's your brother. I want you to tell him to stop. Writing to my son. Contacting him.' She drew a sharp breath. 'Tommy is all I have. And I will not have anyone filling his head with bullshit.'

'But he's trying to protect him. To protect *you*. Don't you see?'

'No. No, I don't see.'

'After the attack. After that man came to your house. Tommy found us. He told me what he'd threatened. That Freddy had to get out of the country. What would happen if he didn't.' The image of the terror written on the boy's pale face came back to her. 'We think... look, we don't know. All right? But just before New Year my father died. In suspicious circumstances. We think it may have been Judd.'

'Your *father*?'

'Don't you see, now? Freddy must be assuming they have your place watched. Dominic Foley, the barrister? He mentioned a private detective. It's the sort of trick they go in for, snooping on the mail. Freddy sent similar postcards to my grand-uncle. Captain Jack Montagu, care of the Royal Hospital, Kilmainham. From Southampton. Then from Cape Town. Don't you understand? He's trying to prove he's out of the country.' Her brow frowned, and her voice dropped. 'He's laying a trail of breadcrumbs for him.'

The floor manager of the hat shop, sometime secret author of Gaelic poetry and of women's erotic fiction, considered this. 'Well he can do all that without involving my son. I want you to tell him.'

'I can try. I don't have an address, just post restante. But I *will* try.'

'I'd better head back.'

'One other thing. Look, it's. I want to. The thing is,' unusually for Kate Hart, words were faltering against one another. She reached inside her bag for a leaflet, which she pushed awkwardly toward the other woman. 'This concerns Tom. His... *condition*.'

Mrs Kinkaid eyed her suspiciously. 'Tommy has consumption.'

'I know. That's what I'm getting at. There's a place. Newcastle. In Wicklow. So you could visit.' She tried to read the expression on the other's face. Indignation? 'A National Hospital for Consumption. It's state of the art. They take people, so long as it's still in the early stages.' In the face of the other's silence, she was stumbling over each phrase. 'The focus is on nutrition. A good, healthy diet. Cod liver oil. Vinegar rubs, exercise. And fresh air. Plenty of fresh air.'

With the back of her hand, the mother pushed aside the leaflet.

'Or if that didn't suit. If he was too far gone, say. There's another. Altadore Castle. A private sanatorium. You take the train as far as Greystones. So once again, you wouldn't be...' This was hopeless. At every word, the resistance stiffened. 'If it's a question of money...'

The leaflet was thrust back into her hand. 'I have to go.'

By half past three, though the sun was scarcely less intense, it was time to resume the trek. O'Byrne estimated they were an hour's ride from the farmstead.

While they still were under the dappled shade, he'd taken from the mule's pack the hunting rifle Hart had picked up in Johannesburg. He himself always carried a Colt; a professional necessity with so much dynamite on site.

He checked the rifle's site, the loading mechanism. 'Have you tried it?'

'Not in anger.'

'Shells?'

Hart located a box and passed them to the geologist, who nodded, knowingly. 'One thing I'll say for your Afrikaner; he's raised cradling a gun the way you might be raised holding… I don't know, a hurl? A hockey stick?'

'A fishing rod, maybe. I was no great shakes at sport.'

'My point being, he can bring down any of the twitchy wildlife they have hereabouts from half a mile with a single shot. It's a point of pride. Do you remember how much target practice we had on our way down to the Cape?'

'I don't remember any.'

'My point precisely. Right,' he said, slipping a round into the chamber. 'You see that seed gourd dangling from yonder branch?' he passed back the rifle. 'That's your enemy, peeping out from behind a rock.'

'One shot?'

'That's the goal.'

The stock, impetuous as a colt's leg, kicked back as the first report echoed about the valley. From the indifferent gourd, not so much as a twitch. He showed O'Byrne the twitch in his hand. 'Can you fellas do something to distract me? It's when I concentrate that I get the jitters. Then at the moment of truth, it seizes up entirely.' He looked to the journalist, prostrate by the great tree. 'Here. Do you want a try?' A.T. Wall, who was out of sorts, passed up the opportunity with a snort.

The Irishman-gone-native quizzed his former officer as he lined up the next shot. 'You really think our sergeant at arms would follow you half way around the world on account of an old grudge? Havelock-Saunders I can understand; he has a case to win. But Judd?'

'I'm convinced of it.'

'Then there's something you're not telling me.'

'I always liked you, O'Byrne. You're perceptive.'

'So tell me.'

'Let's say in Judd's case, he has a personal score to settle.' The second round winged the gourd and set it oscillating. 'This goes back years. 1904. I'd been making my slow and tortuous way back in the direction of home. Port to port. Three months here, six months there. Working passages on packets or tramp steamers. Now I was on a sloop *en route* for Gibraltar. Somewhere off Tripoli, I came down with one of my bouts of malaria. It comes back once in a while, like a memory you can never shake. Harmless enough in itself. But a fever on board ship? That wasn't something they were willing to countenance. I'm not blaming them. They set me onshore. And being feverish, and in a strange port, it wasn't long before I was robbed. Left destitute. To cut a long story short, I all but starved.

'I was saved, if that's the word, by a Bavarian. Maybe damned would be nearer the mark. Never mind his name; this is not his story. The brig he captained was sailing in the wrong direction. A crew of cutthroats. Thirteen of them. Bound, eventually, for Constantinople. But if I remained in Tripoli,

I would die a miserable death. That much I knew. What his cargo was, what the *Pothorst* held in the depths of its hold, didn't bear much looking into. In Tobruk I oversaw crates of carbines being unloaded. I knew well enough, had there been a contract, it would have been signed in one's own blood. I'd get as far as Constantinople, then cross on foot to Greece and landward up through the Balkans. If my mind wasn't made up, my body was. *Trust not to rotten planks...*'

'Antony and Cleopatra.'

'Top of the class! Needless to say, I never got that far.' A shot tore through a leaf, well wide of the mark. 'In Tyre, Fate took a hand. From the fo'c'sle, as we tied up, I saw standing by a wharf a gaunt figure, done up like a Bedouin. Despite the costume and the distance and the four years that had passed, I recognised him instantly, as though by a supernatural force. Our mutual friend was deep in converse with the Bavarian. Would he be joining the *Pothorst*? If he was, I doubted I'd ever see the Straits of Bosporus. I ducked low, decided to bide my time.

'We had the afternoon to ourselves. Four hours' shore leave. I had no interest in brothels. Opium, perhaps. Many months before, a surgeon on a packet had prescribed laudanum against the nightmares, and the shake in my hand. But I had little ready money. We were to receive our wages only once we got to Constantinople. None of the crew trusted me, and the Captain wasn't the man to give an advance. Besides, after Tripoli I was wary of the backstreets about the waterfront.

'Over a hookah in a tearoom I fell into conversation with an official I took to be the harbourmaster. Originally from Smyrna, he said. He was keen to practise his English which, all things considered, was as precise as his moustache. They're a hospitable people, the Turks. He was a long-time admirer of the Royal Navy, he informed me. The *Pax Britannica*. Needless to say, Lance Corporal, I kept schtum about the particular brand of *Pax Britannica* we'd witnessed down here. For my part, I wondered what formalities would be required to jump ship and remain in the Levant.

'As I was mounting the gangplank that evening, I happened to glance into the mess area. The Captain was deep in conversation with two men: one a middle-eastern merchant dressed sumptuously, like one of the Magi; the other Caleb Judd, still done up like a Bedouin. The guttural snatches I heard were not in any language I recognised. Before I moved on, I saw a wallet stuffed with paper money pass from our Captain to the merchant.

'Late that night, I was disturbed by sounds in the hold. Whispering. Whimpering. I lit a candle. Through cracks, I could make out that, on this final leg of the voyage, the cargo would be human. Not slaves, either. At least, not adult slaves. These were children. Boys. Girls. The whites of their eyes were filled with terror. It was a blow, quite literally a physical blow to the solar plexus. I couldn't breathe. I was sickened to the core. But what to do? Even if I made up my mind to blow the whistle, it was past midnight. Where now my harbourmaster? Where, the police? The customs men?

'But could one trust the officials in this ancient waterfront? Were they not likely in on the act? And all the while, playing against the petrified faces I'd seen in the hold, came an ancestral whisper—*there is no one lower than a snitch*. In my school it had been hammered into us. I'm sure it was the same in yours.

The sorry history of our national insurrections, undermined by spies and informers; informers and spies. No surprise to us that Dante places Judas Iscariot in the very lowest circle of hell.

'I knew I had to get off that brig. And this is where a Guardian Angel must have been looking out for me. As I stepped from the gangplank, I collided with Judd. Quite literally collided. Our eyes met. If he recognised me, if he expected to see me, I couldn't say. I can only say I scarpered. And as I ran, I ran into a squad of armed Ottoman police. To the rear of them, my harbourmaster, dressed differently now. They were raiding the brig, had been tipped off about the human cargo.

'Though even that isn't quite right. Someone's palm hadn't been greased. Our Bavarian Captain had tried to pull a fast one on the wrong official. Who knows? The harbourmaster was no mere harbourmaster. He was a government agent. And one of some standing, evidently. Whatever standing that was, it put him in a position to cut me a deal. I would need to turn evidence. A formality really—the crew and the shore operation, in which Judd was second in command, were beyond guilty. My first-hand testimony would merely be the oil to make the food palatable. That was how he put it. I've come to believe it was an act of mercy on his part. He'd taken pity on me. After all, there was little I could add by way of testimony. In return, I would walk away a free man. Not only that. He would gift me, not thirty pieces of silver, but the papers of a dead merchant seaman.

'I like to believe it was the terror in the faces of the stolen children that swayed me. It may have been. Who knows? What I do know is that Caleb Judd cursed me as he was dragged from the dock, and swore his eternal revenge. That was the day I was reborn as Jimmy Cade.'

'Quite the story,' said the geologist. 'Now, put down that rifle before you end up winging one of us. Your shots have been getting progressively worse.'

'I'll take a pot,' said Wall. He'd been watching silently from the shade of the baobab. He pulled on his wire glasses and squinted toward the gourd as O'Byrne passed him the rifle. 'Here's the deal. If I hit it, one of yous two is pulling that donkey along.'

They passed the culvert and the path that led up to the ruined farmhouse; Wall, a grumpy Sancho Panza, still taking up the rear. All three eyed in silence the tamarind from which the young girl had been hanged. Now that he knew what to look for, Hart could make out, perhaps a mile further along the plain, a knoll surmounted by trees surrounding what appeared to be a white pergola.

He knew what to expect. The night before, O'Byrne had gone through it with them. It was not a burial site. So many thousands of civilians had died, turned out by the British onto the veldt or rounded up in their disease-ridden camps, that by the time of Jani Esterhuizen's return from the war, there would have been no certainty in disinterring the bones of his family. A mother, four children, memorialised in marble under the inscription:

Ter nagedagtenis aan die Esterhuizen-gesin,
vermoor deur Britse soldate
op 11 September 1900

Though O'Byrne couldn't recall them, their names and birth dates were recorded on the memorial. The girl had been aged eleven, the youngest, eleven months. Hart refrained from asking about the servants and labourers, though he remembered having seen three. O'Byrne was prickly on the subject of the native population. Time enough for that after he'd secured from him the signed affidavit.

After today's visit, after they'd gleaned what information they could from the site and taken a photographic record of the memorial itself, O'Byrne vowed he would put him in contact with several of the Boer *kommandos* who'd taken their revenge on Major Havelock-Saunders' column two days after the massacre. They should at the very least be in a position to link the latter directly to the events at the farmstead.

The sun was long past its zenith as the horses made their slow way up to the memorial on the *kopje*. Looking at its descent and the stretching of shadows, Wall said he'd have to consider where best to set up the tripod. The shot had to be clear enough to submit as evidence in court. Fred Hart held the saddlebag open as the journalist removed the equipment he'd earlier packed.

O'Byrne, meanwhile, had approached the monument, to clear some branches that had fallen across its white face. Quite substantial branches, thought Hart; the trees about the pergola, planted not seven years since, were scarcely more than saplings.

Too late, he saw the wire running from the nethermost branch. Too late, he made to call out. He took a single step from the mule just as a shock of scorching air and earth and debris hammered him off his feet and set the veldt ringing.

234

CHAPTER TWENTY-TWO

A figure fashioned from dust. Every square-inch mouse-grey, but for a mouth-shaped gash to the forehead in brightest carmine. A stunned figure. A man with arms outstretched, blindly blinking.

From the tilted ground, ears muffled as though underwater, Hart obliquely watched the figure stagger forwards, forwards.

His mouth opened on a dense taste of dust and cordite. Had he called out? Had his words been voiced? He couldn't tell. To his left the mule was turtling on its back, kicking to right itself. Some hobble was preventing it. The bloodied gash in its dust-white side had the same strawberry brightness as the man's wound.

A bomb.

Then he mouthed the word, *bomb*. Throat dry as a baked bone. An image came to him. Cathal O'Byrne stooping, reaching a hand for. Glint of a noose of fine wire. *Don't!*

There'd been a bomb. A booby-trap.

He rolled. He writhed, ribcage awash with sudden pain. Wall, still dazed, was sitting cross-legged now, an Indian brave. Hart was aware of the screams of the mule, but arriving as though from a great distance.

He must get up. He had to get up. There was danger, still. Judd. Judd had tried to kill them. Would try again. They were in danger.

O'Byrne? Where?

On all fours he crawled toward Wall. Eyes white as quartz blinked in the dust mask. 'Guns,' he called. Croaked. 'Need to find the guns.' Horses. Where? The other stared at him, a dust deity. 'Guns!' he insisted. But the idol didn't move.

Through waves of pain he levered himself onto his feet. The ringing in his ears pulsed faint then loud, faint then loud. To his left, the mule was struggling within the tether of its own intestines—lurid pythons, glinting metallic. Lunacy had entered the globes of its eyes. Did it know it was kicking against its own innards?

He had to deal with the threat of Judd. But while the mule thrashed and struggled, there was no way to retrieve the rifle.

All about the fractured memorial were strewn fragments of marble, jagged slabs prised from an iceberg. A dusty trunk resolved itself into a torso. Scarcely human.

Christ, he gasped.

He knelt, frisked the waist without looking. Tried to lift. The body slumped. Resisted. His right hand had begun to spasm like a landed fish. All the same, beneath the stubborn weight of dead meat, the mutinous fingers located the Colt.

They unbuttoned the holster, slipped from it the revolver.

But as he pulled it free it snagged. It was tethered to the belt by a leather thong not two feet in length. Instinct, some atavistic impulse, set him to savage the cord with his teeth. Sweet taste of saliva. Of human sweat. At the same moment a shape several yards away resolved itself into an arm and shoulder. The back of a head. A judder bucked his ribcage. Fisted his throat. Emotion, wild to escape. His mouth opened on a dry retch. Eyes, blinded.

An acrid jet spewed out. A second, so powerful the gut itself struggled to escape.

Spent, he toppled forwards. Forehead on the corpse, he gulped bitter air.

A hand clutched his shoulder.

Wall's. Flesh tones tigered the dust where he'd drawn fingers across his face. He knelt beside Hart. Gently he removed from his fingers the thong and doubled it over. Within its loop, he sawed at the leather with an open penknife until it gave.

Hart put his left hand on the reporter's shoulder. He levered himself to his feet. Wiping at his eyes with his sleeve, he looked for the first time out across the plain. At a distance of perhaps a half mile, the three horses stood, uncertainly.

Far beyond them, scarcely the size of an ant, a horseman was traversing the horizon beneath a declining sun.

The horses had been spooked, by the explosion and by the screaming of the mule. It took them a good half hour to calm them sufficiently to retrieve them. It took another to scratch a rude trench in the dry earth sufficient to bury the remains of their colleague.

It fell to Wall to put an end to the mule's struggles. When

Hart raised the gun and aimed at its elongated head, his hand seized up, and he couldn't trust it to dispatch the animal with a single shot. Then there was the onerous task of removing the packs from beneath the corpse, strapping them about O'Byrne's horse and salvaging what remained intact. It was fortunate that the journalist had removed camera and tripod just prior to the explosion.

By the time all this was done and Wall's gashed forehead washed under a canteen and padded with a clean neckerchief, the light to the west was rapidly losing its lustre. After Hart had carried out a full recce of the place, they decided to spend the night in the outhouse of the ruined farmstead, the very one from which the shot had been fired a decade before. Its roof was largely intact, three of its four walls were of unbroken stone. They would take turns to keep watch over the entrance.

Had the horseman on the horizon been Caleb Judd? If so, why hadn't he waited around, to finish them off in the wake of the blast? But then, who knew how many days that booby-trap had lain there, in wait.

The sky was a jewel box of stars. Having chewed and swallowed his portion of a loaf of dry bread, Hart began to gather scrub and straw and scrap wood for a fire against the falling temperature.

'You sure that's a good idea?'

'Our friend?' He blew on the kindling, watched the flame catch eagerly. 'There's something I haven't been entirely open about.'

'Oh? And what might that be.'

'I've been laying a trail for Judd to follow. Right from the very beginning.'

The reporter sniffed ostentatiously and dispatched a gob of phlegm into the fickle darkness.

'Even before we set sail. I sent letters home. Postcards.'

'Postcards.'

'I'm assuming Havelock-Saunders and his cronies have a watch kept on the mail. I wanted no impediment on what information they might glean. The first one I sent, from Liverpool, was simply to prove I'd skipped the country. Edmond is convinced Judd killed our father to flush me out of hiding.'

'I heard him say as much.'

'I wasn't about to take the chance he might repeat the performance. I'd have to send another postcard from somewhere farther overseas. Get out of the Isles. That was the message he'd sent me through Kinkaid's boy. So I wouldn't be able to show up as a witness, if and when the affair comes to trial. But after that? Judd is not the man to rest easy until he's had his vengeance. So a plan began to come together. This place, here. Far enough away that my family would be safe. But near enough that he'd feel compelled to follow. Ten years I've been on the run.' He watched his colleague lean his head back on his hands, his gaze on the rafters. The flame had by now grown sufficiently that the dark eyes of the horses glinted like glazed fruit.

'This ends here,' he added, by way of conclusion.

'You might have warned us.' The journalist rolled on his side and looked directly up at Hart. 'You might at least have put O'Byrne in the know. It's one thing saying how you felt in your water Judd might be hereabouts. Quite another that you dared him to follow.' Eyes back on the rafters, he concluded,

'You had a right to put him on his guard, so you had.'

'You think that hasn't been running through my head?'

'So the fire. That's to let him know that we're in here like sitting ducks. That's your plan is it?'

'I'm going to make up a bundle under a blanket. Make it so it looks like a figure, asleep. The other one of us will toss and turn, presumably. Maybe snore. Up in the loft, there above the horses, there's a sort of a cubbyhole. Decent view out over the yard as well as in here. We take turns, squatting up there with the rifle. Waiting for Judd to show his face.'

'While the other one of us is bait in the mousetrap.'

'Whoever is lying by the fire has the Colt primed under his blanket.'

'Brilliant.'

'You've got a better plan?'

'The man I remember was a crack shot. At the Orange river I seen him take down three spurfowl in succession in three single shots. Those two bundles, so thoughtfully illuminated by your fire. He'll have them nicely peppered before ever we see hide nor hair of him.'

'How would he manage that? There's no clear shot at the fire except he comes in through that doorway.'

'Says you.'

'Judd may have been a crack shot, I'm not disputing that. He's not Mephistopheles.'

'If you say so, boss. And I say, good luck to you. But if it's all the same to you, I'd just as soon spend the whole night on watch stuck up in your cubbyhole. Stead of lying here stretched out like a target in a funfair.'

'As you wish.'

The night was growing steadily colder. Having made up the second bundle to resemble a sleeper, Hart threw some more brushwood on the fire before settling under a blanket beside it. Instantly, he was overwhelmed by a wave of exhaustion. It was brought on as much by fraught emotion, by the horror of having re-assembled a quartered cadaver, as by the physical heft of the labour. Images of earth-covered body parts were intermingled with flashes of a devil charging out of a mist, cutlass in hand.

He was startled awake by an almighty din. A gunshot resounding throughout the interior. A ricochet buzzed past his ear like a dangerous insect. The horses neighed and reared up wild as a mountain torrent. He jumped to his feet as, beyond the glow of embers, a figure crashed messily from the loft to the floor.

Hart sprang against the wall to one side of the entrance, the Colt hard against his breast. After a count of three breaths, he chanced a peek. Outside, the night had bleached all colour, flattened everything standing into silhouette. No movement. No sound, not even the ratchet of insects. The horses, too, seemed to be alert now, listening.

In the stillness, he mentally traced out the trajectory the girl's shot must have followed to have taken down Havelock-Saunders' mount. Behind him, he heard a clatter and cough, then a piteous groan. 'What? Happened?'

He glanced back. Wall, dazed, was squatting beneath the loft, massaging an elbow.

'You fell asleep, that's what happened.'

The reporter shook his head, as though he were having the greatest difficulty processing the information. 'There was a shot,' he insisted.

'Yeah.' Hart surveyed the abandoned farmyard once more before striding across to where the rifle lay. 'There was. It was you fired it.' He checked the lock, ejected the spent shell. 'Mercy of God you didn't kill one of us.' He walked as far as the horses, and with a fistful of dry grass gave each of them a calming rub. 'With respect, I'll take the next watch.' He proffered the revolver by the barrel. 'You can have this fella.'

'I'm not lying there by what's left of your fire, to be shot at.'

'Take your blanket into a corner if it makes you feel safer.' Hart was awake now, or in that strange state of unreality when all chance of sleep has flown. As well to sit out the rest of the night in watchfulness. From his earlier survey, he knew that the cubbyhole in the loft offered views both over the yard and doorway and, where slats had come loose in the roof, out over the back where the approach ran, below the tamarind and the three giant aloes.

He climbed up into the loft and, cradling the rifle, settled back against the gable. It was that indecisive time, perhaps an hour before sunrise, when ambient light begins to quench the fainter stars. One still dangled brightly, up to the left of the tamarind. The morning star? Or perhaps Jupiter—it was hard to imagine anything else quite so bright.

He drew out the spyglass he'd found in the mule's saddlebag. If it was Venus, hanging low above the northeast horizon, presumably it would have the form of a crescent moon; whereas Jupiter would be round as a thruppenny bit. *When a new planet swims into his ken*—Keats or Shelley? The point of light held within the lens' circumference was indeterminate, a teary blob that wobbled like frogspawn. As he let the spyglass fall away, it dragged across the dark silhouette of the tamarind.

There was something there. Something that shouldn't have been. He returned the tree to view, instantly dropped the telescope, scrabbled backwards.

From the tree, ghastly as a Goya woodcut, hung a human shoulder and arm; beside it a headless torso, suspended by a leg.

CHAPTER TWENTY-THREE

The jibes had been going on for the better part of an hour. Not jibes, precisely. Taunts. A solitary voice, goading. Provoking. Never rising to a shout. The taunts circled compulsively about one syllable as though tethered to it. *Rat.* Every time as though it had been spat.

Come on out, you rat. You're going to die here, Hart, like the rat you've always been.

Rat, lowest of all life forms.

Judd must have come right in against the back wall of the outhouse, not to have to raise his voice. There was no clear shot at that proximity. Meanwhile, they were holed up inside the outhouse, like two proverbial rats. Who knew what confederate he might have brought with him, covering the only exit?

Once in a while, the challenge varied. 'Go on away, you,

Mister Ay Tee Wall. We've no quarrel, you and I. I'll grant you safe passage out. Just so long as you go unarmed, mind. You have my word on it.' Then, when no reply was forthcoming. 'I'm not saying you aren't a rat, hey. Everyone in your profession is. Goes with the territory, you might say.' Then, after a further hiatus. 'That said, it'd suit me to have a witness, to report to the wide world the sorry death of yon sewer rat.'

Every so often, Hart and Wall exchanged glances. Or bent their heads in colloquy. As the morning wore on, it was becoming ever more patent how completely the trap they'd laid for Judd had backfired. For one thing, it was more than twenty-four hours since the horses had had any water, and between them they had less than half a canteen remaining.

His back to the wall by the entrance, the small man called out, 'can I at least take a gun?'

'Can't have you do that. Can't have you plugging me in the back while I'm taking care of your buddy so I can't.'

'And how do I know you won't shoot me in the back, as I ride past you?'

'If I was going to shoot you, you'd be dead already. The same goes for your ratty friend, hey.'

The two men in the outhouse swapped puzzled looks. 'Yeah?'

'Whenever you were gathering wood for your fire. Or while you were taking turns squatting away up there in the loft like stool pigeons. Would've been an easy shot so it would.'

The two exchanged grimaces. 'Then why *didn't* you?'

'I told you already. I've no quarrel with you. It's the tout I'm after, so it is. Only shooting would be far too good for him.'

245

Hart took up the argument. 'That didn't stop you killing Cathal O'Byrne. And then stringing him up from a tree like a traitor.'

A silence followed; Judd composing a response. 'That was by way of an accident. An act of God, you might say. All the same, I wasn't sorry, whenever I dug up that wee hollow ye scratched out for him.

'He was one of your kin, Lieutenant. Sneaking away, the both of yiz, like rats in the night. Then having the Boer sit in ambush on us a couple of days after. He got what was coming to him so he did. But I'll tell you one thing. I was glad it wasn't you that blast got. Because it made up my mind for me. I'm going do this with my own two hands. That's the why I didn't take you out with the rifle and you gathering in firewood.'

'A.T. Wall had nothing to do with any of that business here. He'd already left 'B' Company at that stage.'

'Aye. I already said. Mr Wall is free to go on his way.' Then an afterthought. 'Only, be sure to set down too: not only did yon rat desert his men on the eve of battle. Clocked me over the head with a rock when I wasn't looking, then skulked off into black night with that other rat of a corporal you're shedding tears for. A few years later, your buddy turned tout against the entire crew of a ship he was on. Did he mention that to you, hey? Turned informer so he did, and landed me along with them in a stinking pit in Syria for years on end. Be sure to remember that when you report his inglorious end, won't ye now?' There was a rumble, as of someone clearing their throat to spit. 'Suppose I were to let him live. He'll only turn tout again. Grass up the very men of his squadron he was supposed to be looking out for. Because once a rat, always a rat. That's the way of it. No screed of honour in him. Because the first rule of soldiering, you have your buddy's back. It has to be. What goes down on campaign stays on campaign.'

Hart flashed his eyes at his companion. 'Go,' he hissed, a hoarse whisper. The other looked hard at him, shaking his head. Was it desperate valour, or simply that he couldn't make up his mind to trust the word of the cold-blooded killer outside?

'Go. It might be your one chance.'

'You'd take his word?'

'In your position, I think I would. What choice do you have?' And as the short man hesitated, 'there'll be other records beyond that ruined monument that a massacre took place here. The date of it. The names of the victims. Their ages.'

'Teaching granny to suck eggs, now?'

'All I'm saying, we need you alive, to carry this to a conclusion. You might track down those Boer fighters O'Byrne was saying took part in the ambush. Gather their testimony.'

The journalist turned his head in the direction of the entrance. 'How would it work?' he called.

'You ride away,' came the reply. 'You throw out the rifle where I can see it, you ride away, far as the kop. Take that spyglass with you. From away up there, you can watch what happens away down here.'

Wall looked directly at the former lieutenant. 'I throw out the rifle.' He pivoted back toward the opening. 'Doesn't leave much of a look out for my companion.'

There followed another protracted hack and spit. 'In the first place, your companion as you call him has a wee revolver. You think I didn't know? In the second place I told ye. If I wanted to shoot him, he'd be dead already. But that's not the way. By rights it should be a drowning, that's what you do with a rat. But that's hardly practicable in this parched country. Out here, the best I can offer is to slit open his throat for him, the way he can think on his treachery as his miserable life ebbs away. Then maybe I'll string up his remains beside yon other rat, with a sign hung about his neck warning anyone else is ever thinking of turning deserter or informer.'

All the while Wall led O'Byrne's horse away tethered to his own, Hart's muscles were rigid, his back pressed to the wall where he hunkered. He was awaiting the shot. But the hooves receded, and no shot rang out. He estimated by the shortening of the shadows about the doorway that it must be approaching noon. 'So what, now?' he called, looking down at the gun cradled on his lap. 'How does it work?'

'Aye! Well you may ask.' There followed an aspirate cackle, an approximation of mirth. It made him wonder if he'd ever heard the other man actually laugh. His own mouth was dry as sandpaper, but he mustn't touch the canteen. It was hanging out of temptation's reach, from a nail on the far wall. The former Sergeant might be sadist enough to keep him holed up here until, by slow degrees, he succumbed to thirst.

There was a clatter from the doorway. He crouched lower, gun pointed at the dazzle of daylight. Something snaked through the air, then twisted across the dirt floor. A belt. On the belt, a holster. From this protruded the bone handle of a knife.

Gradually Hart slid himself upright against the stone wall. He reached out into the oblong of sunlight with a boot and heeled the belt into the shadow where he stood.

'Now,' called the voice, which appeared to issue from

248

just outside the entrance. 'I'm going to give you precisely one chance to walk away from here alive. One. You take it, or you die here like a dog. That's a promise so it is. That means you have to ask yourself. Am I man enough to take that chance?'

Hart squinted into the sunlit glare. Could this be a trick? A stratagem, distract him and then shoot, a belly shot maybe, wound him mortally and leave him die a lingering death.

'See, I don't believe you are man enough. Oh, I heard all about Valetta. That old salt you stuck. I don't think he even knew you had a knife, hey. He didn't die, by the way. You couldn't even manage that. But a real fight? Man to man? No. I don't think so.'

Then he hadn't died! That was one less sin to bear. A night that had been obscured for years in a fug of opium fumes.

'But this is one situation you can't weasel out of. Sneaking away. Turning snitch. So you've two choices, the way I see it. Let me sum it up for you. Man up, or die a rat in a trap. Your choice.' A silence whose strain hurt the ear. 'Come on, Hart. Your wee boyfriend is waiting.'

'So, what? I throw out the gun. That your idea?'

'You throw down yours. I throw down mine.'

'Why would I trust you?'

'At the risk of getting boring, because if I'd wanted you shot, you'd be dead already.' Another silence, interrogative, underscored by the rhythmic scratch of insects. 'Here. Let me make the decision easier for you.' At once a deafening report set the interior resonating. Hart threw himself to the dirt. His eyes flicked from the doorway, where a wisp of blue-grey smoke was unfurling, to a trickle at the far wall. The canteen had been holed, and was piddling water onto the dry dirt.

'Don't think you can just gallop out of there, hey. The first shot would take down the horse. Probably break your leg. Then we'd have some sport.'

The thought had crossed Hart's mind. Make a mad dash for it. But even if, against all the odds, he escaped, what then? Wake one night, with a blade pressed to his throat?

'I'll give you one more wee consideration,' sang the voice, 'to whet your courage on. Whenever I took your ole man's venerable head between my hands and wrang his scrawny neck for him, it was your name was the last thing I whispered into his ear. *You've your Freddy to thank for this, sir.* Aye. That's what I told him.'

At once Hart was on his feet, hands trembling. He took the Colt by its barrel and hurled it out into the daylight. If he was to be shot, so be it. With his left hand he swept up the belt, with its insidious cargo. He then strode blinking out into the sunlight.

CHAPTER TWENTY-FOUR

They sat, in the uncertain June sunshine, beside the Basin off Blessington St.

'Are you any good at riddles? Tell me,' posed the old soldier, pointing with his cane over the expanse of water. 'How does it come about that Dublin's hydrophobic citizenry—I have in mind those fine gentlemen and lady drinkers who would never knowingly allow a drop of pure water to pass their lips—how comes it then that, unbeknownst to them, they daily dip their beaks into that reservoir?'

The boy looked up at him curiously, shook his head.

'What if I were to tell you that that's the very source from which Messrs Power and Jameson draw for their whiskey distilleries?'

This was rewarded by a wan smile, one that the old man knew was for his benefit merely. He drew from his pocket his briar and a pouch of tobacco. From the latter he removed a pinch, rolled the tawny fibres to loosen them, then tamped them down with a thumb into the bowl. He held a match above the last, drawing and puffing severally until he was satisfied it had caught. 'We all miss him, you know.'

The lad flinched. 'I just don't see how that bastard can have won the case, is all.'

'The odds were stacked against when the author of the article wasn't alive to defend it.'

'But the judge himself said your man was lying.'

'Havelock-Saunders?' With his free hand, Captain Jack tapped the newspaper folded in his jacket pocket. 'What the President of the High Court said in summing up was that the plaintiff's evidence was inconsistent and as such not entirely to be trusted.'

'Comes to the same thing. It's just a posh way of saying it.'

'Yes. Perhaps you've a point.' The boy was cute, right enough. 'I think, all the same, that our Councillor may find he's won something of a pyrrhic victory. In the first place, with all this washing of dirty linen in public, the army may wish to institute its own court of inquiry as to the events of that infamous day. And then there's this. It's what I believe they refer to as a nice legal quibble. The amount of damages our friend Will Brayden initially offered him, you see, was far in excess of the amount of damages actually awarded. That being the case, when it comes to the small matter of costs…'

But the youth was too fidgety to sit still. 'If they didn't believe him, how come he was awarded anything? That's just plain stupid.'

'I daresay. Nevertheless. It's a trifling sum. It shows in what esteem the Councillor's reputation is generally held.'

Tommy Kinkaid gave him a comically contorted look, as much as to say, what world do you live in when you can call a hundred pounds a trifling sum?

'Neither the plaintiff nor the defence was in a position to prove their case definitively. Affidavits are all very well. But with both principal witnesses deceased, our side only had Private Molloy to give a first-hand account. And a damned good thing we did have him. I'll say that for Foley, he's like a Jack Russell terrier when it's a matter of following a scent. But set against that Mr Havelock-Saunders was able to produce two troopers who swore blind that Freddy's squadron was nowhere near that farmhouse on the day the alleged massacre took place.'

'Alleged!' Tom Kinkaid had stripped a switch from a shrub and was whipping the water's placid surface. A scald rose to his face, remembering how the lawyer with the frog eyes and horsehair wig had probed and goaded and theatrically doubted his word, when all eyes in the courtroom were fixed on him. Even hers. 'I let him down.'

'Bah! You mustn't think that. You were under oath.' He drew on his pipe. 'All in all, I believe Fred would have been well satisfied with the account you gave of him. The man you knew as Jimmy Cade.'

'But that lawyer fella made me say things I didn't want to. And anything I did say he twisted.'

'I expect that's the job of Counsel for the Prosecution.'

'But it meant it came out a lie. He made out that I'd seen Jimmy... that according to me, he was some sort of dope

253

fiend. That the whole episode might just as easy have been a nightmare brought on by drugs.' He flung the stick out over the water. 'But I never said that.'

'I know you didn't.'

'And that judge was on his side, he was. He kept telling me I had to confine my answers to the specific question your man was putting.'

'They'll do that.'

'But I took an oath to tell the *whole* truth. How can you tell the whole truth if you're not being allowed to tell it?'

The retired captain drew deeply on his pipe, his eyebrows raised somewhere between contemplation and admiration. The boy wasn't finished. 'It's because his own son was injured in that African war. Bertie Nuzum.' He frowned, angry as any child at a perceived injustice. 'I thought you couldn't be the judge once you had a personal interest in the outcome.'

'His son was injured in that same campaign, yes. And it's true he'd been a comrade of Fred Hart's. And indeed of your father's.' The stem of the briar acted like a pointer. 'Hard to say how that might influence him one way or another, though.'

Young Kinkaid assessed this. 'The Ma knew him of an old day. Says he was always an oul stick in the mud.' Then he squinted over at him, shrewdly. 'How much will costs run to?'

'Can't say. Many times the hundred pounds' damages Havelock-Saunders was awarded. You may be quite sure of that.'

Tom Kinkaid began to wander away from the bench. He was dwelling, as he often did, on the details of the account A.T. Wall had given them of the knife fight. How the former lieutenant had told him just before he'd left the outhouse, *this*

254

stops here. How, from the destroyed monument on the top of the hill, he'd watched Jimmy Cade step out into the sunlit arena of the farmyard. Within the circle of the spyglass, he could make out a belt dangling from one hand, for all the world like young David holding a sling. That was one thing you could say about the little man in his green corduroy suit; he gave you a picture you could see in your head. An important tool in any journalist's repertoire, the boy imagined. Just as it turned out to be a trump card for a barrister to play, in the game of which side could make the court believe their version of events.

As an aid to words, he'd acted out the parts. This one-man show, Tommy suspected, was for the benefit of the sister, Katherine, whose mahogany eyes had remained intensely on him throughout the performance. Wall stood away from the table before them, hands spread. Then he'd described how Hart stepped out from the cover of the shed to where he knew Caleb Judd awaited him. How preparations were made, Judd unbuttoning but not removing his jacket, and wrapping a linen shirt three times about his left arm. To serve as what he termed a 'fender', to bat the opponent's blade away. Hart in like manner twisted the belt tightly about his left fist.

The performer showed his audience how each held the left forearm aloft, a bar to protect the knife. Jimmy Cade had once told him that he'd never been in a knife fight, though he'd witnessed several. Clearly, he'd taken any lessons on board. Their preparations made, the two men crouched, then slowly began to circle one another, wary as scorpions. A deadly game of feint and parry ensued. How long it continued he couldn't 'vouchsafe'—that was his word. Then all at once they were upon one another, grappling like wrestlers. When they separated, Judd turned his back and strolled away, cocky as a matador after a pass. Hart was left clutching at his thigh. He sank onto one knee (the reporter did likewise). But then rose again, and once more made ready.

Another slow circle. Thrust, parry. Feint. Thrust, parry. Feint. Then they're upon each other again. This time, he succeeds in bringing Judd to the ground. They roll. They grapple. This time, when Judd turns his back and walks away, he's holding his own right arm. But it takes Hart a full minute to get to his feet. Even without the spyglass, one could make out the blood patch spreading over the linen of his shirt.

The third time they come together and go down into the dirt, he sees that Hart's hand is desperately reaching for something beyond them. 'I made a promise. I said you'd have the whole story, Miss Hart. Exactly as it played out, nothing mitigated, nothing glossed over.' The warning didn't raise so much as a flinch on her countenance. 'It took a few seconds for me to make out in the telescope what it was he was reaching for. A gleam, there in the sun. The revolver. It lay on the ground where earlier he'd flung it out. Judd must've been equally aware, because he was reaching along your brother's arm, preventing him. Then he was up on his feet and dragging him backways.'

Here he left a pause, took a sip of water.

'He flipped him, and pressed a knee into his chest to pin him there. To dispatch him with his hunting knife. I seen your brother's hands come up, joined together as though in supplication. What I hadn't taken in was that the gleam was no longer lying in the dust. Because there it was, the gun, between the imploring hands.

'Now, I'd seen him trying four times to hit a gourd the day before. I'd also seen how he was unable to dispatch a mule at point blank, to put it out of its agony. His hand, you see.' The reporter held up his right hand, an exhibit. 'It would seize up on him. Refuse to obey. Lock, or go into spasm. Or shake like an aspen. It was why it was myself was entrusted to pen them letters he sent you. Was it in spasm, now? Refusing to close on the trigger? I saw Judd push the hands to one side, lean in close. I saw his long, wicked blade glint in the sun. Then it come down into the side of your brother's neck. Just there. It's where I found the mortal gash, when finally I got down to him.' He paused. 'I'll spare you the details of the condition I found him in, Miss Hart.'

'Don't. I've already seen a dozen gory deaths in my imagination.'

'As you wish. He was still breathing when I did get down. Or sawing air. Judd had left him to die, knowing he wasn't long for the world. The jugular had been cut, you see. The dirt underneath his neck was slick and blackened. At a gash to the windpipe, blood bubbled. Though he wasn't a Catholic, I whispered an act of contrition in his ear. It was all I could do for him. I hope I did right?'

Another drink of water. Had his story finished? Evidently, not quite.

'But going back to before I got down to him, just after the knife did its deadly work. There's a delay between the flash of lightning and the thunderclap. There was a delay in what happened next. They were now lying, one atop the other. Nose to nose. Intimate as a courting couple. Something gave a kick. A jolt. A second after that, I heard the gunshot.

257

'Nothing happened. I wiped the sweat out of my eyes. They were stung so blurred I could no longer see clearly. But when I could, Judd was back on his feet. He'd turned away. I saw him fling away the gun, far out of reach of your prostrate brother. He was now making slowly to where he'd tethered his horse. My first feeling was... *relief*. I'll explain. You see, Miss Hart, he'd sworn he was going to string up your brother's corpse beside the body parts of O'Byrne. A warning to informers. Who knows what sort of outrage and mutilation he'd planned to carry out on it, first. So to that extent, yes, I was relieved to see him walk away.

'He got up onto his horse. A piebald, like a tinker's, or an Apache Indian's. It took him an effort to mount. Or it's more, there was something clumsy in the manoeuvre. He lay sideways across the saddle before swivelling, then pivoting upright. I had the impression his right arm was out of action. Slowly they began to trot away, he and the stallion. I was eager for them to be gone. So I could go down. See if anything could be done. He got as far as the tamarind, where pieces of O'Byrne were still strung up. Where the girl had been strung up. Just after they passed it, he tilted sideways, then crashed down, startling the mount. The boot must've been caught in the stirrup. I couldn't tell you, Miss Hart, whether or no he was dead before he hit the ground. All I can tell you is that when finally I came across the corpse away out where it had been dragged by the panic of the horse, eyes and mouth were wide open. There was already the first of the blowflies crawling across the cheek. There was no life left in him. I could see where a bullet had traversed the body.

'I left the corpse there, where it lay. And I left the horse to wander out on the veldt. I had enough on my plate, leading the other two horses the long trek back. It was a labour of Hercules, I can tell you, getting your brother's body up and over and then secure athwart the jittery beast that had been his mount. After the autopsy, Miss Hart, I seen he was given a proper Christian burial.

'Maybe a week later, when a couple of local police went out to recover the remains of O'Byrne and to find Judd's body, there was nary a sign of it. I can only assume some wild beast dragged it away, because like I say when I left it, it was stone dead. After a few pointless hours, they gave up trying to catch the pied horse, still with its saddle on it, which knew to stay just out of reach.'

So he'd done for him with that shot, thought Tommy. Judd. His mortal enemy. But there was something that disturbed in the account. He'd looked to Katherine Hart, but if she was bothered by it, it didn't show. Had her brother, in the last, not acted dishonourably? Wasn't there a code of honour he'd broken, introducing a gun into a knife fight? Even allowing for the fact that his opponent was a sadist and a killer. Or was it that the bull might try at the death any trick to bring down the matador?

He looked back to the white-haired man, his eyes shut and face turned to the sunshine. At the month's mind for Fred Hart, if that's what it was, he'd been dressed in full regimentals. He was a retired military man. An officer. Surely he'd know if a point of honour had been traduced. He was just on the point of asking when a voice carried over the open water. 'Hey! Kinkaid!'

It was Soot Kelleher, flanked by one of his sidekicks.

Pisser O'Gorman. A lackey like O'Gorman, the expectant leer on his sycophant faces, drew far more opprobrium from Tommy than Soot himself. The pair were sauntering in his direction with lazy intent.

He looked back to the bench, but Cpt Jack, taking the sun, remained oblivious to their approach. Backs to the Basin, the pair were by this point hovering some ten or fifteen yards from him.

'Hey Kinkaid. Is it true your Ma writes dirty bookes?'

Now the plain fact was that, bizarrely, this information had come out in the course of the trial. After he'd taken the stand, the barrister with the frog eyes had put it to him directly: 'Are you aware that your mother is the author of salacious material?' The defence lawyer had objected: the question could have no conceivable bearing on the case. 'I'm trying to establish, your Honour,' sighed frog eyes, 'the degree to which the witness's awareness and credibility are to be relied upon.' Objection overruled. The judge instructed him to reply to the question, which the lawyer drolly repeated.

Tommy looked up at the gallery. In the midst of the crowd, which had become animate, his mother's face was immobile as a statue's. Behind her sat Br Colman, erect and grave.

He'd looked down at his shoelaces. Shrugged. 'I don't know what salacious means.'

There was a round of tittering, cut short by the judge's glare. He invited Counsel to rephrase the question. 'Are you aware that your mother is the author of *lewd* material?' His mother's features remained stony. '*Bawdy*?' prompted the lawyer, eyebrows hoisted.

'Yih.'

'Yes. I see. And could you describe for the court the kinds of stories that might entail?'

Objection! The witness has already given an answer to the question. This time it was sustained. And that was the end of that. Or should have been, if a couple of gossip columns in the gutter press hadn't seized upon the detail.

'Yah! Little Tommy Kay! His mammy writes smutty bookes, she does.' Safe behind Soot Kelleher's shoulder, Pisser O'Gorman was leering like a gargoyle.

An image flashed through his head; Jimmy Cade as a schoolboy, putting down his forehead and charging the lowest of the bullies. For which they'd dealt him the worst beating he'd ever got. Landed him in the infirmary.

'That your grandpa? Hey gramps! You know your daughter writes smutty books, yeah?'

Two years of humiliation, of anxiety and dull torment lay coiled inside. He saw in the corner of his eye the old man rise. Hold aloft his walking cane. 'You insolent young pup!' he sputtered. Soot guffawed. It was trigger enough. Trigger enough to uncoil the loaded spring of his body. His lowered head caught his arch-enemy square in the ribs. The momentum carried the latter backward over the low wall of the reservoir.

Even as they crashed through the surface of the water, and in full knowledge that following on the action he was about to face the worst drubbing of his life, Tommy Kinkaid, for one glorious instant, tasted the delirium of freedom.

GLOSSARY OF GAELIC, HIBERNO-
IRISH AND AFRIKAANS
EXPRESSIONS

P23—ⅽⱡⱥⱰᵳ̇ⱶⱸⱥⱮⱨ Sᴏⱡⱳⱳⱱ—Sword of Light, a nationalist newspaper edited by Padraig Pearse.

P23 and 56—'what's this it was?'—this syntactical form is still in common usage in Ireland, as in James Joyce's *Ulysses*.

P24—Ⱡⱸⱥⱴⱨⱥᵳⱡⱥⱱⱱ Ⱶⱥⱱⱨ ⱸⱱⱱ ⱴⱥⱱ̇ⱱⱸ/Sⱼⱱⱱ ⱱⱥ Ɱⱴᵳⱥⱼⱨᵳⱸ Ɱᵳⱱⱱⱱⱥⱡ—Library of St John the Baptist/Christian Brothers School.

P27—SᵳⱥⱱⱮⱸⱥᵳ ⱱⱥ Sⱥⱸⱱ̇ⱨⱱⱡⱼⱸ—Irish (ie Gaelic) Grammar

P29—ⱸⱱⱡⱱ Rⱳⱥ—Red-haired Elspeth or Elizabeth

P29—Ɱⱥᵳ ⱥ ⱴⱨⱸⱥⱱ̇ⱨ Ⱡⱥⱱⱥⱱ̇ⱨ ⱱⱥ ⱨⱸⱱⱱⱱⱱⱸ ⱥᵳ Ⱡⱸⱱⱱⱸⱥⱱⱱ ⱱⱥ ⱽⱽⱥⱽⱨᵳⱥⱽⱨ.—Like the flush of TB on the city's cheek.

GLOSSARY

P47, 104, 210 and 233—'yous'—a Dublinism for you (plural)

P48 and 226—'look it'—an Irishism for 'look'

P49—oul wan—'old one'—an Irishism for mother (or, occasionally, wife).
P49—'he takes any sit'—'sit' was contemporary Dublin usage for a position or post.

P65, 223 and 234—*kopje*—In the context of the Boer War, a "kopje" (literally 'cup') was a small, rounded hillock or outcrop, often rocky; a common feature of the South African landscape.

P66—*stroom, meer*—stream, lake
P66—*uitlanders*—foreigners. The lack of voting rights extended to 'uitlanders' exploiting the recently discovered Transvaal goldfields was used as a pretext for the Second Boer War.
P66—*Zarps*—The *Zuid-Afrikaansche Republiek Politie* (ZARP) was the police force of the Transvaal Republic.

P79—Connṁaḋh na Ṡaeḋhilṡe—a Society founded in 1893 to promote the revival of the Gaelic language.

P80—beiḋh Feaṙ móṙ le ṙá aṡainn maṙ aoi aṡ an cionól maiḋin amáṙach—we'll have a famous man as guest at assembly tomorrow morning.
P80—Scoil Éanna—St Enda's, an Irish Language school founded by Padraig Pearse
P80—éisciṡí anois!—Listen now!

GLOSSARY

P80—Ar aghaidh libh, a bhuachaillí táim in éad libh.—Let's go, boys. I'm envious of you.

P98—ní mór seilbh a choimeád air—You have to keep hold of it.

P98—brostaigh ort! Anois, buail é—Hurry up! Now, hit it.

P98—muise ní raibh sé sin thar moladh beirte—That effort wasn't up to much (lit., beyond the praise of two)

P98—ná bí ag faire ar nós cuma liom—Don't be waiting as if you didn't care.

P98—togha fir—Good man

P98—thar an trasnán leis!—Over the crossbar with it!

P98—óinseach!—(female) fool

P98—dúradán—wimp

P98—éist liom anois—Listen to me now.

P98—An dtuigeann tú?—Do you understand?

P128—bithiúnach! Coimeád do chlab dúnta—Keep your mouth shut, you scoundrel!

P128—clár dubh—blackboard

P129—maith an fear—Good man.

P129—brostaigh ort, tá an príomhoide ag fanacht leat—Hurry up, the headmaster is waiting for you.

P156—bulling—Irishism for angry.

P157—'on foot of'—an Irishism still in common use meaning by reason of or as a consequence of.

P176—'make a hames of'—Irishism for make a mess of.

GLOSSARY

P208—*Staan op jou lui swart baster!*—Stand up you lazy black bastard!

P210—*bittereinders*—'Bitter enders' were the Boer faction determined to fight on to the end. They were opposed by 'Joiners', some of whom, siding with the British, took up arms against them.

P216—*Hoe gaan dit?*—How are things?

P223—*plaasopstal*—farmstead

P233—*Ter nagedagtenis aan die Esterhuizen-gesin, vermoor deur Britse soldate*—In memory of the Esterhuizen family, murdered by British soldiers.

P245, 246 and 250—'whenever'—Throughout Ulster, an odd linguistic tell is the use of 'whenever' where 'when' would normally be used. Eg 'Whenever my father died…'

P259—month's mind—A memorial service held approximately one month after a person's death. It's a Catholic tradition throughout Ireland to commemorate the deceased, the service frequently followed by a social gathering for close friends and family. As Fred Hart was Church of Ireland, Kinkaid's assumption here may be inaccurate.

A NOTE ON THE IRISH INVOLVEMENT IN THE SECOND BOER WAR (1899-1902)

Irish regiments had a long tradition in fighting alongside English, Scottish and Welsh regiments throughout the British Empire all the way through to Irish independence in 1922. Thus when the Second Boer War broke out in 1899, the 5th 'Irish' Brigade in South Africa contained units from the Royal Dublin Fusiliers, the Inniskillings and the Connaught Rangers. From 1900, these regular forces were supplemented by volunteers who joined the Imperial Yeomanry in large numbers in the wake of the three disastrous defeats of 'Black Week' (10th—17th December 1899), when all three columns dispatched to relieve the sieges of Kimberley, Mafeking and Ladysmith were defeated by the Boers, an irregular army of militiamen organised into *kommandos*. Irish casualties were particularly severe *en route* to relieve Ladysmith at the battle of Colenso on Dec 15th.

HISTORICAL NOTE

Not all Irish citizens were enthusiastic about what was widely viewed as a power grab against two republics whose independence had been secured just twenty years earlier as a result of the First Boer War; prior, that is, to the discovery of vast gold deposits in the Rand region of the Transvaal. The Irish republican agitator John McBride organized a Transvaal Irish Brigade to fight alongside the Boer *kommandos*, and these distinguished themselves in particular during the siege of Ladysmith defending the Boer artillery emplacements, though they took no part in the later, guerrilla phase of the war that succeeded the fall of Pretoria in June, 1900.

The amnesty that concluded the war in 1902 was extended to all those who had taken arms against the British forces, including Major McBride and his Transvaal Irish Brigade— he would later be executed by the British in the wake of the Dublin Rising of 1916. The amnesty did not extend to those soldiers who had deserted the British Army.

DEDALUS IRELAND

Dedalus Ireland combines Dedalus' commitment to European fiction with the literature of the UK's nearest European neighbour with whom we share our language and a lot of our history.

Titles published so far:

Pure Innocent Boy — Patrick Doherty
Take Six: Six Irish Women Writers — edited by
                                        Tanya Farrelly

JABBERWOCK — Dara Kavanagh
Prague 1938 — Dara Kavanagh
Scorched Earth — Dara Kavanagh
Le Fanu's Angel — Brian Keogh
The Failing Heart — Eoghan Smith
A Mind of Winter — Eoghan Smith
A Provincial Death — Eoghan Smith

Forthcoming in 2026:

Wild Iris — Ruth McKee

JABBERWOCK by Dara Kavanagh

Imagine if Flann O'Brien, with a little help from James Joyce, had rewritten *Alice in Wonderland* or Laurence Sterne had sent Don Quixote on a voyage alongside Lemuel Gulliver, then you have entered the world of JABBERWOCK — an anarchic novel full of delights and fromulous pleasures.

It tells the story of Ignatius Hackett, who rises in 1920s 'Dubilin' to the top of the journalist tree before he is undone by words and has a spell in Dean Swift's Mental Asylum. With Europe on the brink of war, his life takes a turn for the better when his journalistic skills are remembered and he is dispatched across the water to investigate a spate of verbal outrages in a topsy-turvy world in which fonts and footnotes flourish while puns and paradoxes proliferate at an alarming rate. Spurred on, he travels to France and into the dark heart of Germany, and gets caught up in a sinister chess-game of police and informers, of spies and revolutionaries behind which moves the shadowy Ouroboros Brotherhood. Who can be trusted, when words themselves are no longer content to be bound in dictionaries, but are in danger of being pressganged as wonder-weapons in the new World War?

'JABBERWOCK fizzes with wit and ingenuity — a linguistic riot of hiberno-Anarchy.'

Ronan Hession, author of *Leonard and Hungry Paul*

£12.99   ISBN   978 1 915568 41 0   442p   B. Format

Prague 1938 by Dara Kavanagh

"The streets of Prague take centre stage in this smorgasbord of a novel: coming-of-age, familial upheaval, political unrest, artistic intrigue, rag order existence, the folly of youthful infatuation, the warp and woof of flight to a new world; and all of it played out under the looming shadow of war, of a world approaching the precipice. This is elegant, vibrant and read-on storytelling at its very best." Alan McMonagle

"There are many direct cultural references in the book, which make it a rich feast. Some of the chapter titles also have amusing literary echoes, Pequod Mutiny, for example, and Through the Looking-glass and Endgame, which tie in nicely with the chess theme. This all reveals a wonderful playfulness on the part of the author, something I love to find."
Fionnuala Mc Mmanamon in *Books Ireland Magazine*

"...magnificent *Prague 1938*, an immersively convincing voice describing a vanished, polyglot world... it is not just its Mitteleuropean setting that made me think I'd stumbled on a recently rediscovered manuscript of Stefan Zweig or Joseph Roth, but the immersively convincing voice of Kavanagh's prose in describing this vanished, polyglot world. Leah Meisel's gang of thieves has none of Dickens' picturesqueness, and as Prague starts to fill with refugees, '...hopelessness, too, has its odour... a mixture of woodsmoke and incontinence and wet cloth and acrid perspiration'."
Katherine Mezzacappa in *The Historical Novel Review*

£9.99   ISBN 978 1 912868 51 3   280p   B.Format

Take Six: Six Irish Women Writers
edited by Tanya Farrelly

Take Six: Six Irish Women Writers features work by six award-winning Irish women writers: Rosemary Jenkinson, Geraldine Mills, Mary Morrissy, Mary O' Donnell, Nuala O' Connor and Tanya Farrelly.

'In this powerful anthology, Tanya Farrelly curates six short stories spanning dystopian futures, where daughters are outlawed, to quiet acts of voyeurism, all threaded with tension and ethical ambiguity.'　　　　Adam Wyeth in *The Irish Times*

'Farrelly's editorial vision is cohesive, intelligent, and subtle. Rather than assembling a showcase of virtuosity for its own sake, she brings together writers whose stories reflect one another in tone and temperament. The stories are not showy; they unfold. Each narrative, in its own way, attends to the small decisions that shape or deform a life.'

Ruby Eastwood in *Books Ireland Magazine*

'…a literary ride of hell, heaven, bombers, Keats, flotsam, a crap mother, sex in the city of Belfast, love triangles and a certain poetry that comes with shared experience of place and time.'　　　　Angeline King in *Fortnight*

£11.99　ISBN　978 1 915568 64 9　296p　B. Format